NOX

A ROYAL PROTECTOR ACADEMY NOVEL

RANDI COOLEY WILSON

Published by SECRET GARDEN PRODUCTIONS, INC.
Editing by Liz Ferry of Per Se Editing
Cover design ©Hang Le byhangle.com
Book Formatting by Type A Formatting

NOX (A Royal Protector Academy Novel, Finale)
Randi Cooley Wilson
Printed in the United States of America
Second Edition January 2019
ISBN-13: 9781793056818

ROYAL PROTECTOR
ACADEMY

ALSO BY

RANDI COOLEY WILSON

THE REVELATION SERIES

REVELATION

RESTRAINT

REDEMPTION

REVOLUTION

RESTORATION

DARK PARADISE

**THE ROYAL PROTECTOR ACADEMY
NOVELS**

VERNAL

AEQUUS

NOX

A KING RISES NOVELLA

DARK SOUL SERIES

STOLAS

VASSAGO

LEVIATHAN

CONTEMPORARY ROMANCE

IF | A NOVEL

THE MONSTER BALL ANTHOLOGY

ISLE OF DARKNESS

HAVENWOOD FALLS NOVELLAS

COVETOUSNESS

INAMORATA

GYPSY HEART

PRISON OF ASRIA

For anyone who told me I could not,
because I did.

The calm had brought a sort of courage and hope with it.
Instead of giving way to thoughts of the worst,
he actually found he was trying to believe in better things.

Frances Hodgson Burnette
The Secret Garden

TRISTAN GALLAGHER

When you are the heir to a legacy,
always read the fine print on the family crest.

Because the symbol alone will seduce you.
It will lure you in—have you believe that you are
invincible.

Yet, it's in the smallest of print where you learn of the true
duties and obligations of your rise to power.

Honoring bloodlines comes with great sacrifice,
none greater than to sacrifice in the name of love . . .

PROLOGUE

TRISTAN

I need to get the fuck out of here. As I take in the damage to Serena's bedroom, a dark, ugly sigh escapes me.

The destruction I've caused feels symbolic—like I've ruined the last part of humanity the gargoyle princess created in me. And in its place is an empty shell of the being I might have become, but no longer wish to be.

Her room at the Royal Protector Academy mirrors my current emotional state—ripped apart. Gutted. Destroyed.

Exhaling roughly, I attempt to clear the dismal thoughts threatening to push me further into this black hole of despair. I rub my hands over my face and remind myself that I don't wallow in self-pity.

Protectors take control of the situation.

Seek revenge.

And endlessly fight for what's ours.

With a final decision, I turn to my brother and best friend, Zander. I study his face, longing for a simpler time —when we were children, running carefree among the forest through my mother's realm—instead of the nightmare we're facing.

Zander was once the second in command to the woodland realm's royal guard, under our father, Rionach.

After Rionach's death, he was to step in as commander of the Lion Guard. That was before I renounced the throne, giving up my satyr birthright to become the king —for her.

Given Zander's pure satyr bloodline, my brother will make a more noble king for the realm. He understands the kingdom's needs more than I ever could. And honestly, at his core, Zander is a much better being than I will ever be.

Even so, it's written all over his face. He doesn't want to be the king of the woodland realm any more than I did. And now that we've assumed reign and protection of the water realm, he's got that much more to rule over.

He'd much rather lead my army and protect me.

The irony in all this is that he can't protect me.

No one can. Because the gargoyle blood that runs through my veins won't allow me to be part of that world anymore. Neither will my love for Serena St. Michael, the heir to the gargoyle race. My reason for existing.

"Set up the meeting." My tone is final as I change the course of my fate forever.

Zander dips his chin at my declaration before reluctantly taking his leave. Once the door is closed, my focus darts around, landing on the remains of Serena's bed.

A vision—a distant memory of promises made between us—hits me hard in the gut, like a punch.

"I can feel it, Tristan. We're becoming something else. Something bigger than we even know."

"Maybe it's time to walk away, then," I mutter.

"Let me in." She whispers the plea.

I wince. "Why? You'll leave me. Hurt me."

Her eyes water with unshed tears as she shakes her head back and forth. "I won't."

"Everyone else has, Serena."

"I'll fight for you in a way that no one else ever has."

Her ghost flickers in and out, triggering another memory. A conversation we shared before she disappeared.

"Tell me this is real," she pleads. I'm afraid that this . . . unknown shadow is going to descend on us and take you away from me. Leaving me alone."

My fingers stroke her cheek as I stare at her intensely, allowing my thumb to run across her bottom lip. "Trust me," I whisper, "nothing is going to happen to me, or you."

I release a bark-laugh at the promise. It was a lie then. And after what I just instructed Zander to do, it's a lie now.

With a firm resolve, I walk toward the door and yank it open. Zander is leaning against the wall with his arms crossed. His expression is one of concern mixed with determination. Relief floods through me, knowing he did it.

I pull out a cigarette, light it, and inhale deeply. It's been months since I've had one. My eyes close as the nicotine invades my head, relaxing the edginess rattling inside me.

After a moment, my lids slide open and with an exhale, I lock my attention on my brother. "You ready for this?"

"You're smoking again?" Zander accuses, eyeing me.

"Are you going to lecture me?" I challenge.

After a quiet moment, he shakes his head. "I suppose when the love of your life goes missing and you're about to make a deal with the devil, a cigarette is a trivial matter."

I shake off the reminder of what we are about to do and take long strides toward the front door of Serena's suite, with Zander following closely behind. He shadows my steps protectively, having my back—like he has my entire life.

He taps my shoulder, causing me to face him.

"Are you sure you want to do this?"

"Wants and needs are interchangeable at this point."

He frowns. "What about your future?"

We fall silent for a moment as I take another long hit off my cigarette, blowing out my words on the heavy trail of smoke. "I have no future without her, Zander. I'd rather have Serena live a long existence hating me for what I did to protect her, than have her not exist at all."

Zander scoffs. "You're an idiot."

"I love you too, man."

"I mean it. That girl is head over heels in love with

you," he points out. "Which is why, when Serena finds out that we did this, she is going to punch us both in the face. You for doing it and me for allowing you to do it."

"Then we'll make sure she gets both our left sides, so our bruises match," I reply, motioning for him to walk through the open door.

He does so, mumbling something under his breath about being too good-looking to be sporting bruises.

With a final look around her suite, I close the door and officially walk away from the past—to give her a future.

THE SLEEK BLACK car drives up to the edge of the darkened meadow. With the press of a button, Zander shuts off the engine, but keeps on the headlights.

As we wait, I take in the pitch-black grassland in front of us. The only sign of life is a few shadowed cattle swinging their tails as they chew the dry desert grass.

My attention falls to the clock on the dashboard—it's an hour past midnight. Above us, the stars dance and sparkle brightly in the night sky.

Even the moon keeps its eyes on us tonight. Its whitish slivers cut through the inky darkness surrounding us.

"Why here?"

"It's near Kur," I reply.

"Of course, *he* would make us wait in a field of cow

shit. Fucking asshole," Zander grumbles from the driver's seat.

"He'll show his face when he is ready to," I advise.

Zander looks around, his features scrunching as he examines our surroundings. "Another uninspired shithole."

My brother hates visiting the earth realm. He prefers the beauty and glamour of our home in the woodland realm.

His face suddenly becomes tight as his focus locks on to three figures appearing out of thin air. In silence, we watch the crimson auras approach, gliding in a V shape toward us.

"Here we go," I mutter, and we open the two front car doors, sliding out and stepping in front of the vehicle, breaking up the headlights' beams.

Casually, I lean back on the hood and cross my arms, calmly waiting while the beings come to us. Zander stands in a warrior pose at my side—ready to fight and protect.

"It is not often I am summoned by a satyr prince." The deity's old-world-accented voice booms in the silence.

I don't acknowledge the tone of his words, which make it sound as if I am a lesser being. There is no need to prove myself anything other than what this piece of shit assumes me to be. He knows why we are here; the deal has been laid out.

He stands tall, long black hair blowing in the night breeze. His hard, rectangular face is pulled into a tight expression as he watches me. The Hispanic man to his left and Asian female to his right each keep an eye on Zander and me, disdain and loathing etched into their features.

"Your fast rise to power in the underworld has been impressive," I state. "The hushed rumblings of your justice- over-mercy approach have made you a god in their eyes."

"My bloodlines make me a god, satyr prince. My creed is a simple warning for those I hunt and extinguish," he responds with an air of arrogance.

Peering at the three warily, I assess them. There is something about all of this that rubs me the wrong way, a gut feeling that at the end of all this, it is all going to go to shit, but I have no choice. I'll pay any cost to protect her.

I stare at him, and he at me. A power struggle at its finest has the two of us evaluating one another, untrusting.

"You look a little worse for the wear, satyr prince."

I grant him an unfriendly smile. "Sleep eludes me."

The female narrows her eyes, sliding her gaze to Zander. "From the looks of it, your army's commander has been getting his beauty rest. Then again, Zander, you always were a pretty boy," she taunts in a seductive voice.

Zander's smirk has a wicked undertone. "You never complained about my looks when I was between your legs, Tova." *Christ. Is there anyone my brother hasn't bedded?*

"Fuck you." Her expression is one of pure fury.

The Hispanic guy grabs her, preventing her from leaping forward and attacking my brother.

7

"Enough of the pleasantries," the guy holding Tova growls out, annoyed with the drama simmering.

"Helios commanded my presence," the leader states in a deep, authoritative voice. "No doubt, at Aoife's request," he adds.

I don't respond to his unconcealed displeasure at being called upon by the sun god to meet Zander and me.

"To be clear, I am not a hellhound. I don't come when beckoned. Especially when summoned by my brother's nymph whore. A brother whom I despise with a passion."

My lips press together. I know better than to defend the honor of my old lover, Aoife, a magical tree sprite.

In our world, nymphs, especially mistresses of deities such as the god of the sun, are second-class entities.

"Then why are you here, Nox?" I growl out.

Nox stands deathly still, his eyes black orbs burning into me, filled with intrigue and vengeance. A look I'm sure has struck fear into the heart of many a dark-souled being.

"I owe Helios a debt." The deity's voice is lined with disgust. "Acceptance of your *task* is my repayment to him."

The muscle in my jaw tightens as I try to keep my breathing controlled—striving for a cool indifference to all of this. If I were a better man, a better being, I would walk away from this deal and find another way to keep Serena safe. But I'm not. The truth is, I'll pay any price, suffer any cost to make sure she is protected. Even this.

"The terms are clear then?" I confirm.

Nox's mouth twists into a suggestive smile. "The

terms of our oath are clear, satyr prince," Nox announces. "And just so there are no misunderstandings, once I have eliminated the dark-souled threats to your princess and her race, you will make good as you have promised."

I pull out my dagger and slice open my palm, allowing the crimson liquid to rise to the surface. "I swear my oath to the gods. If I break my vow, I pray that I may die and return to the land from which my bloodline was created."

Nox releases his dagger from its sheath. A snake coils around the onyx handle as he, too, slices his palm, allowing the gold liquid the deity carries in his veins to seep out.

Without hesitation, he slides his hand over mine, mixing our bloodlines—the god of night and the prince of the woodland realm—sealing my fate and our pledges.

"Your prayer is a waste of breath. Betray me, satyr prince, and I will not rest until not only do you cease to exist, but also the entire protector and satyr races," Nox threatens.

Within seconds, the three deities disappear, leaving Zander and me alone in the pitch-black field, the moon now hidden behind darkness. It must have sensed my sealed fate and, saddened, gone into hiding—like I should probably do.

As my wound heals, I wipe the small amount of mixed blood still lingering on my skin onto my jeans.

"You don't have to do this," Zander says bitterly.

"It's done."

"You can undo it," he barks. "You can save Serena another way. This way . . . will break her heart and spirit."

"She's resilient and capable of surviving whatever is thrown at her. Serena St. Michael is the heir to the gargoyle throne. She was born to rule. Her bloodline alone dictates her endurance." My response is automatic, harsh, unfeeling.

His eyes narrow in disapproval. "Heed my warning," Zander says with icy vehemence. "Because this oath is going to come back to haunt you when you spill all of our blood."

With my other hand on the handle of my dagger, I sigh and lower my voice. "As my brother, I need you to trust in me. Rest assured, the only blood I spill will be my own."

Frustrated, he roars into the darkness before calming enough to say, "You're so damn arrogant."

"That I am." I wink at him. "Now, let's go grab Magali."

"Why?" he barks at me.

"We have one final stop to make this evening."

"Where?"

"England. The London clan's flats."

BEAUTIFUL MESS

TRISTAN

I t's been said that the darkness you know is better than the darkness you don't. Icy pinpricks of dread and adrenaline wage war with my constant fatigue. The throbbing ache of Serena's absence drags me into my dark thoughts. The voices inside my head mock me. Reminding me of my failures.

Serena and I were young and naïve to think that love trumps all. It doesn't. Love is blinding. And destructive.

Outside, lightning crashes and thunder rumbles. But even the rain can't wash away the damage we've created.

Sighing, I attempt to quiet the mocking whisper in my head. I know she's gone, yet I swear I hear her soft murmur calling to me. Pleading with me to bring her home, which I am trying my damnedest to do. "Hang on, raindrop."

"Tristan?" Zander prompts.

I blink, slowly coming out of my own mind as I absorb my surroundings. After a measured moment, I push away the trepidation clutching my chest caused by the gargoyle princess's absence. With each passing day, the empty space beside me, where she should be, elicits more anger and hurt.

Without Serena, there are holes in my soul.

They release the light but leave the dark.

Rage consumes my every fiber as I look around the room. A sea of familiar faces stare right through me, waiting for my response. Without her here, I've become distracted.

"Time is of the essence," Asher St. Michael, leader of the London clan of gargoyles, states with finality.

"I know," I reply coolly.

"You have a choice, Tristan," Zander states.

"Wrong." I stare at a saddened pair of crystal-blue eyes watching me. A single tear falls from them, as Serena's mother, Abby, studies me. "If I really had a choice, I would have chosen to never love her in the first place. I would have chosen my kingdom and kin first." My answer is directed at Abby more so than Zander. I shift my gaze, meeting his. "If I had a choice, I would have walked away to protect her from all this. When it comes to love, fate gives us no choice."

Asher takes a step forward. "Gage came to us. We charged you with Serena's protection at his request. In exchange for a place . . . a home for you within our clan. You've failed to protect my bloodline. The heir."

Ignoring the remark about my biological father, Gage Gallagher, I force myself to be humble. King of the gargoyle race or not, Asher is right. On all counts except one . . .

"Serena is more than just your bloodline," I argue.

The protector considers me. "You do not fear the end of your existence?" he asks me. The question is rhetorical.

Slowly, I turn my head and meet Asher's gaze. He's watching me, as if I'm a new creature he's encountered. He doesn't understand the way I love her. None of them do.

They won't ever accept or allow it.

They won't allow us—not anymore.

Under my protection, I loved and lost her.

And it hurts like hell.

"Death is welcome. Stone petrifaction is welcome. It's a life without Serena's existence I fear," I reply with resolve.

"It's your existence I am worried about, if you go through with this deal with Nox," Zander interjects.

"I didn't start this war. Asmodeus, Kupuva, and the dark army did." I meet his gaze. "But I am prepared to finish it."

"Seeking Nox's assistance was unwise," Zander argues. "The demon hunter is unpredictable. Trusting him," my brother holds my eyes with a steely gaze. "It'll bring certain death."

"Maybe my time has run out," I counter, unfeeling.

"What. The. Hell. Did you just say?" Serena's aunt McKenna roars. Her hands barrel into tight fists as she stalks toward me with furious, narrowed sapphire eyes.

Both Zander and Asher try to step between us, preventing her approach. I stop them, holding my palm up.

Understandably, her wrath has been constant since we arrived at the St. Michael flats in London, England.

From the moment the gargoyle warrior opened the door and narrowed her gaze at me, she has been going on and on about my incompetence and lack of proper protector training. Kenna is pissed at the world, and most of all me.

I back up as she grabs me by the shirt and pushes me against the wall. The hard, rough brick bites into my back as the gargoyle presses me against it harder. Kenna and I are matched for height. And even though I may have a hand up on her in strength, she has me beat at pure intimidation.

I could fight back, but I owe her this.

I owe the entire London clan this.

"Serena is our blood. And if you love her, then stop being a fucking pussy-ass and moping around as if someone ripped out your heart and then stepped on it," she spits out.

"Kenna—" Eve, Asher's human mate, gently sighs out.

14

"Shut up, blood of Eden," Kenna yells at Eve. "No one gets to defend the traitor's bastard son," she snarls.

By *traitor*, she's referring to my biological father, Gage. He's looked down on amongst the gargoyle race for not taking on protector assignments. And he has a reputation for being reckless since the death of his mate.

Kenna's gaze searches my empty stare as I let her rant.

"Tristan wants to embrace his gargoyle bloodline? Then he can defend and protect himself. Isn't that right, *asshole?*"

I don't bristle at the crude nickname. I'd made the mistake of falling asleep one night with angry, drunk, female protectors surrounding me. Which led to Serena's unvoiced roommate and best friend, Magali, taking a permanent marker and writing *asshole* across my forehead, then texting every being across all dimensions the photo.

Mags cringes in my peripheral vision, before she signs that she is sorry to me. I try to offer her a reassuring smile.

Eve pushes her way into the sliver of space Kenna has allowed between us. The tightness causes her back to press into my chest and pushes me even farther into the wall.

Asher steps closer to us, clenching his jaw at his queen's choice to insert herself into this. I exhale a shallow breath, because Eve needs to stay the hell out of it. She won't.

If I've learned anything from spending the last few weeks with the St. Michael clan, it's that they love hard—and fight harder.

"Move. Now," Kenna snaps at Eve.

"No."

"I mean it, Eve."

"Make me, cupcake," Eve taunts.

"Tell your human shield to fucking move, Tristan."

I grab Eve's shoulders and guide her out of the way, stepping in front of her before the two get into a fist fight.

Asher's jaw flexes and his teeth grind together as he storms over and grabs his mate's wrist, pulling her away.

"Stay the hell out of it, siren," he barks.

"I will not." She slips away from him, crossing her arms.

"Everyone just calm down," Keegan, McKenna's mate and Asher's older brother, sighs. He looks exhausted.

"Does no one listen to me anymore?" Asher looks around the room. "I am still the king of this race, am I not?" he poses. "If I want to protect Eve while she is trying to defend Tristan, I'll do it. If I want to stone petrify Tristan for losing my niece on his protector watch, then I will do it. I'm the king. Rules don't apply in this room, and right now, I am tired, hungry, and pissed off at that asshole," he rants, pointing to me, just to clarify which asshole he's talking about.

"Damn, this family is violent when hungry. And crazy," Zander states. "Is it wrong that I kind of like it?" he asks Magali, who rolls her eyes at him—she's used to his antics.

"Christ, someone get Asher a goddamn Snickers bar," Gage throws out from his corner near the door. "And

Keegan, tell your mate to back the fuck off Tristan already."

McKenna's eyes narrow before she spins to face Gage. She takes two strides in his direction before Asher steps in front of her, shaking his head twice. The warning stops her.

"You tell her." Keegan folds himself into a chair next to his youngest brother and Serena's father, Callan.

"Enough," Callan's quiet voice has the same effect on all of us as if he'd shouted the word. The entire room falls into a tense silence as his gaze lifts, meeting mine. "Where the hell is my daughter, Tristan?" he barely manages to ask.

I lick my lips and wince as I try to stand to my full height. My voice cracks. "As I said before, I don't know."

Callan's attention slides to Abby for the briefest of moments. Her face pales as her gaze falls back to the table.

In an instant, Callan is pushing out of his chair and into my face. His forearms are firmly pressed across my neck. I don't flinch as they jam into my throat, crushing my windpipe and stopping air from flowing.

Just yelling at me isn't going to appease him. If our roles were reversed, I would do the same—probably worse —because she owns every piece of me, not just a father's heart.

"I should just end your existence right now." He releases a laugh that is anything but amused. "Give me one good reason not to do it." He pushes into me farther. "Just one."

"I love her," I rasp, holding his steely gaze.

Callan's eyebrows shoot up.

Next to us, Asher groans and takes a step out of the line of fire, causing me to snap my attention to my left at Gage.

Gage keeps his face impassive.

Zander and Mags are silent.

"You . . . *love* her?" Callan repeats, sounding pissed off.

"By the grace, Tristan. Teleport," Eve whispers.

"Yes."

Callan replies with a quick snap. "In our world, love is shown through protection. If you truly loved Abby's and my daughter . . . Serena would be by your side right now."

"Stop," Abby pleads quietly. "Babe. Just. Stop."

Callan and I just stare at one another, his eyes empty and cold. Something I've never seen in them. Usually, they're carefree and sparkling, filled with warmth and love.

"You will never be good enough for her," he says in a hoarse yell. "This clan will find Serena. And when we do, you will return to the woodland realm and take your place without so much as another look in her direction." He lowers his voice. "And if you think otherwise, I'll end you."

He shoves into me one last time before stepping back.

"Won't happen," I bite out, rubbing my throat.

Callan lunges for me again, but is stopped by Asher.

"Walk away, brother." Asher grabs Callan by the shoulders and directs him toward the door, where Keegan is now waiting to escort him out of the room. "Take him," he directs Keegan, who grabs Callan by the elbow and pulls him out of the conference room, with Kenna following them.

Asher turns and faces me, the anger fading slightly from his expression and voice. "My brother is hurting, but he has spoken his wishes. You'd be wise to listen to them."

Eve steps to her mate's side and interlaces their fingers. "No. He wouldn't. Now, come on. Callan needs you." She guides him toward the door, grabbing Gage on the way out.

I motion with my head for Zander and Magali to follow.

After a moment, they reluctantly do, leaving me alone.

Abby clears her throat.

I turn to face her, having not realized she was still in the room.

"Tristan," she says in a shaky voice, "Asher is right, Callan is hurting. We all are. That said, my daughter is very strong-willed. She is after all, a St. Michael." She forces a smile. It doesn't reach her eyes. "As protectors, we make choices. Some are good. Some are bad. But we are all responsible for the decisions we make. Even Serena."

My face pinches at her words.

Her expression softens. "It's not your fault."

"Isn't it?"

Abby frowns. "There are no faults in love."

I shake my head, disagreeing. "My love for Serena blinded me. It became a distraction from my duties and vows. Even now—" I inhale through my nose. "Even now, she is all I think about. That isn't love, Abby. It's obsession."

"What you two share is a strong bond. A connection. A love so deep that no other being in existence can break it. Even her father, regardless of his crazy demands or wishes."

"Everything is a mess."

A sadness settles across her features. "Sometimes, love is a beautiful mess. But it's worth every messy moment. Have faith. You will find her. And when you do, you both will become the royal protectors I know you can be. Together." Abby takes my hands in hers. "You and Serena are the future. As one, you'll carry on the legacy. Trust in that. In her. In love. In our—*your*—clan."

"I'm numb. I can't feel her. Why can't I find her?"

Her smile is sad. "Because she isn't ready to be found."

2

SILENCE

SERENA

Someone once told me that time moves at different paces, depending on circumstance. For some of us, it's slow, methodical. For others it it's over in the blink of an eye. Either way, they pointed out to me that before we've even had time to fully exist, life is over.

And most of us miss out on everything that is truly important to us. I'd always thought the idea of time slipping away from me was nonsense . . . until now.

Silence surrounds me.

The longer I sit here, the louder the silence becomes.

Sometimes, in the darkness of my seclusion, I whisper to the shadows that watch me, hoping that Tristan might be listening and hear me asking him to bring me home.

The sounds of moving water and a steady breeze calm me. The constant humming of nature is the only thing preventing me from becoming fully broken as the feelings and memories of Tristan—permanently ingrained in my mind—taunt me. Daily. Hourly. Every minute and second that ticks by, my every thought is haunted by him.

I pretend that with time, the memories will fade into background noise. It's a lie I tell myself to keep myself from slipping away.

Closing my eyes, I inhale and focus on the energies the earth and elements are giving off, grounding and healing myself. The winds shift along with my erratic emotions.

The frenzied rhythm of dragonflies zipping around the forest pulls my attention away from the remorse settling deep within my core as I begin to second-guess myself.

A cool breeze wraps around me, lifting strands of my long hair, forcing me to try to capture and tame them.

Sliding my eyes open, I gaze out at the babbling brook as the water laps over my bare toes.

The stars and moon hang low, their reflections floating and dancing across the liquid's rippling surface. The effect offers me a brief moment of pure, untainted peace.

Crickets sing their lullabies through the trees and the sadness descends again. As time slips by, I have come to terms with the fact that what Tristan and I share has come to an end. And my clan—the royal protector family I am part of—I don't want the London clan to know my secrets.

They won't understand or forgive what I've done in the name of protection and love. Neither will Tristan.

So, I will let him go, knowing I get to keep a piece of him with me. My fingertips brush over the mark behind my ear. The Sun of Vergina. Tristan's insignia. The same one he wears around his neck, branding him nymph royalty.

The way he'll forever be safe in my heart.

Another light gust of wind brushes over me, pushing in a thin layer of fog, blanketing me. I should go. The sliver of time I've allowed myself to spend here each night while I heal may be good for my body, but it isn't good for my mind.

It's just making me more lost and scared.

Tristan isn't coming for me.

Not this time.

Memories of us float around my head, or maybe they're images of what could have been. I have no way of knowing which, because what might have been was taken away from me the night that Freya switched places with me and left me to die. In that one moment in time, everything changed. And now, nothing will ever be the same. Ever.

"I'm sorry I couldn't get to you," I whisper to Tristan, even though the attempt to get him to hear me is futile.

"Are you giving up on me?" a deep, familiar voice asks.

An odd feeling crawls up the back of my neck, tightening all the muscles in my body. My breathing stops, but the movement of the wind and crawling fog make me feel as though I'm swaying. The motion twists my stomach.

Slowly, I turn and my eyes meet a warm cognac gaze.

"Tristan?" I barely whisper.

"Raindrop."

My lips part as I scan the forest behind him.

"Sorry I'm late," he states in a quiet tone.

"L-late?" I stumble. "How are you here?" I ask, confused.

His lips twist as he squats in front of me, silently.

"Am I imagining this?" I ask quietly, confused.

His heated gaze roams over me. It's hard to tell if he's angry or happy to see me. He ignores my baffled state.

"Come home, Serena."

My heart stutters at the desperation in his voice.

"I promise to do better." His voice cracks. "Be better."

"Tri—" I stare at him, breathing him in.

By the grace, I love this man with everything I am, which is why I can't go back. Not yet. I need to protect him.

"We'll start again," he whispers. "I'm not afraid."

"I am," I admit.

He leans closer and I hold my breath. "Whatever it is you're scared of . . ." He bends in further, toward me.

"Stop," I plead.

If he gets too close, my resolve will disappear.

With one final tilt, he takes my face in his warm palms, lifting my gaze to his. "On my honor, I will protect you. Us."

His proclamation stirs something familiar in me.

It's a protector vow—a London clan decree.

My fear becomes palpable.

He's been with my clan, which is dangerous.

I shake my head. "You can't protect me. Us."

"You can stop running," he mutters across my lips.

"I have to let you go," I say, though it kills me.

He searches my eyes. "You can let me go, but that doesn't mean I'll go. Fight for us. For me, as I will for you."

"You need to stop fighting," I beg.

"No."

"Tri—," I start.

"I need you to come back to me."

"I can't."

"Why not?"

"If I do, it will destroy us."

"If you don't come home, it will destroy me."

His forehead drops to mine and right before our lips are about to touch, he dissolves into the shadows. Disappearing.

Leaving me to face the darkness of the night.

3

THE SPACE BETWEEN

TRISTAN

I wake up screaming her name—like I have every night since she disappeared. Wildly, my eyes dart around the dark room, seeking her out. Images of her slide through my mind and choke the air out of my lungs. Her smell, the warmth of her touch, her palpable fear, it all felt so fucking real.

Blinking my eyes several times, I try to release the dream and return to the here and now. Beads of sweat trail down my neck as I attempt to calm myself, allowing reality to seep in. With each erratic breath, my mind begins to understand that the vision wasn't real. Serena is still gone.

The reminder makes everything worse. Panic and dread claw at my throat. The pain of her absence is indescribable, like my body and heart have been torn in half.

Memories of the dream-like vision flash across my

mind, causing a searing ache to build at my temples and tears to burn at my eyes.

The dreams are coming more frequently now, as if something is pulling me to her. And after each one, it takes me longer to center myself—to bring myself back to reality.

A silver-blue-tinted beam of moonlight pushes through the closed curtains. Staring at it, I rub my face, trying to ease the ache in my heart, which is pounding in my chest.

Flashes of sapphire eyes flecked with cognac swarm me. My vision blurs and my stomach roils with the image of the girl who changed me. The girl I never wanted, but desperately needed. The girl who is my reason for existing.

With a gasp, I feel my heart stutter again. Seconds later, I slide out of bed and stumble over to the one spot in the room I know will provide me a false sense of security.

As I sit, I push myself back into the darkened corner. With a rough exhale, I welcome the shadows of night that have fallen across the room. The walls on either side cocoon me. Shelter me. And help me to ground and center myself.

The distress starts to fade slightly from my veins.

Only to be replaced by emptiness and loneliness.

I try to take in a deep breath, to calm myself down, but the air won't fill my lungs. The visions always leave me mentally exhausted and on an adrenaline high, all at once.

A tall form bursts through my bedroom door, stopping briefly before it carefully approaches me with its sword raised. I know it's not a threat, it's just my brother, trying to protect me from the unknown that haunts my dreams.

"Tristan," Zander whispers, lowering his weapon.

Pressing my back against a wall, I nod my understanding that it's him and not a ghost from my past.

He walks up to me, squatting down in front of me before he slowly exhales and pushes his hands through his dark hair. "You all right?" Zander asks, his gaze gliding over me, filled with worry. "Did you have another dream of her?"

Eyeballing me, he waits for me to say something, but I am still not fully present. The visions take me to another place. Another time. One where I am with her and only her.

At my lack of response, Zander snaps his fingers in front of my face, causing me to focus on him—in the now.

I stare at the dark circles that have settled under his eyes. He hasn't been sleeping—because of everything that has happened over the past few weeks.

Things haven't been easy for either one of us after losing Zander's father and my stepfather, Rionach—my mother Queen Ophelia's true love. The only father I knew.

Then I renounced the throne, handing it over to Zander to inherit—for Serena. Only to have her stolen from me, and my brother pleading for me to embrace my birthright.

My oath with Nox, coupled with my visceral reaction

to Serena's disappearance, isn't providing either of us a breather.

I squeeze my eyes closed and reopen them, before jerking back against the wall, needing it to anchor me at the reminder of it all. So much sadness and loss in a short time.

"Was it Serena?" he mutters.

Hearing her name on his lips makes me want to commit murder. It's both unwelcome and wanted simultaneously.

Where the fuck is she?

"I can't decipher if it was real or not," I struggle to speak.

I hate this feeling of being weak.

Loving her makes me both.

Weak and strong.

Love is meant to be freeing, but right now, I just feel trapped—as if I'm drowning and no one can save me.

Zander studies my face for another moment before his hand grips the back of my neck and he pulls me forward so he can speak quietly in my ear. "I've got this. I've got you, brother. I'm holding the life raft, just swim over to me."

Taking in a deep, cleansing breath, I dip my chin in acknowledgment of his words and desire to help me. He needs to think I am okay, so he'll stop worrying so much.

"You need to back off. I'm starting to think you like me as more than just friends. Or brothers," I attempt to joke.

It's fake, but he needs the lightness right now.

Relief floods Zander's face. "There you are, man."

A weak smile pulls my lips upward. "I'm here."

"Shit!" His eyes widen. "I need to call off my back-up."

My gaze narrows. "What?"

Magali enters the room holding a large bucket of water and my attention slides between her and my brother a few times. "Planning to douse me with water?" I accuse.

Zander smirks. "Ice water. It was a just-in-case."

I just stare at him, mouth agape, brows raised.

"What?" he shrugs. "Kenna suggested it."

Sighing, I lean my head back against the wall. "Of course she did." The adrenaline slowly ebbs from me, causing me to become tired as my body crashes. "I guess cold water is better than you trying to make out with me."

Magali moves gracefully across the dark room, using her gargoyle senses and heightened eyesight to navigate.

"Hey!" Zander points at me. "You leaned into me last night," he lowers his voice. "And we agreed never to speak of it. Yet, here you are, bringing it up in front of my girl."

Magali shakes her head and places the pail down so she can sign. "Satyrs or not; you're brothers. It's gross to joke."

"Not by blood." Zander argues, provoking her.

"Still . . . ew!" Her face pinches at the thought.

"He's just kidding. After my reaction to my dream last night, Zander offered his hand to help me up. I leaned in to take it and then he accused me of trying to take advantage and put the moves on him." I explain to her, irritated.

Magali looks Zander over before bursting into laughter.

"What?" Zander waves over himself. "I am damn good-looking. And hard to resist. You should know this, Mags."

She smiles and waves off his antics. "Idiot."

I can't help but watch the way he studies her. All the humor has left his face, replaced by pure obsession at the way her smile beams around us. A look I'm familiar with.

It's the one you get when you are completely in love with the other person smiling back at you. My brother is officially gone. In this moment, his mind, body, soul, and quite possibly his entire heart all belong to Magali.

Zander turns to me and offers a sly wink. And just like that, a small sliver of light peers through the dark chains that have a hold on my soul. With a slight shake of my head, I stand and he takes a step back, giving me needed space.

A heavy knock on the door has all our attention shifting to the intimidating gargoyle, dressed in all black, walking through it. Sea-green eyes search around the room.

Gage's gaze lands on me and something flashes in his expression, before it's gone and his stare turns vacant and cool.

His voice is firm as he announces, "We found her."

MY MUSCLES TENSE as we walk down the hallway to the private room she's in. I steal a glance at Gage. He's relaxed, smoking a cigarette. It's obvious he's ready for what we are all about to find behind the steel door we're approaching.

Right before I am about to burst into the chamber, a strong hand wraps around my shoulder, squeezing, causing me to stop and turn my focus to my left, toward Zander.

"You ready for this?" he asks.

"No," I growl out.

"Remain calm, Tristan. Whatever you do."

My eyes meet Magali's, and she offers an encouraging smile.

A quiet plea for me to keep my cool and a level head.

"I'll do my best," I manage through a tight jaw.

"Do better than that," Gage interjects, and kicks open the door with his foot. It slams against the wall, bouncing with a loud thud that vibrates through the concrete cell.

The minute I see her, rage consumes me.

"Holy shit," Zander blows out at my side.

Clenching my jaw, I look around the steel box of a room.

The London clan stands in a U-shaped formation behind her. Their steely gazes fix on me as I step into the space and squat down in front of the familiar woman tied to the chair.

My stomach clenches at the sight of her. Once, it brought me joy. Now, it only makes my blood run cold.

With every ounce of self-control I have, I gently push away the long, straight strands of black hair sticking to her damp face as I take in her bruised and mangled appearance.

I straighten my shoulders.

"Maria," I manage.

Her swollen eyes widen in shock when they meet mine.

"Tristan," she cries out, with a Hispanic accent.

I don't speak as I stare at the fae whom, over the years, I'd trusted with my home in the woodland realm. My housekeeper and, once, my friend. The fairy who joined me when I took over the Royal Protector Academy as chancellor.

The very same one who broke my trust by going behind my back and conspiring with my betrothed, Freya, scheming to kidnap Serena.

As I stare at her now, I recall how she brought me coffee that day, only to drug it and use it against the woman I love.

My love was handed over to a demon lord who wants her dead. The fae in front of me is the reason for it all.

"Nassa came across her hiding in Brazil," Gage states.

"How did you find out her location?" My voice is tight.

"The sorceresses of the Black Circle used a location spell. It wasn't working prior to now because she had a shield up, charmed by dark magic. Yesterday, the shield dissolved without her knowing it, leaving her vulnerable and leading Nassa and me to her," Gage explains, indifferent.

Black magic. As we thought, she had help hiding.

"Where the fuck is Serena?" I ask Maria in an even, steady tone, piercing the air around me with a cool finality.

My former trusted kin yanks her head away, falling silent. I stand taller, crossing my arms at her defiance.

Unspeaking, she stares at the cement floor; the light gray is stained with spots of crimson. The stains don't look fresh, but the state of her face leads me to believe otherwise.

"If you don't answer my questions, you will leave me no choice but to allow the royal protectors in this room to punish you for your treachery against their heir," I explain.

Slowly, Maria raises her head, locks eyes with me, and whispers. "At the Midnight Temple, in New York City."

"LIAR!" I shout, startling her. "We checked. She isn't there. As your future king, I demand to know where she is."

A cruel smile twists on what was once her pretty mouth.

"You denounced the throne; therefore, you are no longer slated to be my king," she draws out, exhausted.

I lean into her face. "Lucky for you, I don't hit women. But so, help me, if you don't start talking, I will cut your heart out with a fucking spoon. Try me. Go on. I dare you."

Watching me, she presses her lips before she speaks again. "I am under no obligation to you," she taunts.

Without warning, the handle of a dagger slices through the air and connects with Maria's jaw, causing a loud popping sound to echo around the chamber, followed by a cry of pain. Her eyes water as blood drips from her lips.

"You might not hit women, but I have no problem kicking her sorry ass," Eve states, now standing next to me.

All attention in the room, including mine, slides to her.

Eve shrugs. "What? I can't get a little rough?"

"You're super violent for a human," Zander points out.

"I taught her that," McKenna beams.

"That was fucking hot, siren." Asher smiles at his mate.

I turn back to Maria. "You've given me no choice here, and you know it," I threaten. "Your loyalty should have been to your realm. Your kin. The woodland queen and me. Instead you've chosen to betray and forsake it all, for what?"

"Freya was to be my queen. I stand by my allegiance," she mumbles through her broken jaw and the dripping blood.

I snap and yell, "Freya is dead! Your *queen* still reigns."

"Where is she, Maria?" Gage's cool voice asks.

"I'm telling the truth," she mutters, spitting blood everywhere. "I was there, with Serena in the club. I was sent with her when Asmodeus took her—to take care of her."

My eyes shift around, meeting the other protectors' confused expressions. "Asmodeus and the Diablo Fairies want her dead. Why would he bring you to look after her?"

"It was a condition of Freya's," she croaks out.

Freya hated Serena, because I love her. She would never think to have someone look over and protect her.

"We searched the club. Gage's partner, Nassa, was inside turning over every corner of that fucking building. And guess what? There was no sign of her. Explain that."

"She escaped," she whispers, and my heart stops.

Asher's wide-eyed expression meets mine.

"What the fuck did you say?" I lean toward her.

"She. Escaped. She isn't there," she manages to push out.

"If this is true, Serena is probably still in New York," Asher interrupts. "I'll call Marcus; he's the leader of the Manhattan clan of gargoyles. He might be able to help."

"We'll go with you." Callan's voice is void of emotion.

I nod my head in understanding, and the St. Michaels all march out like warriors. As they do, my eyes meet Magali's and I motion with my chin for her to go with them.

In response, she narrows her eyes at me, letting me know she isn't interested in my directions, nor is she planning to listen to me.

I know where things are going to lead with Maria and I don't want Serena's best friend here to witness it. I'd never forgive myself if Magali was a part of the end result. Or saw what I am truly capable of doing when pushed too far.

After a brief standoff and a dramatic foot stomp, Magali sighs heavily and reluctantly gives in, following Serena's clan, leaving Zander, Gage, and me to finish this.

"How?" Gage demands.

Maria's head lolls to the side.

"How did she escape?" he repeats.

With the last bit of strength she has, she lifts her head.

"Maria?" I prompt.

A single tear runs over her dislocated chin. Her eyes challenge. And I know that whatever else she knows, she isn't sharing with us, but instead will be taking to her grave.

I flex my hand into a fist.

Gage's hand appears in front of me, holding the lighter.

My eyes hold Maria's terrified stare as I push away the guilt of what I am about to do. Normally, I would show kindness and mercy before ending a satyr life. Not this time.

It's been too long since Serena was taken from me.

At Maria's and Freya's hands.

The ache in my chest grows.

I take the lighter from Gage.

Without hesitation, I flip open the top and show Maria the flame. Fear crosses her expression. I stand taller and toss the lighter onto her, without bestowing her the grace of killing her before burning her to death. My revenge.

Hair, clothing, and ropes all catch quickly. The flames spread fast, silencing her screams. The sound of the metal lighter hitting the cement is the last sound I hear as I turn and walk out with Gage and Zander as we let the flames climb and consume her. How's that for fucking mercy.

The darkness that has been slowly killing me and the anger eating away at my soul—they ease for the briefest of moments, granting me peace for the first time in weeks.

Gage steps in front of me, catching my eye. "When we are wronged, we tend to justify the choices we make. But justifying those choices doesn't make our actions right. It just makes it seem right. In the event your satyr empathy is rising, Tristan, remind yourself that gargoyle justice was served," he states. "An eye for an eye. The protector creed."

I don't respond. Death and revenge are nothing new.

Zander shuts the chamber door.

The sound of it closing is the most gut-wrenching sound in existence, sealing another chapter of my past and securing another part of my future.

4

DARK KNIGHT

TRISTAN

The feeling of relief I felt hours ago, after ending Maria's existence, left me as quickly as it appeared. I lick my bottom lip as I try to stand to my full height, while I focus on breathing in, instead of pain. In and out. Easy and steady.

The sharp, fiery pain I am now feeling—courtesy of Kenna's knee meeting my lower region—is causing my vision to swim and making me light-headed.

"By the grace, Kenna," Abby scowls at her cousin.

"What?" Kenna snips back.

Abby's eyes grow soft as she looks at me, her focus on my crotch. "I would like to have grandchildren someday."

Kenna snorts. "Well, then, you'd better get used to disappointment. Not only does he fight like a woodland fairy, but he has no balls. And this is a *training* session."

"I have balls," I croak out. "They're just in my throat."

Kenna swings her daggers in the air, pointing them at me—again. "I'd be happy to dislodge them for you . . ."

Abby's shoulders square as she narrows her baby blues at me. The look is one Serena used to give me when she was pissed off at something I'd done. It's unnerving to see it.

"Didn't you train our protectors at the Academy?" Kenna taunts. "No wonder they are afraid of the dark army."

"The gargoyles at the Academy are prepared for battle. Just as my woodland army is," I argue. "They're capable."

"You need to fight like a protector," Abby points out. "Not like a woodland prince. There's a big difference. Especially when faced with demigods and demon lords."

Grunting, I push my shoulders back and stand taller.

"What my cousin is saying is stop fighting like a fucking fairy," Kenna adds, and I clench my jaw so as not to attack her.

"Tristan looks pained. Why?" Asher watches me from the doorway with a mixture of amusement and curiosity.

Seeing my discomfort, his mouth moves into a barely-there smile; it's hard to tell if it's sympathetic or mocking.

"I'm fine," I grumble.

"His balls need time to redescend," Kenna announces.

After a few beats of silence, Asher casually stalks into the room. With a tilt of his head, he motions to the ladies to leave. There is an uneasy silence that settles around the training room before anybody moves. When they finally do, Kenna bumps into my shoulder as she walks past me toward the door. I don't react, receiving her cold eyes as she exits.

"You'd be wise to protect your assets around female gargoyles. They take pride in targeting them," he suggests.

"Speaking from experience, Your Highness?"

His smile widens. This time I am certain he is mocking me. "I'm still recovering from my last sparring round."

I drag my hand along the line of my jaw, watching him.

At the motion, any smile left on his face slides away.

"I've spoken with Marcus. He has intel. You and Zander will leave tonight for New York City—to meet with him."

"Wait, what about Asmodeus? A delay in dealing with him before he and the Diablo Fairies attack the Academy again is a grave mistake and error in judgment," I argue.

"Maria's mention of my niece's alleged escape changes everything. You will bring her home first. Marcus has information which might prove to be helpful," he reasons.

"I'm not su—," I start, but Asher cuts me off.

"This clan prefers Serena be under our roof and protection before we put an end to Asmodeus," he states.

"Callan made it clear that his *clan* would bring Serena back. Not me." My tone is cool, confident, as I hold his gaze.

"My brother suffers from low blood sugar and says stupid shit because of it. As your king, my word is final. *You* will go and retrieve my niece. That is how I want it. Yeah?"

"Why?"

Asher takes a few steps until he's invading my personal space, lowering his voice. "Because it is you that loves her. And because you are the one who lost her. Therefore, it will be you retrieving her," he explains. "We on the same page?"

"What if I can't?"

"Can't? Or won't?"

"What if I'm done? With her. With the protectors."

Asher frowns. "You know, I've known Gage for a long time. Before he turned into this—being who simply exists. And you—you carry not only his blood but also his fuck-the-world attitude. You are a lot like him, Tristan—whether you care to acknowledge that fact or not. Both of you act like you don't give a shit about anything or anyone. The truth of the matter is, you're just as haunted as he is. Your thirst for revenge just as unquenched. Your loyalty and love run deeper than most. The death of Camilla broke Gage. Those of us who love and honor his friend-ship allow him to lash out. To be distant. To hurt. And to push us away. We accept this in Gage because we were unable to stop the brutal way his love was taken from him. But understand this: the London clan will NOT make that same mistake with you. We don't turn our back on family. No matter how much of a pain in the ass they turn out to be. Being Gage's blood, and Serena's love, makes you a part of this clan. Like it or not. It doesn't matter that she is gone, or that Gage has not claimed you. He came to us and vowed, on his honor, that you would protect our bloodline. In our world, honor is everything. It's binding. Like your link to her. There is no *done*, here, Tristan. You are bonded to her."

I look away. "Our bond is broken."

"Bullshit!" he shouts, forcing my gaze to meet his again. "You're an asshole for thinking that. You aren't listening." His index finger points straight at my heart, digging into it. "You know where she is. Listen to the deepest part of your soul. She calls to you. Your heart and mind know."

"And if she doesn't want to be found? By me. Or you?"

Asher tips his head sideways, studying me from a new angle. "You think I haven't been where you are? That Eve didn't want not to be *found* once or twice? That she never ran, or hid because she was fucking terrified of what we are? Or what we had to face in order to be together?"

I feel the urge to respond, but don't.

"I know exactly what you are feeling right now. Which is why you—and you alone—will go find Serena and bring her back to her family. Because when you love someone as deeply as we do, there is no price you wouldn't pay. Prove to us all what kind of prince and royal protector you are."

A spark of anger fires through me. "And if I don't?"

He leans into my face. "Then you both cease to exist."

I hold his gaze and dip my chin in understanding.

"Now, if you will excuse me," he backs away. "Callan has been baking all afternoon and there are some dark chocolate chunk cookies with my name on them," he wiggles his brows before walking toward the doorway. Right before he's about to exit, he taps the frame with his hand and looks over his shoulder. "Oh, and Tristan. A word of advice—don't eat the oatmeal raisin cookies."

My brows pinch. "Why not?"

"Callan bakes when he's upset, and while making that batch he kept mumbling under his breath about what a shithead you are. I think he may have taken to your new nickname and laced the dough with a laxative," he explains.

My eyes widen. "This clan is insane."

Asher gives me a cocky smirk, as if this amuses him.

"We love dirty. And fight dirty. Welcome to the family."

I GLARE AT MY REFLECTION, staring back at me from the tinted window. A light blanket of rain has crept over the vibrant city, making the place seem eerie as it blurs the vivid lights.

Zander drives us into the underground garage of the Ansonia Building, on the Upper West Side of New York City. Once we're parked, I throw a questioning glance at him. He replies by nodding his readiness, and both of us open the car doors and exit the SUV.

We walk through a set of glass doors, which opens into a glamorous lower lobby. The guy behind the desk greets us and after we sign in, he motions toward a black-and-white-tiled corridor, leading to the posh elevator, which we take up to the penthouse. Seconds later, the elevator dings, alerting us of our arrival, and the doors glide open.

Zander and I step out into a modern entryway. Our boots are heavy on the hardwood floors. An oversized gilded mirror faces us from behind a wooden table. It's showy. Just like the entire entryway and building—overdone and insanely ornate to the point of being gaudy.

My face pinches at the flamboyance of the entrance.

"Not your design taste?" The question is posed with a slight Roman inflection from the vampire approaching us.

Neither Zander nor I respond to the bloodsucker.

He pushes his wavy, neck-length hair out of his gray eyes, taking us in before his focus slides to the mirror. "No. I wouldn't think it would be. The woodland bloodline in you prefers something—rustic. Am I right, satyr prince?"

"That title no longer represents who I am," I reply.

My statement snaps his attention to me.

"We're here to see Marcus," I state, bored.

"I know why you are here," he responds, facing us.

"Apologies, gentlemen. You'll have to forgive Stephan's inquisitive nature. He tends to be overprotective of those he loves." An African American gargoyle approaches us.

"You must be Marcus?" Zander interjects.

"That I am. Leader of the Manhattan gargoyles.

This," he looks over at the vampire, "is Stephan, my mate. Welcome to our home," his voice is smooth.

"Pleasure," Zander dips his chin respectfully to both.

Marcus's chocolate gaze studies me. Like he's waiting to see what I'll do next. Behind the warm twinkle in his eyes, my empath abilities pick up that he's hiding something. I remain stoic as he assesses me. I'm not here for pleasantries.

A small smile crosses the gargoyle leader's mouth when he sees I won't be respectfully greeting him or Stephan.

"You are here about Serena?" The gargoyle leader asks.

"We are," I confirm.

"Aren't you going to *invite* us in?" Zander asks Stephan, chuckling at his own joke. "See what I did there, vampire?"

Stephan tilts his head. "My, my. How clever you are."

Zander smiles brightly. "The ladies certainly think so."

"Lucky for them then, that you exist," Stephan retorts.

"That *is* what I keep saying," Zander admonishes.

"Join us, please." Marcus motions toward the large open living space adorned with high ceilings.

Each wall is full of glass doors opening to terraces that grant perfect views of the New York City skyline. It's open and bright. All around us, beings are laughing and talking. Their gestures are big and loud as they carry plates of food and glasses filled with crimson liquid and wine into the room.

The moment we step into the filled space, all talking

and laughter stops. At the stillness, I straighten my shoulders and glare harshly through each and every individual watching us.

Zander's hand grips my shoulder. "Easy, brother."

Marcus's guests literally part like the Red Sea as we follow him and Stephan through the lavish apartment. As we pass, some beings dip their chins respectfully, while others nervously look away. A few curse under their breaths at our mere disgraceful presence.

Zander and I are, after all, satyrs. Regardless of my protector, or royal, blood. Our race is considered inferior among the supernatural worlds and beings living in it.

Once we are in what appears to be an office, Marcus shuts the door and the room falls silent as we all settle in.

"Did we interrupt a celebration?" I ask, not caring.

Marcus lifts his chin toward the door. "This? No. We throw these extravagant gatherings once a month to show support for the supernatural community here in New York. It's our way of keeping communication and information flowing between the races. A ruse for intel, if you will."

"Seems like a lot of effort," I reply.

"And yet, as you will soon see, it works," Stephan says.

Marcus watches me with a strange curiosity. His gaze is unnerving, too knowing and focused on me for my liking.

"What is it that you know about Serena?" I question.

"Right to the point, sans pleasantries," Marcus replies.

"I don't have the luxury of time for pleasantries."

"You are angry that you are here?" he surmises.

"I should be at the Midnight Temple, asking the demon lord what the fuck he knows. Yet, here I am."

"You'd be wasting your time with Asmodeus."

"And why is that, Marcus?"

With a heavy stare directed at me, he pauses before speaking. "Asher said the clan has proof that leads you to believe Serena was being held at the Midnight Temple," he recounts. "And then, it was suggested the princess escaped."

"We have confirmation she is no longer there," Zander steps in and answers on my behalf, sensing my irritation.

"An escape from the demon lord is an impossible feat."

In my peripheral vision, Stephan twitches at Marcus's statement. It is the slightest movement, but the nervous tremble doesn't go unnoticed by me. I make a mental note.

"Serena is often underestimated," I reply.

Surprise crosses Marcus's face. "Is she now?"

"She is one of the best royal protectors in existence."

"Is that so?"

"Yes. That is so."

"So, then, you love her?"

My entire body seizes, curious as to why Marcus is asking.

"It's a simple question. Do you love Serena? Does she own your soul? Your heart?" Marcus pins me with a look.

"We are here at the request of the London clan, to retrieve the gargoyle princess. That's it," I lie, not trusting him. "You would do well to respect me and not pry further."

"Whom do you think you are fooling?" Stephan asks.

"I beg your pardon, vampire?"

"I can smell her blood running through your veins, gargoyle. Even your satyr line can't mask it," he snarls.

"Ah," Marcus smirks. "You are her bonded protector."

"And intended," Stephan adds.

I press my lips together and narrow my eyes before speaking.

"I am. Both."

"And yet, you've lost her."

"I did."

"And now, you want her back."

"I do."

"The question is, why?" Marcus's attention glides over me. "You have a haunted look and dark circles beneath your eyes. Your lips are pressed into a hard line, silently daring anyone to question or attack you. When you walk into a room, it's as if you own the entire world. As if everyone automatically becomes lesser than you—a satyr. You reek of royalty, and yet, the darkness in you is overwhelming."

"I am not here for a therapy session or to be analyzed."

"Neither am I. If you wish to be my future queen's dark knight, then I need to make sure you are here for the right reasons. We protect our own. Even *from* our own," he says.

51

"Are you suggesting that I lost her on purpose?"

Zander shifts to stand slightly in front of me, ready to step in.

"Did you?"

"No. I fucking didn't."

Marcus shrugs. "Then you are a shitty protector. How am I supposed to trust that if we help you locate Serena, you will safeguard her this time? Let me be clear— Asmodeus and the Diablo Fairies are not beings to fuck around with. The St. Michaels know this, and yet, they trusted their blood and legacy to you. A Gallagher. One that is half satyr," he adds. "You have been nothing but reckless with Serena's trust and heart. She has my loyalty and protection. Even if I need to protect her from someone who claims to love her."

His words strike me with such resentment that the only reaction I am capable of is anger. "Keep speaking to me like this, and I will cut your tongue out with my sword. Serena is mine! Mine to protect. Mine to love. Mine to speak of."

"Tristan." My name is a warning from Zander.

Something red flashes in Stephan's eyes, but Marcus holds his palm up, preventing his mate from doing what-ever it was he was planning to try to do to me. Of course, they'd be fiercely protective, but this seems like something more.

I step closer and lower my tone to a cool but vicious one. "While I appreciate the loyalty you are showing to your *future* queen, have some fucking respect for the royal protector standing in front of you. I am her intended."

"Are you claiming her?" Marcus asks.

"That's a little personal, dude," Zander throws out.

"I am. Have. And always will. She. Is. Mine."

Marcus tilts his head, his eyes slowly inspecting me from head to toe. His face a mask of complete indifference. After a moment, his shoulders relax and he bows slightly toward me. "Apologies for my behavior. I had to be sure."

"Be sure of what?" I roar, annoyed with his games.

"That you truly will keep her safe. Even from her own."

Though my emotions are in overdrive, I attempt to keep calm, realizing Marcus was testing my loyalty to Serena and to the gargoyle line. Something I respect as a prince.

"Is she in danger from the protector race?" Zander asks.

The room falls quiet, but the air is electric, like someone opened the door and let mountains of tension seep in, as everyone awaits my next words.

Dipping my chin, I exhale slowly. "Even from her own."

Marcus's expression morphs into one of relief.

I glare to my right, but Stephan keeps his face impassive.

Marcus holds his hands up in surrender. "It is true.

Serena did manage to escape her captivity from Asmodeus."

My head snaps to attention. "How do you know that?"

He shoves his hands in his front pockets. "Stephan and I found her. After she had just run away from the Midnight Temple. The vampire underworld got word to us that the gargoyle princess was stumbling around Central Park—lost and . . . highly medicated. The vampires picked up on her royal protector bloodline and alerted us of her location."

"Hence the party," Zander says under his breath.

"Intel. It's the only way to maintain control and protect the city and the humans residing in it," Marcus replies.

"Where the hell is she now?" I step closer, anxious.

"I don't know."

"You guys . . . *lost* her?" Zander questions, shocked.

Marcus and Stephan both throw my brother a look, as if to say, "Are you two really questioning whether *we* lost her?"

"When we found her, she was sitting under a tree; her legs were scraped and bleeding. She had a cut lip, broken ribs, and bruises all over her body." He winces and I cringe at his description. "Her blood reeked of drugs. There was so much in her system, she should have ceased to exist."

I take in a sharp breath. "Why didn't she heal herself?"

"She couldn't. The drugs prevented her from doing so."

"Fuck." I swallow back the fear in my throat.

"That's why you can't feel her, Tristan. Whatever was, or is, in her system blocked the bond," Zander deducts.

"Is she okay?" I demand.

"When we last saw Serena, she was here in our home. Safe and healing in a stone state sleep," Stephan answers.

"Why didn't you share any of this with Asher when he called?" I growl out. "Her clan has a right to know."

Marcus hangs his head. "Stephan and I needed to get the drugs out of Serena's blood so that we could put her into the deep sleep so she could heal herself." He throws an apologetic look to his mate before returning his focus to me. "The only way to do that was to drain her blood, cleansing it of the drugs, and then replenish it during the sleep."

"What the fu—" I twist and take a step in the vampire's direction, but Zander steps in front of me, holding me back.

"Easy, Tristan," Zander coos.

"You fucking bit her!" I shout at Stephan.

"He had no choice," Marcus steps in. "Let me explain."

"Let you explain why your leech of a mate bit mine?"

"Keep calling me names, and I will bite her again just for the hell of it," Stephan threatens in a calm, cool tone.

"You son of a bitch," I push closer, but Zander holds me.

"Enough! Both of you." Marcus pulls my attention to

him. "In the park, we injected Serena with a heavy sedative."

I inhale through my nose. "Why?"

"We knew she'd fight us. She was set on getting back to you, Tristan, and we needed her to cooperate in order to protect her. Her physical health was bad, and time was of the essence," Marcus rushes. "We brought her here, and, yes . . . Stephan bit her and pulled enough of the tainted blood out of her system to let her to begin to heal. She didn't feel it, and she wasn't aware of the bite thanks to the sedative."

"The St. Michaels need to know this," Zander argues.

Stephan moans. "As second in command to Lord Valentin, leader of the vampire world, I am not permitted to bite another supernatural creature without their permission. Let alone a royal heir—under any circumstances. Even this. The act is punishable by death."

"My friendship with the London clan won't save my mate if they found out what he did," Marcus points out.

I look at Zander for help figuring this all out.

"You let her almost bleed out?" he accuses. His eyes drip black as they pierce Stephan. "You could have killed her!"

"I didn't. I just released enough blood to allow her to heal," Stephan answers quickly. Confident. "On my honor."

His vow gets through and we all take calming breaths. After a moment, Zander grants them a cocky grin, no doubt counting the seconds until we can punch in their faces.

"So, she just healed and walked out of the place. What if she was recaptured?" Zander challenges.

"She didn't walk out," Stephan scoffs.

"Then how did she leave if she was still healing?" I ask.

"According to our source, Serena teleported out of the room Asmodeus held her in," Marcus answers. "That's how she managed to escape. The security cameras we have here in the house confirmed she did the same while still in a stone state sleep, after she healed for a few days."

"Teleported?" I parrot, confused. "Serena can't teleport. I can, but she—" I stop myself as realization dawns on me.

"Holy shit!" Zander releases.

"I could teleport, but when she disappeared, my ability did as well." I meet my brother's gaze. "She pulled my gift."

Zander's eyes widen. "The link isn't dulling. It's strengthening. Which means your dreams aren't visions, they're quite possibly Serena reaching out for help through your bond," he points out in one long breath.

"She's dream walking to you?" Marcus probes.

"I don't know what that is," I drop my tone.

"It's something protectors can do. We can enter another's mind and manifest in some form in a dream to communicate with each other. Whoever initiates the dream can pull the other being into it by manipulating it and the link," Marcus explains. "So you are there with them."

"That's why it feels so real, because it is," I whisper.

Zander stretches his neck from side to side. "She's trying to let you know where she is, so you will find her."

My face pinches in irritation that I didn't know this before today.

Marcus lowers his voice. "You should try to recall some of the elements from your dreams of her, Tristan. They could be clues to where she is."

At the suggestion, I shoot him an annoyed glare.

The leader of the Manhattan clan rolls his eyes in response. "She'd go somewhere safe. Or somewhere only you and she would know about. It's how protectors think."

Forcing myself to ignore the way he's schooling me on the protector race, I try to recall the dreams. Water, a warm breeze, and dragonflies cross my memory and then it hits me, like a quick punch in the gut. *Holy shit.*

I know exactly where Serena is.

5

BIRD IN A CAGE

SERENA

The wind rises as I stare out into the dark abyss. Liquid silver eyes glimmer at me from the shadows. "Your fate has found you," they whisper. "You must decide. It is time."

Without warning, they disappear, leaving me frozen and unable to take my eyes off the spot where they were staring at me through the dimness of the dark forest. I want to collapse under the pressure, the weight, the fear. I don't.

The scent of fresh rain and moss, mixed with pine and decaying wet leaves, rises from the damp earth, jolting me to move forward. I stumble amongst the tangled roots, as a gentle wind sweeps through the trees, until I see the rock.

Climbing onto it, I sit and press my back against the rough bark of the tree behind it, while attempting to clear my mind. To detach myself from the world and just be still.

To heal.

After a while, I sense the air around me shifting. The breeze picks up, carrying with it the scents of spice and citrus. The combination paralyzes me. I close my eyes and press myself further into the tree, trying to disappear into it.

The sound of heavy boots approaching has me panicked, causing the wind to swirl and become more aggressive all around the forest. As an elemental gargoyle, my emotional state affects the weather. And right now, chaos is about to ensue. My hands fist in my lap and my pulse picks up.

"Stop," I beg in a quiet plea.

The boots stop moving toward me. They listened.

Which means he isn't a figment of my imagination.

He's real. And here.

"Is it really you?" I whisper.

I don't open my eyes.

I don't want to see his face.

The minute I do, all I've been fighting for will be lost.

Everything about him makes me lose sight of what's important. What's best for me. And, right now, he isn't it.

Yet, every fiber of my being wants to run to him.

"Serena." My name is barely audible.

The desperation in his voice slays me, and my heart makes the decision for me as my lids slowly flutter open.

The pained expression that crosses his face is terrifying.

We look at each other for several seconds, unmoving.

I can see Tristan's internal struggle, the desire to grant me space mixed with the need to snatch me up in his arms. With a long shallow exhale that is full of nerves and fear, I watch as he tilts his head and points at himself.

"I'm here, raindrop," he announces, his voice cracking.

My eyes dart around the forest, trying to decipher if this is real, or another one of the many visions of him I have conjured up. Moments later, they land back on Tristan.

I study his expression, which is full of trepidation.

His gaze falls from mine, slowly grazing over and taking in every piece of me, until his attention is back on my eyes. And my heart goes haywire at the way he's looking at me—with a deep sense of relief and peace, mixed with promises and love. All lined with fear.

"Hey," he whispers.

At the sound of his voice again, the fog holding my mind and body hostage lifts and clears a bit, showing me reality.

"Hey," I croak out.

Tristan's entire body sags in relief at my reply.

"Are you really here?" My voice breaks with emotion.

He brightens, as if I just gifted him the world, while his eyes fill with tears. "It took me a while, but yeah, I'm here."

The tension grows between us.

Our gazes never deviate from each other.

My focus remains solely on him, and his on me.

I don't move.

I simply sit and wait for my mind and heart to catch up.

Tristan takes one measured step closer to me and stops.

The smaller distance he's put between us causes the walls of my chest to feel as if they're closing in on my heart.

"You ran," he says matter-of-factly, without judgment.

"I had no choice. Asmodeus would have killed me."

"I know."

"I once had a professor at the Royal Protector Academy," I explain, since it's him I'm speaking of. "He taught me that if I was not able to use my powers, and if hand-to-hand or weapon combat wasn't an option, the only way to not get myself killed right away would be to run."

Tristan swallows, taking me in, and I relax a bit.

"So, I ran."

His beautiful face softens as my words sink in and his stare bores into mine, trying to see inside me. "This *former* professor of yours . . . he sounds fucking brilliant."

I shrug. "Rumor has it he slept with his students."

"Only one. And if memory serves me, we never slept."

My lips part and I stare at him while we recount our history. His cognac eyes are filled with unspoken emotions as he looks at me. Without warning, I feel a tear trail down my cheek at the familiarity and normalcy of our banter.

It's real.

He's real.

Tristan's jaw twitches as he initiates our game. He takes

one more slow, predatory stride toward me. And then stops.

"What are you doing?" I whisper my line.

"Approaching you." His tone is low, lulling.

This time, he doesn't keep advancing as he usually does.

I frown. "Why did you stop?"

"This time, it's your move, raindrop." He waits.

His words rattle me. He's letting me decide. Every time before, he's chosen for us. To be mine. Now, it's my choice.

Run away from him.

Or run to him.

"I want you to be free," I plead. "To have peace."

"You are my peace."

"I stayed away to protect you," I explain.

"From what?"

"I had hoped you'd return to the woodland realm. To reign over your people. Asmodeus and the Diablo Fairies are not your problem, Tristan. They're mine. I need to shield you from the darkness they bring—I bring—to you."

"I don't need your protection."

"Yes, you do," I state.

"No, Serena. I don't. You forget, I have an entire army at my disposal, the Lion Guard. And Zander to lead them."

"They're not enough to defeat Asmodeus."

"I also happen to be a kick-ass gargoyle."

"You're arrogant; you know that, right?"

"I am very aware of my accomplishments, raindrop."

The desire to run to him physically hurts me. But the expression he's giving me, it makes me want to kill him.

"Don't look at me like that. I don't need your pity."

"I wasn't offering it."

"Your expression says differently."

"It's nice to see you so focused on my good looks."

"I'd forgotten how annoying you are. And how emotionally draining it is to breathe the same air as you."

"Most beings find me charming and irresistible."

My eyes remain locked with his. "I'm not most beings."

"No. You're not." His tone is final.

I'm afraid to move. Afraid to breathe. Afraid he will change his mind. I need Tristan, like the air that I breathe, but I also needed to give him the option of walking away.

He doesn't.

He's still here.

"So, this is it?" I ask, pointing between us.

"This is it."

"You and me?"

"Until the world implodes and we cease to exist."

"How romantic."

"I warned you, I'm not a romantic kind of guy."

"No? What kind of guy are you?"

"The kind that would light the world on fucking fire to find you. The kind that would renounce the throne, his kin, his family and his very soul to be with you. The kind that would take his last breath protecting your existence."

At his words, my heart slams into my chest. "Do I look like I need your protection?"

Tristan tilts his head. "It would seem that since I renounced the throne, I no longer have an army. So, truth be told, it's me who is in need of safeguarding, raindrop. And I want to live a long time, so I need the best protector in existence—that would be you."

With a measured pause, I flatten my palms on the rock and slide off it. On a quick exhale, I force myself to take a step toward him, knowing what it means—I choose him.

Tristan's jaw tightens, his face conveying a mixture of emotions. None of which I can decipher, but all of which are overwhelming, causing me to just stand in front of him.

Guilt gnaws at my chest. I never should have stayed away from him. I should have gone back to him, as soon as I was healed and able to do so. My heart sinks even further.

Tristan's focus is locked on me. My knees buckle as a pained expression forms on his features when I don't move.

His eyes close. "Again," he pleads quietly.

Without thinking, I take another slow step toward him.

"Again," he mouths.

The beat of my heart against my chest increases with each second that ticks by before I take another measured step in his direction. Toward safety and love. Toward home.

"Again," he breaks.

I close the last bit of distance between us, pushing into

his space. My shallow breaths fall across his lips. With his eyes still closed, he senses me and tilts his chin toward me.

Changing our roles in this ongoing game of ours, I gently grab *his* waist this time and tug *him* to me, lining up our bodies as my fingers dig into *his* sides.

"Caught you," I mutter, and he sucks in a sharp breath.

Without opening his eyes, Tristan lifts his hands and runs the backside over my cheeks. The cool metal of his rings sets off warm sensations throughout me, as they always do. When his long lashes flutter and his lids lift, his eyes are hooded as he stares deeply into my gaze.

Never in my life have I wanted to feel something as badly as I want to feel his lips on mine. One of his hands moves to my chest, the beat of my heart pounding violently under his palm.

And I relish his touch.

Slowly, Tristan slides his hand upward, until it's at the base of my throat. I watch intently as the empath in him reads my emotions.

He moves closer, pressing his body tighter to mine. The overwhelming need in each of us to see if the other is real has completely taken over both our senses.

I don't think about the invisible lines that we are crossing. I no longer care for them. All I care about is that he's here, with me. Forever.

"I love you," I say shakily across his lips.

With one hand still wrapped around my throat, he tilts

his face closer to mine. With the fingers on his other hand he grazes my jaw, slipping that hand behind my neck.

His palm conforms perfectly to the back of my head, as if it was made to hold me like this. He pulls me toward him and I willingly go, understanding now he's really here.

My fingers dig tighter into his waist. The desire to crawl inside of him and live there, to be safely protected, claws at me. His breath falls in waves against my lips and his forehead falls to mine.

A deep rumble is released from his chest.

"By the fucking grace, don't ever disappear on me again, raindrop." His voice is full of emotion as he presses into me.

"I won't."

Desperately needing relief, I lean into his lips, but he pulls away the slightest amount. Frustrated, I narrow my eyes and move toward him again, but this time he tightens his grip on my throat and head, holding me away from him.

"I love you, Serena St. Michael. With every breath that I take. *You* have become my only reason for existing. Don't ever leave me to exist alone again, because if you do, I won't fucking survive it. I won't. Do you understand?"

"I swear to you."

"Always fight for us."

"Always." I search his eyes.

Tristan smiles and it makes my chest ache with a

familiar warmth. His mouth connects with mine and something in me breaks completely, becoming his entirely.

My soul lifts. It's as if every pent-up, denied feeling I've had over the course of these past few weeks is suddenly released.

Finally, I'm no longer trapped like a bird in a cage.

6

I FOUND YOU

TRISTAN

Serena's hands wrap around me, her hold unforgiving. As if I'm anchoring her, keeping her grounded. My grip tightens against the back of her head, pulling her closer, knowing she needs it. Maybe even more than I do. For the first time in weeks, I'm finally at peace. I found her.

My lips close over hers, over and over again, and with each stroke, our kisses become more desperate. Her hands slide up my back, and my hands slip down to her waist, then over the curve of her ass, lifting her up. She wraps her legs around me as our kiss escalates, becoming more need-filled.

I walk us over to the rock and without removing my lips from hers, lower her onto it. Nothing in my life has ever made me feel as good, yet ache as much as the way I feel about her. She releases a small gasp and I inhale it.

After a few more kisses, my brain takes over. I tear my mouth away from hers. Both of us gasp for breath as the desperate grip she has on me keeps me locked against her.

Refusing to let our mouths reconnect, I am torn between wanting to take her right here and waiting until we've had time to talk over what has, and will happen, with us.

"We can't do this here," I force out, dropping my forehead to hers and closing my eyes, basking in her scent.

Exhaling rapidly, she doesn't attempt to kiss me again. I can feel her energy shift from want to confusion.

"I just found you and I'm certainly not going to take you here. In the open. Where you first met Freya. After all she's done," I pant out and open my eyes, wishing I hadn't.

At the mention of the water princess, Serena frowns and slowly releases the grip she had on me. Her eyes glass over, and the fog I'd seen in her expression earlier has returned.

"Hey," I say in a firm tone. "Stay with me," I demand.

Her eyes shut tightly. A single tear crawls down her cheek as she covers her mouth with her hand and tries to scramble away from me. I cage her in, not letting her go anywhere. I drop my mouth to the side of her head and press my lips against her ear. "I'm here. I've got you. You're safe."

Seconds later she takes in a deep breath and nods, letting me know she is okay and ready to face what is ahead.

In one fluid motion, I lift her up, turn us around and sit on the rock with her on my lap. I push the auburn hair out of her face and wipe away the remnants of the tear, while searching her gaze, which is back to being focused on me.

"The brown flecks in your eyes are deeper now."

"Are they?" she replies, quietly.

I prevent myself from growling and screaming "*mine*" when I see the color of my eyes invade the blue of her clan's. When a female gargoyle is mated or bonded, she takes on the eye color of her protector, and fuck if I don't like my hues swirling through her irises. She owns me.

Swallowing, I hold her gaze. "It's how I knew that Freya had glamoured herself to look like you. It's how I knew that she wasn't you, raindrop. My color wasn't in her stare."

Her eyes narrow. "What?"

Christ. I forgot she doesn't know everything.

"What are you talking about?" she probes.

My gut twists and turns before I give in and talk. "I'm not sure how much you remember, but Maria and Freya were working together against us. This entire time. You were right," I hold her gaze. "Maria wasn't to be trusted."

Her eyes turn into dangerous slits. "No shit?"

I can't help but smile at the sarcasm. It's nice to hear.

"Freya befriended Maria long ago and over the years the two became the best of friends. In an effort to get you out of the way, Maria drugged the coffee you drank the day you disappeared. When you passed out, they had Freya take your place, glamoured to look like you. After a bit, Zander and I realized that Freya wasn't you and took care of it."

"She used our own tactic against us?" she snarls. "I swear to all that is holy, when I see her, my daggers will be the last thing she feels. Both her and Maria," she vows.

The fire is back in her eyes and I relax, knowing my girl is slowly returning to me. I reach for her and untangle some leaves from her hair before leaning forward and kissing her on the top of her head. "She's dead," I say in a smooth tone.

Serena stares at the leaf I flick to the ground. "What?"

"Freya is dead. So is Maria. Both by my hand."

Out of the corner of my eye, I catch her eyebrow raise. "Tristan, you shouldn—," I cut her off.

"It's done. No more talk of it."

"But Queen Ophelia and the woodland rea—,"

Leaning forward, I rub my nose in her hair. "I'm half gargoyle. We believe in, and enforce, an eye for an eye."

She sighs softly. "You are also a satyr prince."

"Which is why I'm so good at giving you orgasms."

A slow burn appears on her cheeks.

At the sight of her blush, I focus on just breathing.

My throat constricts, my lungs seize, and my heart soars because it hits me hard that I love this intelligent, attractive, vulnerable warrior. With everything I am. And I will destroy anyone or anything that tries to hurt her.

"You want to talk about it? Are you okay?" I ask, the meaning behind my words heavy as I prepare myself.

I need to know what Asmodeus did to her in captivity.

She looks sideways at the forest. "I will be. I promise."

"Tell me what you remember," I encourage.

"I woke up in a dark room, with broken ribs and a cut lip, heavily drugged. Before that, everything is a blank. After, I just remember trying to escape—to get back to you. But . . . I was so tired, Tristan, and I couldn't heal myself. I kept stumbling and tripping. I managed to get out of the building and into a park, surrounded by trees. Then, Marcus and Stephan found me," she trails off, watching me.

"How did you get out?" I ask, already knowing.

"I teleported."

The idea that she pulled my gift evokes a powerful reaction inside me, pride. I dip my head and remain quiet, so as not to freak her out even more as she confirms what I knew.

"I don't know how I did it, but I did it three times at the Midnight Temple and once in Marcus's home," she whispers.

I watch her play with her protector bracelet. It's a habitual gesture of hers, signaling she is trying to ground herself.

"Say something," she pleads, quietly.

"Like what?"

"Like . . . you're pissed I stole your protector ability. Or

73

you feel angry that even though we share the protector bond and Sun of Vergina prophecy link, you don't want to be forced into a forever with me. And now, with me taking on your eye color and gifts it's happening. Just, say something. Anything."

"Forced in——," I laugh under my breath. "I'll say this, raindrop, it's apparent that you have excellent taste. Your newfound gift just goes to show that you are attracted to someone with strong survival skills, intelligence, and most important, physical prowess," I reply with a wink.

I think I hear Serena snort-laugh, but it's faint.

"You're mocking me," she protests.

"I am. Now, let's talk about why you chose this forest, of all places, to hide out in. The one spot on campus that Freya brought you to when you first met her." I state.

"What makes you think I was hiding?"

I study her. She holds my eyes and looks away.

"I know you. Better than I know myself," I point out.

"I needed to heal. I was under the assumption that the Academy was the safest place to do that, but . . ."

"But what?"

"This place on campus drew me to it. I can't explain it."

"Maybe you chose it because it was the one place that you knew I would find and save you from, as I attempted to do before," I offer, reminding her of my failed attempt to save her when she came here with Freya that first time.

"Do I give you the impression I'm a damsel in distress,

or in need of saving?" She repeats the line from our first encounter here.

"Never. But you are scared and recoiling."

"Asmodeus wants to end my existence. He declared revenge on my family and the protector race. He wants to destroy the Royal Protector Academy and all it stands for."

"I'm aware."

"I thought—think—maybe it's best if I stay away."

"There'll still be war and bloodshed," I counter. "It's all semantics. If you continue to stay away, Asmodeus will attack the Royal Protector Academy and the gargoyle race. With or without your presence. This threat is not aimed entirely at you. You are a target, but not the whole."

"How can we possibly stand against ancient evil like Asmodeus and the Diablo Fairies and win . . ." she trails off.

"By doing so together. As one. Aequus," I remind her.

The forest around us is silent except for the light hum of the vernal purple dragonflies flittering through the night's dark sky.

"For what it's worth, I'm sorry, Tristan."

"What exactly are you sorry for, raindrop?"

"Bringing war to your realm's borders and spilling satyr blood. Destroying the possibility of peace with the water realm. Rionach's death. Being the reason that you denounced the throne. The pain," she mutters. "All of it."

"There is nothing for you to be sorry for."

She looks down. "I feel like . . ."

"Like what?"

"One way or another, I'm always breaking your heart."

My heart freezes in my chest and I stare at the woman I love, sitting in front of me. Taking her in, I remember why I've done what I have. Why I woke up today with fae blood on my hands. For her. I do this all to keep her safe. To make sure that she has an existence even after all this shit is over.

"No," I say quietly. "Just the opposite."

She reaches up and traces the outline of my jaw. "I need you to give me something I need more than air right now."

"Anything." I twirl a piece of her hair around my finger.

"Reassurance. Never leave my side again."

I watch the pulse beat at the base of her neck. Her life. And with as much courage as I can muster up, I lie to her.

"I promise."

7

THE RETURN

SERENA

I grip the broken piece of wood in my hands, allowing each finger to push into it as I get my breathing under control. Looking around, I take in the mass destruction, wondering what the hell happened to my bedroom here at the Royal Protector Academy, in the suite Magali and I share.

Lamps are shattered. My bed and furniture look like they got into a clawed fight with a wild animal—and lost.

Everything is ripped and shredded to pieces. I frown.

Tristan's appearance in the doorway has me turning around and staring at him. His ability to make me feel both comforted and terrified all in the same mind-numbing breath is unnerving. For so long, all I wanted was for him to see and accept all of me, overcome our pasts, and power through whatever our families have planned for our future.

Right now, in this moment, all I want is to be invisible to him, because the look on his face will haunt me forever.

Anguish.

The lines around his hollow eyes are so much more pronounced than I'd realized earlier. He looks exhausted.

He doesn't look carefree anymore—he just looks pissed.

"I, uh," he draws out. "I had a bad reaction to your disappearance," he explains in a detached voice. "Sorry."

My lips part. "You did this?"

He looks directly at me. "With my bare hands."

I take a second glance around in disbelief before throwing the piece of wood down on the pile of rubbish that used to be my bedroom. "It looks like a tornado leveled it."

"A tornado did." He pauses. "Me."

Every word he says causes me to feel numb.

Tristan's gaze becomes distant. "It had been absolute torture. Not knowing where you were, if you were alive or not," his voice is hoarse. "If you were coming back to me. I couldn't feel or reach you. Then you started dream walking to me, and the visions were so real. I didn't know at the time that they were. I simply interpreted them as unattainable desires."

My eyes meet his again, and guilt rushes up my throat.

"I wasn't lying to you, raindrop, when I said if you didn't come back, it would destroy me. It almost did. Almost."

At his confession, I panic.

Without warning, I'm suddenly in the bathroom.

Confused, I look around and pinch my brows, wondering how the hell I materialized in here. Then it hits me—I teleport now when my emotions become heightened. *Crap.*

I really need to learn how to control it. Or figure out how to give Tristan his gift back. *By the grace.*

After a few seconds, I lock myself in—unable to face Tristan anymore. I just need . . . a moment.

Staring at my reflection in the mirror, I exhale.

I stole his gift of teleportation. This is what I meant when I said that I feared I'd always break his heart. No matter what I do, or how good my intent is, the cost of being with me is too much for him to pay.

I turn on the shower to tune out the sounds of my own thoughts. Weeks. I've been gone weeks. And he's suffered.

Tristan pounds on the door. "Open the door, Serena!"

"I just need . . . a second," I yell.

"Serena," he growls, and pounds against the door again. "Open the damn door. We need to talk."

I shiver and watch the steam from the hot water cover the mirror. I'm a mess. Within seconds, Tristan's boot kicks through the doorway, making a huge hole in the door.

Splinters of white wood fly everywhere.

His hand pushes through the opening and he unlocks the door, slamming it open. With a smirk, he lets himself in the bathroom, gently closing the broken door behind him.

"Sorry. I can't teleport anymore," he says offhandedly. "Add a new door to the list of things I'll replace," he adds.

I spin to face him and stumble back against the sink.

"A door replacement would be great, since this one no longer offers any sort of privacy," I mumble, and try to appear unaffected by his magnetism.

"Raindrop." Tristan's eyes zero in on my face.

"What?" My voice sounds breathy.

"Don't run out on me. Ever." He says in a tense voice. "If you're pissed about the mess—," he continues, but I interject.

"I could give two fucks about the furniture, Tristan. It's just . . . stuff," I shout, annoyed that he's focused on that.

"Then what?" he growls back.

"I hurt you," I whisper. "And . . . I keep hurting you."

Tristan shortens the distance between us, pushing into me and bracing his arms on either side of me on the counter.

His scent mixes in with the heavy steam that has settled around the room. My knees weaken at the smell.

The hole in the door is not allowing enough of the heavy mist to escape and give me a chance to breathe.

Tristan's mocking eyes crinkle at the edges in a smug expression. "I'm not hurt. I was just terrified of losing you."

"Your mother was right; love makes you weak. We shouldn't be allowed to love one another. Neither of us can afford that luxury. The price is too high for both of us."

"To be with you, I'll pay any cost."

"Tri—"

"Love is our fate. And we are going to embrace it and fight for it. For each other. As one. Do you understand me?"

"But—," I attempt, but he shakes his head no.

"We have a dark army, led by a demon lord, coming after not only you, but our kin. You can't throw a shit fit every time you get upset. I am fine. You are here now. I went batshit crazy when you went missing. But you're here. You're safe. With me. You don't have to run from me."

"I ran because you taught me to," I argue.

"To stay alive, yes. From me, because you think I am better off without you, no. In the future, I can't be worried about you disappearing again because you think you are protecting me. Especially when I'm the one who is supposed to protect you. This back and forth ends tonight."

I lift my chin as tears clog my throat. "Fine."

"Good."

"But . . ."

His lips part. "But what?"

"We protect each other. As equals, aequus."

"Agreed." His tone is overly pleasant.

My eyes narrow into slits. "That was too easy."

Tristan grants me a polite smile. "I am a satyr and as such, I have been accused of being a lot of things over the years. *Too easy* is not one of them."

"Being a satyr isn't as bad as you make it seem, Tristan."

He winces. "You're right. It's far worse."

"Thank you for letting me protect you." I answer without thinking, immediately regretting it and wanting to take it back. There are probably many things I should be saying, but thanking him for letting me protect him is not one of those things.

"No thanks are needed, raindrop. You are a well-trained royal protector. Aside from Zander, you're the only one I trust my existence with. Then there is the business of you being able to teleport and me not being able to anymore. So if I need a quick getaway, you are it. Therefore, I think that you should stick close by and never, ever leave my side."

I laugh with a bitter edge.

"That funny?" His breath falls across my lips.

"A little."

"One more thing."

"What?"

He moans. "You smell good."

"Are you trying to distract me with compliments?"

"You're mine to compliment whenever I want to."

"Again, with this archaic declaration?"

"Archaic or not. You. Are. Mine. To protect. To love. It's you and me. That is nonnegotiable. So, if you're getting grandiose ideas of walking away, in the name of saving me from something that you think you are causing, but you aren't, I'd rethink your strategy. Aside from my heart and soul, you have my eye color and my gift of teleporting. That makes you mine, raindrop. The. Fucking. End."

Frustration rumbles in my chest as I stare at him.

"Fine," I reply. "I think I can handle being *yours*."

A playful gleam crosses his expression. "You can't."

I open my mouth to argue but he cuts me off, leaning closer, bringing his lips toward me until his mouth brushes mine with the lightest of touches.

"One more thing." His breath tickles my lips.

I lose my ability to breathe. "Anything."

"You should shower."

"Why?"

"We leave in an hour."

"We aren't staying here?" I ask.

"No."

"Why not?"

"For one," he eyes twinkle. "Your bed sucks. It's like sleeping on broken pieces of wood. And second, this place is a mess and, sadly, I no longer employ a housekeeper."

"Very funny."

"I can be."

"I'll continue to wait for you to prove it."

A muscle flexes across Tristan's jaw as his cognac eyes bore into me. "Why don't you want to go home?"

"If we go back, they won't ever let me leave again."

Tristan frowns. "Your family is worried about you. I promised them I would return you after I found you."

"Then unpromise them, Tristan. I am not going back."

"You will. You are. Even if you hate me for it."

His expression is one of finality mixed with pain.

He interprets my silence as acceptance and gives me a jerky nod and walks back to the door. Tristan's hand hovers over the handle briefly. "And Serena. When we do return, it's as mine. Not theirs. Not anymore." With a final sharp look back at me, he lets himself out of the bathroom.

I stare at the broken door and, with a relieved sigh, slide down the sink's side and collapse onto the tile.

That's it.

Tristan's words are meant to be final.

He makes it sound so easy.

As if all the ugliness of the world doesn't exist.

The ugliness that my clan vowed to protect me from.

Once I return, they will all blame Tristan for everything that has happened, which means they won't let us be together. No matter what he thinks or declares to me.

My fingertips run over the silver protector bracelet sitting on my left wrist. The gift from my aunt Eve is designed with intricate flowers and vines around the band.

Tilting my head, I study the details closer. Before this moment, I've never noticed the irony of it. My protector band was designed with elements from the woodland realm.

Flowers and vines.

Tristan's realm mixed with mine.

The realization suddenly fills me with determination.

I refuse to go down without a fight.

For myself.

For Tristan.

For my kin.

I resolve to finish what Asmodeus started.

Only this time, I'm going to end his existence and finally stop the Diablo Fairies' threats against the gargoyle race and the Royal Protector Academy.

And when I do, my clan will let me go.

Return to the life I want.

Return to Tristan.

8

THE REASON

TRISTAN

I half-expected Serena to follow me out of the bathroom with her daggers lifted and aimed at my back after my caveman declarations. Instead, she pads down the hallway and throws me a bright, easy smile. *Strange mood shift.*

As my gaze falls from hers, it hits me . . . it's not so strange. I blink rapidly and try to swallow. My body begins shaking with pure need and lust as she approaches me wrapped in nothing but a towel and messily styled hair.

She must have read the panic in my eyes, because she smiles even bigger as I stare at her like a lunatic. Like a man who has never seen a half-naked woman before in his life.

"Do you want to shower with me?" she asks, sweetly.

"What?" *Did my voice just become higher-pitched?*

"I'm assuming we have a plane to catch and that time is important. I want to be sure you have time to shower too."

"Plane?" I repeat automatically, and shut my eyes.

"To. London."

"London." I rub my face.

"We could save time, by showering together."

I take her in. She approaches me and climbs onto my lap.

"Now you want to go home?" I try to figure her out.

She shrugs casually. "Sure. Why not."

"Why not," I repeat, confused.

Her eyes glisten with secrets as she leans in and wraps her fingers around the leather necklace I wear, which has my insignia, the Sun of Vergina, dangling from it. "I'm yours. This makes you mine too," she pulls at the necklace.

I eye her, because I know she's up to something.

Serena tugs it, pulling my face closer to hers. "It also means I will protect you. Even if it's against my family."

I sigh against her mouth. "I'm going to need your protection when we return and your father sees me again."

Her face pinches as she leans back. "Again?"

"We have a lot to catch up on, raindrop."

Glaring at me, she tenses. "This sounds bad."

"It's not bad, it's just . . ." I exhale. "Don't freak out."

"You can't say don't freak out and expect me not to."

"I've been in London for the past few weeks."

"Okay." She says in a bland tone.

"With your family," I add, and her brows raise. "Zander suggested it. I wasn't exactly in a clear state of mind. We looked for you on our own, but we kept coming up empty-handed. That's when I sort of lost it—" She cuts me off with the narrowing of her eyes into tiny slits.

"Sort of?"

"That is when I lost it." I reword. "Better?"

"Better."

I watch her.

"You've been there this whole time? With my clan? In London?" she repeats. "My dad, and uncles. Aunt Kenna?"

I give her a curt nod and frown as she chews on her bottom lip, sucking it into her mouth only to release it.

"Zander, Magali, Gage, and Nassa stayed there as well."

Her eyes widen. "Is Mags okay?"

"She was a mess, but yeah. Zander watches over her."

After a few seconds, she nods. "Was my clan horrible?"

I bristle. "They weren't exactly happy to see me."

"It's not your fault."

"Not directly, but I should have been more aware. A mistake I won't make again when it comes to you. I swear."

"I didn't see Maria coming either. Or Freya for that matter. If the last few months have taught us anything, it's that we need to go into things with our eyes open," she says.

"Agreed."

"So . . ." she clears her throat. "Gage was there too?"

"Yeah. He, Nassa, and the Black Circle located Maria."

Serena's face falls. "I guess we'd better get back then. Before Aunt Kenna starts an all-out war with everyone."

"Too late for that," I mutter.

She pins me with a look. "My point."

"It will be fine. What's the worst that could happen?"

"Other than death?"

"Other than death."

"Stone petrifaction?"

"Nothing they haven't sentenced me with before."

"They could send you away—from me."

"We've done nothing wrong. The Vergina Sun prophecy has been fulfilled. Our link is strong. They no longer have authority over who or what we are fated to do."

"Stop being so calm about everything," she orders.

"Stop worrying about everything."

"Make me," she dares.

We meet each other's gaze as I lean forward, taking her lips. There are no niceties about my actions. No seduction. Just me doing exactly what she asked me to do—push her mind into oblivion as I kiss the shit out of her. Making her forget the last few weeks ever happened.

She moans when I pull her tighter and let my lips trail over her chin, down her throat. With a salacious look, I nip at the spot on her neck right above her pulse.

Anger runs through my veins as I recall that Stephan

bit her here. There are no marks. When she healed herself they disappeared, but nonetheless, it still pisses me the fuck off—knowing the bloodsucking vampire touched her.

Without thinking, I let my teeth bite into her flesh, followed by my tongue, and lips, bruising her. There is nothing gentle or loving about what I'm doing. It's hard and insistent as I suck and pull at her delicate skin. Marking it.

The harder I nip and draw her in, the breathier she becomes, sliding her fingers into my hair, tugging me closer to her. After forcefully drawing her skin in and out of my mouth over and over again, I run my tongue over the spot, soothing the red mark that has formed, while Serena writhes beneath my mouth.

After a few moments, I let my breath tickle the spot and groan in pleasure at her response to my violent desire to mark her. Pulling back, I take in the skin that is going to bruise and grin as I push her off my lap so she can stand.

"Let's go shower instead of worrying about things we can't control," I encourage.

She tightens her grip on my hand, squeezing my fingers to get my attention. "Thank you," she whispers.

My gaze falls onto her neck, where I've marked her. "If that impressed you, wait until you see my showering skills."

Serena rolls her eyes. "I meant, for finding me. For not giving up on us. For knowing that I needed you."

I grant her a cocky smirk and wink. "Haven't you

heard, raindrop? Being your savior is the reason I was created."

"Is that so?"

"That. Is so. Now, stop talking and let me show you the reason you were created," I attempt to seduce.

9

NO CHOICE

TRISTAN

"I swear I won't hesitate to put a fist in your jaw if you don't release her," I bark out at Zander, who has Serena in a tight hold from the front, with Magali wrapped around her back.

From the moment we stepped off the jet at Heathrow Airport, he and Mags have been suffocating her with attention.

"We need to go," I snap out, annoyed at my brother.

Ever since the two of them pretended to be together, in order for Serena to gain entry to my realm and stop my wedding, they've become close. Too close for my liking.

Magali steps away from her best friend and her nostrils flare at me before she kisses her middle finger and flashes it my way. A moment later she winks sweetly, turns to the driver, and slides into the luxury vehicle waiting for us.

"Let. Go. Of. Her," I order.

"No." The word is muffled because my brother's face is pressed into Serena's hair. "I thought we established she's my girl too."

My jaw clenches. "No. She fucking isn't."

Zander turns with Serena tucked into his chest and glares at me from over her head. "Just five more seconds. I've missed her flowery smell." He inhales her hair.

At the sight, I lose my shit.

Taking a step in his direction, I point at him. "Brother or not, I will kick your ass."

Zander leans toward her ear, whispering something that makes her laugh, and my heart stops . . . because I never thought I would be lucky enough to hear that sound again.

He pulls away from Serena and tilts his head. "Listen, champ," he says to her. "Tristan is making his constipated face again. We should probably stop flaunting our love."

"If you insist," Serena agrees, kissing him on the cheek.

My brother smiles down at her. "You remembered our agreement."

She dips her chin. "Cheek kissing only in front of Tristan."

"See, our love is still strong—better than ever."

Zander's playful gaze meets mine. "Are you just going to stand there staring, or are we leaving? I don't mind an audience. In fact, I tend to perform better when there's one."

Serena perks up and shakes her head. "Stop."

"What? It's true; ask Mags."

Magali sticks her head out of the car. "Ask me what?"

"Your boyfriend is incorrigible," Serena signs to her.

Magali rolls her eyes. "Don't I know it," she replies.

Zander smirks. "You used the wrong sign."

Serena frowns. "No, I didn't."

My brother's fingers lift and he signs, "damn sexy."

"That is not how you sign incorrigible," she corrects.

"No, it isn't. But what you meant to sign is, your boyfriend is damn sexy," Zander argues, walking toward the car. He takes Mags's lips and tumbles into the limo.

Serena turns and smiles at me. "Your brother is an ass."

"No shit," I mutter, pissed at their connection.

Her head tilts and she holds her hand out for me to take.

"You with me?"

I walk to her, grabbing her hand in mine. "Always."

At the feel of her, my anger disappears. I know it's childish and wrong, but I want to be the only one who has this connection with her. And while I love that Zander would take a bullet for her, it isn't his place. It's mine.

I lean forward and press my lips to hers briefly, before slowly backing away from her and guiding her into the car.

Before I can follow her into the car, Zander sticks his head out of the open door, stopping me from getting in.

"Hey, if anyone asks, I am totally telling them I gave Serena that hickey on her neck." He wiggles his brows.

There really is no other choice—I punch him in the jaw.

10

LOVE IS RARE

SERENA

Ever since Tristan stepped foot in the forest, I have been physically incapable of taking my eyes off him. When you are supernatural royalty, most relationships are formed based on wealth, power, protection, or prestige.

Love is rare.

It's just a harsh reality of the world I come from.

Gargoyles are different, though. We believe strongly in family, love, and protection. The three go hand in hand.

It's that belief system that has me praying my family will allow Tristan to stay—even after all that has happened—because I'm positive that my clan, especially my parents, blame him for my disappearance. He was my protector when I was taken, so in their eyes, he failed his assignment.

A wry curve appears on his lips when he catches me staring at him. When his gaze grows intense, I look away.

"We'll be in London shortly," the driver announces.

"Thank you," Tristan replies, using his regal voice.

The chauffeur closes the divider, giving us privacy, and Tristan winks in my direction. I shake my head at his flirtatious antics. While they are adorable, it's not the time or place.

Magali's foot taps mine to get my attention, when I look over, she motions at Zander, who is sulking. His posture is stiff as he looks out the window, no doubt nursing his bruised ego and jaw, where Tristan punched him.

I frown and throw a disappointed look at Tristan, who chuckles to himself just as a dark shadow passes over the car. With his brows pinched, Tristan leans closer to the window, looking up at the sky.

Curious as to what has pulled his focus, Magali and I both peek through the sunroof. Waves of black tint the gray clouds above us. The desperate sound of birds cawing back and forth between each other becomes thunderous, as their irritably loud conversation echoes around us.

I drop my gaze and look to my right out the window to see swarms of crows dipping in and out of one another. Thousands of the black birds are spinning through the sky in a tightly choreographed display. The dark lines make twisting patterns as they twirl in a calculated pattern, crossing one another and surrounding the car.

It would be beautiful if it weren't so terrifying.

"Shit!" Tristan leaps forward and stumbles to me.

"What is it?" I ask as he tackles me.

He knocks on the divider but the driver doesn't lower it. After a moment, Tristan looks over his shoulder, meeting Zander's tight expression. At the same time, the car speeds up and swerves at dangerous velocities. The force causes the four of us to tumble on top of one another in a corner of the back seat as the car begins to spin out of control.

With a guttural sound of impatience, Tristan pushes himself up and kicks the divider a few times before it breaks and we see the front seat is empty, void of our driver.

Fighting the force of the car's motion, Zander crawls over us, squeezing himself through the small space and into the front seat, so he can try to get control of the unrestrained limo.

"Serena," Tristan shouts. "Hold them back with wind."

Focusing my energy, I feel my fingertips begin to tingle and my protector vitality flowing freely through my veins. I strain as the currents lift and move, but then fall quickly.

My minimal attempt at conjuring the breezes isn't affecting the quantity of birds surrounding us. Frustrated, I try to calm myself as the winds disappear completely.

My panicked gaze meets Tristan's.

"Again," he commands. "You can do this."

I look up through the sunroof at the dark cloud of black circling the car. With a quick, angry flick of my wrist I once again attempt to coerce the currents to push them away. For a few moments, it works, and the black bands push back.

That's all Zander needs. He hits the brakes hard and the limo stops, but slides out of control before tumbling onto its side, and we roll. Tristan manages to cover me as we rotate several times before the car comes to a complete stop, upside down. The sound of glass shattering and crunching mixes with the angry screeching of metal bending around us.

With a hard exhale near my ear, Tristan pushes back and looks around wildly before his eyes meet mine.

"Are you okay?" Tristan yells.

Stunned, I remain quiet and motionless.

"SERENA!" he growls, yanking me out of my shock.

"I'm okay . . . I'm okay," I manage to reply.

Tristan blows out a long, relieved breath before sliding his attention to my left. "Magali, you all right?" he asks.

I drop my head to the side and see he grabbed us both, protecting us from the glass and metal twisted around us.

She nods and signs for Zander.

As if on cue, the door creaks open and Zander crawls in.

"Everyone okay? Mags!" he hollers, sounding scared.

"She's fine," I call out for her, since she can't vocalize.

"Fuck. I'm sorry," Zander huffs, grabbing Magali and pulling her to him. "I'm sorry, baby," he whispers to her.

"Zander!" I shout. "She's trying to sign to you that

she's okay." I bark at him because the bear-hug he has her in isn't allowing him to see her hands.

"The wind isn't going to hold them off much longer," I point out. "Can I teleport us out of here?" I ask Tristan.

"My gift only allows one, maybe two of us at a time— and that is with a lifetime of focused expertise. It's still too early for you to really control and manipulate my gift."

"Just . . . follow me," Zander orders, as he makes his way back out of the small opening from which he came.

On our hands and knees, we struggle out of the mangled mess and stumble into the open field. Once we've managed to get a few feet away from the smoking, upside-down, totaled vehicle, we all collapse and take a moment just to breathe, watching the black birds now circling us like prey.

"What the hell is that?" I ask.

"Crows. A shitload of them," Tristan replies.

"As always, your uncanny ability to state the obvious in these situations is utterly mind-blowing." I reply drily.

He chuckles. "I live to blow your mind, raindrop."

I drop my head to the side and catch his amused gaze.

"You're giving me sexy eyes," Tristan purrs.

I blow out a long breath. "I might want to kiss you. You know, for saving both Magali and me from being hurt."

"You're just in shock from the accident. Give it a minute. It'll wear off," Zander interjects himself in our moment.

"The female protector should learn to produce the

devil's wind." A deep baritone intones loudly. "It would have been a better protection for you against us."

At the sound of the rumble, the hairs on the back of my neck rise. With quick glances at one another, we push to our feet.

The crows are now circling the field above us in one large black ring, as a thin and forlorn fog crawls around our ankles, hanging on to the blades of jade grass.

The cloud of dust from the dirt road hasn't yet settled behind a sleek black car idling in the empty field in front of us. Two beings open the two rear doors and slide out, taking their places on either side of the voice's owner, the three watching us with calculating and curious gazes.

"Are we protected?" the lead guy asks, in the same deep baritone he used with his earlier comment about the wind.

"Yes, my lord. There are warriors in the woods," the female on the right answers. "Another handful watching the road. And more at various points within the sky and field."

I take a step toward the three, shaking off Tristan's hand as it snaps out, trying to grab hold of me to prevent me from moving closer to the unfamiliar beings speaking.

"Who are you?" I demand.

The leader tilts his head in my direction, silently assessing me—dressed in all black—like some sort of godlike knight. His battle armor is composed of onyx plates with layers of inky leather sitting underneath. Each graphite shield is artistically sculpted with snakes rising out of what appear to be leaved branches. The armor applied to his body protects his thighs, chest, shoulders, and forearms.

Immediately, I notice his height. He must be at least seven and a half feet tall. Long, soot-colored hair flows in the breeze, reminding me of the dark night. His bleached irises lock onto me, their color like silvery snow, matching that of the moon. The heated judgment in them causes me to shift, and my gargoyle wings to snap out of my back in both protection and warning.

Behind me, I hear the cracking sounds of Magali's and Tristan's wings as they release in warning to the warrior.

In my peripheral vision, Zander steps closer to Tristan's side. "I hate that I'm the only good guy without wings," he pouts. "Guess I'll just rely on my charming personality to get me out of this. Oh wait, I command an army. That's right. I can kick these guys' asses with my bare hands."

"Zander—," Tristan warns.

"And for the record, you *all* have wings. We could have kicked out the sunroof and you three could have flown out of the car, while I teleported," Zander points out.

"Point taken," Tristan mumbles.

"See that, Mags," Zander sings. "Brains and beauty. I am a total catch," he flirts. "Tempted to mate with me?"

My gaze slides to her, curious about her reaction to Zander's teasing. "I'm good," she signs and rolls her shoulders back, ready to take on the threat in front of us.

A throat being cleared forces our focus back to the

three beings watching us, unamused. Their gazes are powerful, like they crave and get off on supremacy and control.

A strong breeze swirls around us—a result of my over-active emotions—causing the warriors to look around.

"An elemental gargoyle. How simply . . . charming," the pretty Asian girl states, unimpressed, her tone mocking.

My attention snaps to hers, and when we lock eyes a cruel smile plays on her mouth, as if she's goading me.

"Elemental gargoyles are greatly underestimated," I retort, taking in her silvery leather clothing and sterling-silver armor plates, which have the same snake design.

The girl's eyes are also the exact bleached color as the leader's. Her elegant straight white hair is cut on angles, falling below her chin, highlighted with silvery-gray tones.

Above us, the circle of crows becomes loud again and their flapping is rapid as they fight to stay airborne against the currents I've conjured up. It tosses them around the sky.

"Tova, call the birds off. They're giving me a headache," a bald, Hispanic man says from the leader's other side.

His snake-designed, medieval armor and leather are bronze-colored. A cobra wraps around his head in black ink. It's tattooed on him to make it seem as if the reptile is slithering downward into the armor, toward his heart.

All three of these beings look like rogue knights. And yet, you can sense the regal authority coming off them, like vibrations. Regardless of their physical appearances, they're ancient, and hold dominion over something dark and big.

I stand taller under their gazes.

"I asked you a question. Who are you?" I repeat with a firm tone, focusing on the leader.

He motions to the woman. "Tova," he states, clipped.

My head tilts toward the bald guy. "And him?"

"Lael."

"And you are?"

"Noxus. Known to most as Nox."

Every hair along my neck pricks with fear as the muscles in my neck stiffen. I raise my chin, trying to remain calm and appear unflustered, unrattled—not an easy task.

Noxus is the god of night and the prince of death. He's known in my world as *the* demon hunter. To be in Nox's presence usually means the end of your existence.

From what I recall of my studies, he is the offspring of the demigoddess Ereshkigal and Lucifer. It's rumored the deity is the darkest-souled of all the demigods. With a fearsome reputation for seeking out and destroying high-level demons.

Legend has it that even Hell shivers in his presence. It's alleged that is how he got his name; he reigns over the darkness, as it fears only him.

"The look on your face, princess, is telling. I assume my reputation is well known among the protector race."

"Your name is both known and feared." My voice is steady, though inside I'm quivering with panic and dread.

"As it should be. I am not one to toy with," he replies.

"Noted," I manage, and Nox slides his gaze to Tristan.

"Fate has dire plans for you, satyr prince," Nox states.

"An interesting sentiment, since I have dire plans for fate," Tristan snarls back at him, stepping in front of me.

I shove away the unease at the familiar way the two are speaking to one another, and deepen my tone as I inquire as to why Nox is here. "Surely the demigods must have better things to do than to seek out gargoyles and satyrs, neither of which carry dark souls."

Nox's stern face pinches and his large muscled body slightly leans toward me, as if he is struggling to keep his composure, while at the same time overawe me. I stand tall, refusing to let him intimidate me. Demigod or not.

"I am the god of night. And a hunter of darkness, not a mere demigod," Nox counters gruffly, with an air of arrogance. "Show me respect, or I will show you your end."

"Do not threaten her," Tristan bites out.

"Do not protect her, satyr prince," the deity advises.

I step to Tristan's side, tired of their pissing match.

"Those of us who stand before you do not carry dark souls," I point out again. "Therefore, we have no business with one another. I suggest you and your minions leave."

A cruel smile seeps onto Nox's lips. "She doesn't know?"

"This should be fun," Zander sing-songs, as if excited.

"Know what?" I ask. "Tristan?" I prompt.

His attention is fixed on the three warriors. "Nox is here for me," Tristan hisses. "Your crows located my soul?"

"They did," Tova confirms.

"They almost killed us," Tristan barks at her in a low resonating voice filled with contempt and mockery.

Lael stretches his neck from side to side with a cool demeanor. "Your fairy brother almost killed you."

Zander steps forward in a threatening manner, but Magali jumps in front of him, pushing on his chest, stopping him. "Hey, asshole, one, I'm a satyr, not a fucking fairy. And two, I wouldn't have had to get control of the vehicle if our chauffeur didn't mysteriously disappear from the wheel."

"Your *driver* was a demon. He is no longer," Lael says.

"My crows are seekers, not murderers," Tova interjects, irritated with the obvious insult to the birds she controls.

"Seekers or not, it was not within your rights to send them to find me," Tristan clips out. "I would have come willingly at your request, had you politely asked it of me."

"Wait. What?" I grab Tristan's hand, forcing him to turn and face me. "What the hell is going on here?"

"I can answer that. Tristan's new *friends* killed our demon chauffeur to get his attention," Zander answers.

"A dark-souled demon," Tova corrects.

"Why are they here?" I ignore Zander, instead

directing my question at Tristan. "For you? And why would that be?"

He closes his eyes for a moment before reopening them and looking into my gaze. "I've decided to commission Nox's army to help us defeat Asmodeus and Kupuva."

My lips part, stunned into shock at his admission. Everything around me becomes silent, except the blood pounding in my ears as I absorb the meaning of his words.

After a few seconds, I come back to my senses. "We already have armies under us, Tristan. The Lion Guard and protector forces can handle the dark army," I argue, scared.

"Not like the Noctis army can."

"Tristan!"

"Stop," he growls back, frustrated with my debating.

"You stop this—whatever you've done. Stop it now."

He steps toward me, leaning over me. "The way to defeat an ancient demon lord is with a deity and an immortal army that hunt and destroy dark souls. It's the only way."

Heatedly, my eyes widen as the rationale behind his obstinacy sinks in. I step closer, lowering my voice. "You've already agreed to this? To work side by side with Nox?"

"Told you she was going to be pissed off," Zander mumbles next to us, causing me to shoot him a glare.

"You knew about this? You LET HIM do this?" I yell.

Zander holds up his palms in surrender. "I told him no."

I swing my attention back to Tristan. "Aside from being unpredictable, Nox has no concept of mercy. Only justice. *HIS* form of justice."

"His form of justice keeps you and the Academy safe."

"At what cost?" I grind out.

"The cost of your existence is insignificant."

"Tri—," I begin, but he cuts me off.

"If it were me, what price would you pay?" he challenges, pausing as he inhales. "What price to save me?"

Annoyingly, Tristan's argument numbs me into silence. He's right. I would do whatever it takes. Anything. Irritated that I don't have a point of contention anymore, I narrow my eyes at him before shifting my attention over his shoulder, locking it on the terrifying demigod behind him.

With less resolve, I try one more time. "Gargoyles do not need the help of dark demigods to protect us."

"Satyrs do," Tristan disputes. "This is the only way I can be sure you continue to exist, and not in fear of Asmodeus or the dark army, Serena," he hisses. "I need his help."

The panic and fear in his voice has me relenting. With a heavy sigh, I drop my shoulders and soften my voice. "If you do this, Tristan, you are making a deal with the devil."

He leans in. "To end evil, you need to fight with evil."

My gaze meets his and I hold his steely focus, realizing he isn't going to relent on this. Rather than continuing to bicker and attempt to win an argument, I clench my jaw.

"The woodland realm seeks Nox's help," he mutters. "For your safety, and that of both our realms," he adds.

Muscles tighten throughout my body at his statement. I may not have had the life experiences Tristan has, but my extensive education and knowledge about Nox is clear: a deal made with Nox seals your fate. And I vowed to protect Tristan, as he has me—unconditionally.

I growl out, "Since you are dead set on doing this—the gargoyles will swear an oath and allegiance to the Noctis army as well."

"No. Fucking. Way."

"Yes. Fucking. Way."

"Sere—"

"Shut up, Tristan!"

His eyes dilate with rage at my outburst.

"If you do this, it's with me by your side. Or not at all."

"It's too dangerous," he lowers his voice.

"My point exactly."

The corners of Tristan's mouth tip up, but it's hardly a smile. There is something truly menacing about his expression. "I'm not here to negotiate with you, raindrop."

"You aren't in a position not to," I debate.

"Is that so?"

"That. Is. So." I step closer and lower my voice. "While half your blood is satyr, the other half is gargoyle. Meaning I'm your future queen, and as a subject of mine, you will show respect for my authority and the political decisions I make on behalf of my kin, my clan, and my realm."

"You're pulling rank?" he asks, taken aback.

"You bet your sweet ass I am."

Tristan sighs, his eyes locked on mine. "You are——"

"Your savior," I finish for him.

"Fucking relentless and stubborn as hell."

"When it comes to you, yes. Without apology."

"Fine." There is a certain finality in the word.

"Do you really think my ass is sweet?" he smirks.

"I do."

After a moment, Tristan shifts his focus back to Nox.
The deity shakes his head no. "We had a deal."

"Which I will uphold," Tristan answers casually.

"The princess wasn't part of it," Nox adds, cryptically.

"She is now."

The air shifts. "You're forcing us to accept new terms, satyr prince. You do know what this means?" Nox bellows.

"I know."

"Then it is done."

"NOXUS!" Tova shouts.

"Silence," he barks at her, while lifting his chin. "We accept the new terms the satyr prince requires," the deity replies with a chill in his tone. "Conditionally," he adds.

Tristan crosses his arms over his chest and a low growl escapes his throat. "State the condition, Nox."

"You and the gargoyle princess will come to Kur."

"No."

"Then we have no deal."

Tristan simply stares at Nox.

"We are to return Serena to her clan," Zander steps in. "It was a vow, and if broken, it will upset political relations."

"That isn't our problem," Lael replies.

"It will be," Zander coughs under his breath.

I step forward and answer. "We will go with you."

Magali suddenly appears in my face, eyes narrowed.

"Are you mad?" Her fingers fly at me angrily.

"Consider this my something stupid for the day," I reply.

"Serena, this is not a game," she bickers.

"I know," I snap back.

"Kur is in the underworld," she points out.

"Then it should be warm," I quip, sighing when she doesn't laugh. "Don't make me command you to let me go."

Magali pushes her shoulders back and throws me her *fuck off* expression. It's a protector challenge. One that I now have to accept as her royal instead of her best friend.

"You leave me no choice."

"There is always a choice," she counters.

"Consider yourself assigned," I manage to push out, and wait, holding my breath, knowing she'll be pissed.

Her expression and fingers become still.

"Go to London and announce the Nox Treaty. Let the royal clan know that the protector race, along with the woodland realm, has declared its allegiance to the Noctis army and the god Noxus, by order of their princess."

Irritation creases Magali's brows. "Fuck you," she seethes.

"I am not asking," I bark out. "It's a royal order."

"I'm not going to be the one to tell your father and clan what shit you've stepped in now," her features soften.

"You will. Because you love me and want to protect me," I reply, hoping she will understand what I am asking of her.

Magali's eyes drop and her expression turns confused.

I step closer and lower my voice. "War is coming."

After a moment of staring at me, she sighs in defeat, because she knows those three words are true.

"You're a pain in the ass," she replies. "I swear to everything gargoyle if you don't return within ten days, I will hunt your scrawny ass down myself. Then kill you with my own two hands. Princess or not. Best friend or not."

"I expect nothing less," I whisper.

Tristan watches us, his look thunderous.

I fight the urge to cower under his glare because there are times when he appears scary fierce and warrior-like.

Just as a lion would.

"I'll go with Mags," Zander throws out.

"No. You will come with us." Tristan's voice is cold.

"Why?" I challenge. "Mags could use the protection."

"Zander is next in line to the woodland throne now. I need him, to allow for certain . . . realm politics and trade."

"It's fine," Magali signs, and offers Zander a sad smile.

He steps toward her, looking unhappy.

"I can take care of myself," she assures him.

Zander takes Magali's face in his palms. "Be safe, my love," he says dramatically, and she rolls her eyes, not falling for his attempt at charming her.

"I'm a gargoyle. I think I will be okay," she offers.

He dips his chin. "Okay. But, in my absence, remember my good looks and my charismatic personality. And also, my thick luxurious hair, which by the way, will never thin, just in case you are concerned for our future kids."

Magali's annoyed gaze slides to mine, clearly unamused with him, and I can't help but smile at the ridiculous, yet adorable, way he's sending her off.

"But most of all, don't ever forget my impressive girth."

Mags keeps a straight face, lifting her fingers as she smiles up at Zander through her lashes. "It would be a difficult task to forget all you've commanded since you've filled my phone with photos of yourself," she teases, before her wings expand and she disappears into the sky.

"You won't be gone long," Tristan points out to Zander.

"Tell that to my girl. For Magali, every moment away from me is pure torture. I mean," he smiles brightly. "Wouldn't you miss me every second if I was your man?"

"Mags seemed okay with leaving you," Tristan says.

"Get in," Lael motions to the black car.

Zander winks at me. "Well, champ, this should be a fun little adventure. I hope they have a duty-free store in Kur."

11

WAR OF HEARTS

TRISTAN

A war against demons and evil? Simple. It's not so easy when you're trying to win a war against the heart. My mind respects Serena as a royal protector. My heart though—her declaration of allegiance to the Noctis army, and Nox, shattered entire sections of my heart.

The damn gargoyle has no idea the lengths to which I have gone, or will go, to protect her. And within seconds, she's destroyed it all.

I avoid her heated gaze as we slide into the back seat of the car. She doesn't move, but her jaw clenches and the muscles twitch as if she is grinding her teeth together while shooting murderous looks at the side of my head.

Resisting the urge to look in Serena's blue eyes, I focus my attention on the field outside the window. Because I know that with one simple look, she will strip me down to the raw reality of who I am and what I've gotten us all into.

Tension falls around us as the car begins to surge forward. Zander moves his head back and forth between Serena and myself before rolling his eyes and dropping his head back onto the leather seat. "Never a dull moment."

To say that the ride to Kur is awkward is an understatement. Every few minutes, Serena glares in my direction. Huffs. Twirls her daggers and glares at me again.

After a few hours, Lael leans toward me. "Try to break our deal, satyr prince, and I won't hesitate to kill you. Ask me for favors and I'll do us both a favor and make your death look like an accident," he threatens me.

"Fuck off," I reply.

Lael snickers.

I send him a warning glare and shift my eyes to Serena.

She's pointing a dagger at him, while looking down the sheath with one eye closed. "Threaten him again, you piece of shit, and I will remove your eyeballs," she growls.

Lael laughs. "Got a girl fightin' your battles for you?"

"Nope. Not a girl." I glare at him. "A royal protector."

He frowns, not understanding my reply.

"Be careful. She'll make good on her threats, so I suggest you play nice with me," I warn him. "And her."

My gaze meets Serena's and she quickly looks away, hiding a smile as she stares outside the window. We pull up to the cavern's opening and a few seconds later, the car stops and our doors open. The fresh air gives us permission to slide out and take in a tensionless breath.

"Thank gods," Zander whispers under his breath.

Serena meets my gaze. "How do we do this?"

"Do what?" I look around in confusion.

"Get into Kur?"

I try to keep from laughing because she's being serious.

"We follow Nox into the cavern," I say, slowly.

"No. I mean, walk? Teleport? Fly?"

I stare blankly at her face and she mutters a curse.

"It's the underworld. I've never been. How am I supposed to act? Do I bow to Nox, or—"

"You're fine. Just act normal," I try to assure her.

"What's the holdup?" Tova barks out, waiting for us.

Serena's face falls.

"Trust me," I wink.

Zander snickers next to me. "Serena normal?"

"Hey, I can be normal."

"In what world, champ?"

Serena glares. "I won't hesitate to pull my dagg—"

I cover her mouth with my hand and smile tightly as I whisper. "Tova is waiting. Let's all calm down and move forward. You are fine. It's just another realm, Serena."

Narrowing her eyes, she pulls her head away from my hand. With a dark smirk, I grab her, lacing my fingers with hers and tugging her behind me toward the cavern opening.

Once we're all standing in front of the cave's dark entrance, Nox lifts his hand. *"Aperire portal,"* he whispers.

Serena snorts next to me.

"Problem?" Tova questions.

Serena scoffs. "Really? Open the door? In Latin?"

"So?" Lael prods.

Serena shrugs. "It was just . . . kind of anticlimactic."

The air in the entrance of the cavern shifts and begins to shimmer with a deep crimson color. Nox motions for us to follow and we walk through it. Once we're all on the other side, inside the underground cave, the deity closes the portal behind us and turns toward a stone wall.

"Ignis." At the command, fire torches come to life around us, providing both light and warmth.

Tova steps forward, handing Nox a staff with a snake on it. She lifts what appears to be a wand and begins to scribble ancient Latin on the cavern's stone wall. When she's done, she takes a step back, admiring her writing, and then nods to the god of night, who steps forward.

"Vitae," Noxus states, and the snake comes to life, slithering and hissing as it sways and stretches in the dark.

"What does the writing say?" Serena whispers to me.

"Zagros Mountains," Lael answers from behind us.

The snake snaps forward and its tongue rolls over the ancient lettering. With each stroke, the symbols begin to shimmer bright pink, flickering before turning a solid red.

When the words glow steadily, the stone falls away,

disappearing, giving way to a scene filled with a rocky mountain terrain rising above desert pastures.

Noxus motions for us to step through the opening toward the Paleozoic rock formation. Once we do, the snake turns back into a staff and the stone wall behind us returns and dissolves, leaving a large grassy pasture filled with animals behind it. The desert sun and hot air surround us.

"Welcome to Iran," Tova says as we follow her, making our way toward the limestone and shale formation.

"What is that?" Serena asks, pointing to the rocks.

"The Zagros Mountains. At the top is Mount Dena and the opening to Kur. We will teleport there," Tova answers.

"I can—" Serena begins, but I squeeze her hand, silencing her. I don't want them to know she holds my gift.

Tova chants, and within seconds we're all standing in front of another cavern entrance at the top of the mountain.

Serena breathes out. "That teleport was insanely fast."

"I know." Tova smirks, unfriendly.

"You'll have to teach me how to do that," Zander says.

"No." Tova's answer is clipped.

"Angry and beautiful," Zander mutters under his breath.

With a wave of Nox's hand, the entrance fills with the colors of the sunset—crimson, auburn, and butter hues.

Serena's lips part in awe as we all walk through the

final portal entrance. On the other side, we end up on a set of high limestone stairs, looking down at the city of Kur.

Within seconds, darkness falls behind us once again as the portal closes. The stairs behind us no longer provide an exit; now they disappear straight into a wall.

I meet Serena's worried expression and try to offer her a reassuring smile—something hard to do, given that the only way in and out of Kur is with Nox himself. But like a true warrior, Serena shakes off whatever nervous energy was flowing through her and masks her indifference.

The ancient city below us is lit in the same sunset hues as the portal opening. Nox leads, the rest of us following.

I watch as Serena's fingers run along the limestone wall as she takes the stairs. To our left is a steep drop into the darkness of the abyss. One wrong step, and the fall would be never-ending. Each stair is only wide enough for one person to walk down at a time, designed that way on purpose.

"Can't you teleport us down?" Zander teases Tova.

"Supernatural abilities and trickery do not work in Kur." Tova doesn't look back at us as she explains this point.

"Why not?" Serena questions, realizing that none of our gifts will work down here.

"Only the deities are powerful in Kur," Tova answers.

"Sounds egotistical," Serena mumbles, and I swear I hear a dark chuckle release from up front, coming from Nox.

We continue down the thousands of steps until we finally reach the last one, landing us at the entrance.

Kur is an archaic city, designed to look like Babylon, which was rumored to be the gateway of the gods.

This version, though, is a shadowy replica, ruled by the goddess Ereshkigal, queen of the Great Earth and underworld, a gift from Lucifer to her for all her loyalty, after his fall. As was Nox, who reigns over Kur, alongside his mother.

We step closer to the towering walls that guard the city and I admire its old-world beauty. Even if it's the underworld. Gold urns blazing with fire surround a stone pathway that wraps around the outside of the city. Tall, thin palm trees are placed in between each urn. I stare at the trees, curious as to how they grow here. As my gaze lifts, I notice that more fire-filled urns sit atop the tall city walls.

We're led to the entrance, a blue-tiled gate that has designs of snakes rising out of intricate branches and leaves.

"Is that the Ishtar Gate? The same as the one in Babylon named for the goddess of love and war?" Serena questions.

"A replica," Nox replies, running his fingers over the tiles. "Kur and the gate are both gifts to Ereshkigal from my father. But unlike the one in Babylon, instead of bulls and dragons decorating the stones, Kur's version has snakes rising out of leaved braches. The symbol you see on our armor and weapons."

Nox faces me. "This gift is a reminder that love and war go hand in hand. Isn't that right, satyr prince?"

I meet his steely gaze. "An age-old, ongoing battle."

"Even in Kur," he adds.

I dip my chin, understanding his meaning.

The deity moves in front of us, taking on a god-like stance. "We shall enter the city, where I reign. You will respect Kur's rules. You will respect me. And you will respect Ereshkigal. I will bring you to my palace, as my honored guests. We will rest and eat. Then we will discuss this war of hearts we are to embark on and my army."

I find it poignant the original Ishtar Gate had dragons on it. Ironically, the reconstructed one in Babylon now has lions. Dragons and lions. Serena's and my clans' symbols.

My eyes glide over to her and I remind myself of why we are here . . . the arrangement I've made with Nox.

The deal that will end my existence.

And secure hers.

12

THE DARKNESS

SERENA

I see the split-second shift of Tristan's eyes as they glance across the courtyard toward me. After a moment, he returns his focus to the book he is reading. It's obvious he doesn't want me to approach him, or know what is going on in his head, because it would only shed light on the fact that he's done something I won't approve of and I'll try to stop him.

He hasn't spoken a word to me since we got to Kur a few hours ago. A smile teases at my lips because the brooding warrior is *reading* as a form of evasion. I leave him be. It's obvious he needs time to think and process. As do I.

I drop my gaze to his hands, staring at the rings encircling his middle fingers. Right now, an eternity separates his hand from mine. I frown, missing the warmth that radiates from his fingertips when he touches me. The warmth I feel in the deepest parts of my core. His touch is always a reminder that we are meant to be together. A team.

Crossing my arms, I take in the ancient walls of the city that surrounds us. Hours ago, Tova showed us to our regal quarters and stepped out while we got settled. Apparently, we are free to roam as we please, since there is only one way into the city and one way out—and both require Nox.

The faux sky appears as if the sun is trying to break through the dawn, but since we're inside a mountain, I can only assume the breaking dawn is a façade, done with demigod magic to appear as if the sun is rising, cresting over the tall buildings adorned with gold urns of fire, one in each corner. Archaic drawings are etched onto the ancient tiles decorating the stone walls.

As I walk through the courtyard, I take in the taller-than-life columns rising to absurd heights from the ground. Each is etched with the snake symbol that seems to be prevalent everywhere Nox is. The columns are surrounded at their bases by lush tropical vegetation and wild desert flowers.

A pool of crystal blue water sits in the middle of everything, with a tall fountain proudly stretching from it, designed as a snake circling the base of a tree. *More snakes.*

Single, lean palm trees are scattered around the city, reaching for the sky, shadowed by temples and buildings. In a strange way, it's beautiful. Reminiscent of a time long gone. A cross between ancient Egypt and Greece.

"The reptile surrounding the apple tree symbolizes the tree of knowledge of good and evil. The courtyard was made in the likeness of the Garden of Eden," Nox points out, having suddenly materialized out of nowhere.

Adrenaline begins to fill my veins as he steps to my side. Nox's looks and reputation are intimidating enough, but as I stand next to his large frame, he seems even more godlike.

"The god of night has a *thing* for symbolism?" I reply with a sarcastic edge to my voice.

Nox shakes his head no. "The fall of humanity."

My fear of him gives way to irritation. One more demigod jealous of humans' free will. "The fall of humanity," I repeat on a sigh. "Are you saying you're another deity fixated on the humans' ability to exhibit free will? To choose if they want to live in a state of constant obedience, or exert their right to design their own fate?"

He studies me in a way that has me feeling transparent. "I forget the gargoyles protect human souls and artifacts, absolutely and without question. Your unwavering loyalty to humans will be your kin's downfall."

His words aren't cruel, more matter-of-fact.

"You make us sound like warriors who are mere pawns."

"Aren't you?" he challenges.

"Pawns? No."

"Soldiers—of an ancient war that is not yours to fight?"

I bristle at his rhetoric, because it's true. Even now. My thumb seeks out the Celtic tattoo on my left wrist. The symbol that binds me to the Spiritual Assembly of Protectors and allows me to accept divine assignments.

Nox follows the action, his expression knowing.

"We all are," he whispers.

I chance a glance at Tristan.

He's watching Nox and me with interest. He doesn't move, just studies us. No doubt listening to our conversation with his heightened gargoyle hearing.

"Even you?" I pose.

"Even me," Nox dips his chin.

"And how would the god of night be a mere soldier?"

"The gods and goddesses created me and bestowed upon me the gift of never-ending darkness. To them, I am Nox—a night hunter. Hired to seek out the darkest of souls and end their existence. It's a way the deities control the balance in the game they oversee between Heaven and Hell. So yes, young one, the fall of humanity is interesting to me. The idea that one is able to control one's own fate—decide one's own destiny is a fascination of mine. Is it not yours? Do you not wish to control your own fate? Away from the Sun of Vergina prophecy, or the London clan's legacy?"

With my attention still on Tristan, I remain quiet, because controlling my own destiny is all I've ever wanted.

I pinch my brows, realizing that even the deities' existences are not their own, which makes me wonder, what makes Tristan and me think our fate will ever be truly ours?

"What's with all the snakes?" I change the subject.

"The serpent is a reminder."

"Of?"

"That which has been forbidden to us."

"Interesting that you've chosen a reptile which is known for cunning and deception to represent Kur," I speak with conviction. "I suppose it makes sense that the dark-souled deities in Kur would worship a spineless animal."

"Immortals deceive too; not just dark souls."

"Some."

"Most. Dark souls simply deceive outright."

"And the others you speak of?"

"The others do it in the way of artful and clever deceptions, like the archangel Michael. Your satyr prince tells me that the angel got a human pregnant. A no-no in the eyes of the council. One that required deceit."

My heart sinks, knowing where Nox is going with this. In order to protect his daughter, my aunt Eve, the archangel Michael made a deal with the Angelic Council and gargoyles. A treaty which, later on, he had to solidify by promising Asmodeus my life, in order to ensure his daughter's safety. To save face, Michael bound Tristan to protect me from the very demon he sacrificed me to.

"That is not deceit; that is love in the form of protection. I doubt too many would object to that form of deception."

"Unless you are one of the two hearts forced to be bound together for eternity." Nox turns to me, to meet his towering gaze. "Perhaps you need another example, such as the same archangel making a deal with the demon lord Asmodeus, promising him an innocent child in exchange for the life of his own blood, all the while threatening a mother with her secrets if she didn't agree to a protection bonding. At least Queen Ophelia had the good sense to go to the deities—to Helios—for guidance and help."

I remain silent.

His recounting of what happened is all true.

Nox steps in front of me, looking around. "Deception in the name of love, or protection, does not deserve justification. Yet, all beings do it. The gargoyle race carelessly places its trust in the divine, while turning a blind eye to the other, darker, fragment of its bloodline."

There is nothing light or pleasant in the way his words come out. In fact, his expression is razor sharp, almost accusatory. The statement hangs in the air between us for a moment before his eyes align with mine.

I lift my chin. "The divine created gargoyles to protect mankind against evil," I point out. "Our protection spirit is tethered to the dragon. Our bloodline is divine at its core."

Nox eyes me, considering my words. "The dragon was

sent by the dark army to attack a man of God. It was Lucifer's way of setting off another war, which means the dragon carried darkness in its veins and soul when it tethered itself to the divine soul. The dark-souled dragon is a symbol which your clan proudly wears and worships. Is it not?"

"You're twisting our history to serve whatever purpose or point it is you seek to make," I bite out, annoyed.

"Do you know why gargoyles do not carry a soul?"

I hold my breath.

"If you did, it would be dark because of the dragon. And that Celtic tattoo that you so adorably rub for strength is the angelic army's way of keeping you protected, so the darkness doesn't take over your bloodline," his tone sharp.

Tristan's gaze finds mine again. I know he heard what Nox said. Tristan's satyr bloodline grants him a soul, a divine one. One of light. Whereas mine would be dark.

Holding Tristan's eyes, I whisper. "Why are we here?"

The question is meant for Tristan, but asked of Nox.

"Your satyr prince commissioned a favor," Nox states.

"Which is?" I query, my focus remains on Tristan.

The book he was reading is now forgotten, closed and placed beside him. He focuses his attention on the demigod and me with an expression that is full of annoyance.

"To extinguish Asmodeus and Kupuva."

"And the Diablo Fairies?"

"They will be reborn as soldiers in my Noctis army."

"What was the cost for this contracted favor?"

Tristan stands and takes a measured step toward me, at the same time his features turn thunderous. He shakes his head at me, letting me know he doesn't want me to push. At his heated reaction, my stomach roils and my heart pounds.

"There is divinity in the satyr's lineage. But it is you who fights as if the blood of the golden gates runs through your veins. I don't blame you, princess. I blame the upper world for brainwashing you into believing that your race is more important than it is. Yet, you do serve a purpose."

My eyes snap to Nox. "Which is?"

"Your existence is worth more to him than his realm."

"What is it exactly that Tristan promised you in exchange for Asmodeus and Kupuva?" I question, angrily.

"A divine soul, gifting me the earth's vitalities."

My lips part as realization falls across me. All the blood rushes to my ears as I watch Tristan take his last furious strides toward us, his jaw tight as he approaches us.

"Ereshkigal, the goddess of the earth, was cursed for her loyalty to Lucifer in the war. Sent to rule over the underworld. Banished from the upper layers of earth. Never to feel the sun's warmth, or inhale the fresh air after a spring rain again. When you take away a goddess's ruled elements, you essentially kill the deity's spirit and reason for existence. Her very soul. My mother is dying a slow, torturous death simply because she once loved another."

"The woodland and water realms are ruled by the

supernatural courts. Even if Tristan gifted them to you, a dark-souled demigod could not reign them," I point out.

Nox leans toward me, lowering his voice. "A dark-souled demigod will not reign. A dark-souled satyr prince will."

My breath hitches as I stare into his empty eyes.

"I do what I must, to defend Kur. I was born into my dark reign. It is my fate. The darkness is what feeds my existence. Ereshkigal was born of the earth. In order to survive, she must return to it. So, yes, I will take the supernatural court's precious realms and grant you your freedom with my sword. In exchange, Tristan will give my mother his soul, freeing her and returning her to the earth."

"ENOUGH!" Tristan roars. "Our agreement is sealed."

I storm to him and push at his chest in anger. "You promised him your soul? The woodland and water realms?"

Tristan narrows his eyes at me, not backing down. He pushes into my space. "Your existence is more important to me than either my realm or divinity."

"Tristan, you can't do this."

"It's done," his tone is final.

All the breath leaves me as I search Tristan's eyes.

Nox walks away from us. "You see, princess, the gargoyle race can't protect humans against darkness or evil," his voice is steady. "Because evil doesn't play fair."

Within seconds, Nox disappears into thin air.

"It's okay," Tristan tries to calm me, whispering.

"You're a satyr prince. Your lifeblood runs through the realm you reign over and vice versa. You've signed away your soul. Without the realm, your soul ceases to exist."

"Which is exactly why I did it."

CHOSEN OR CURSED

TRISTAN

The door slams loudly behind Zander as I slump into the leather couch across from the fireplace. Since we arrived in Kur, I am in a constant state of exhaustion from the endless arguing that seems to be Serena's and my only interaction. She's infuriated with me and what I've done.

Every time she looks at me, she seethes with silent anger and frustration. It's merited, given she doesn't know everything yet. Right now, I'm thankful for the momentary reprieve from her fear and anger caused by her lack of understanding. I stretch my neck from side to side. It cracks with the effort. My muscles protest the movement.

For a brief, fleeting moment, I glance at the fire and contemplate throwing myself into it. But even that feels like it would take too much effort at the moment.

"Listen," Zander says in a quiet voice from behind me. "I haven't been in a relationship, like, ever, but I can tell you this: if Magali found out that I made a deal with someone behind her back, she would cut my manhood off. Which, being a satyr and all, would be a huge fucking problem. Since your junk is still intact, I'd say Serena isn't half as pissed at you as you think. So stop brooding."

"What are you doing in here?" I growl as he takes a seat next to me. The cushion moans under his weight.

Zander chuckles. "I thought you might need someone to point out how much you've fucked this all up."

"Pretty sure I've figured that out for myself."

We both sit quietly, watching the flames dance. After a long silence, Zander sighs and breaks through the quiet.

"What's the end game here, Tristan? We've always had one, but lately, your end games aren't something you share with me." His tone is severe, his eyes clouded with gravity.

I remain silent.

"There is an end game to this plan of yours?"

"What if there isn't?" I reply with lackluster defiance.

Zander glances over at me, muttering a curse.

"I've got this," I attempt to soothe him.

"Chosen or cursed, however you look at it, as prince of the realm, your lifeblood runs through it. Are you really going to embrace the throne and hand over both realms to a dark-souled deity?" He clenches his teeth. "Do you think Queen Ophelia is going to allow this transaction? Without a fight? A war? Don't we have enough shit to deal with?"

I meet his eyes. "It is the only way."

Zander releases a dry laugh. "I hate to tell you this, but our realm will not bow as easily as you assume."

"I never assumed it would."

"You *assume* your plan will work. Like an ass."

Swallowing down my arguments, I shift on the couch.

This is the only way.

I have to believe the end will justify the means, otherwise what is about to come will destroy me. I can't allow myself to fear what is right, to ease those I love.

"There is an end game," I state.

"Then fucking share what it is with me so I know who, or what, it is we are fighting here," Zander demands.

My gaze refocuses on the fire. "You don't need to know *who* we are fighting. Just who we are protecting."

"Right," he snips. "Of course not. Why tell the being in charge of your army about your war strategy? That is just stupid. He's charming and smart. Let him figure it out for himself," he mumbles under his breath, referring to himself.

I ignore his rant. "You're not always charming."

Zander narrows his eyes at me. "Don't be jealous." He faces the fire, watching it. "Life has been one big-ass tragedy lately. I miss when things were simpler. When you were grooming for the throne and I was bedding hot nymphs."

"I don't know if you've heard, but the last time I was in line for the throne, things didn't turn out so well for the future of the monarchy. Besides, those days are long gone."

"What a fucking mess," he growls.

Silently, I take in his words. Mess doesn't even begin to describe what is happening in our world. "I want you to train with the Noctis army while we're here," I state. "Gain intel."

The air around us shifts.

Zander leans forward, placing his elbows on his knees as he shoots daggers into the blazing flames dancing in front of us. "Is that why I am here? As an infiltrator?"

I nod. "We've been approaching this upcoming battle wrong. No one is interested in a united supernatural world. The Lion Guard and the protectors need to be retrained how to survive, not just fight. It won't be long before the dark army attacks again. Being in Kur with an army made up of deities is an opportunity to for us to prepare, given that most likely agreements will not be reached between the realms."

"If you want me to train with the deities, I'll train."

"Learn from them. Absorb everything you can."

The door opens and we both twist to face Serena. She pauses in the doorway, looking at both of us with guarded eyes. They flash with annoyance, trying to figure us out before she steps into the room and the door closes quietly.

"Champ," Zander greets her happily as she approaches us, stepping between where we are sitting and the fireplace.

"Zander, I thought you were coming to see me?" Her eyes flicker to me for a brief second before focusing on him.

"I came to your room to find you, but you weren't there."

"I see." She crosses her arms, her expression hard. "Well, I'm glad you're here then, with Tristan," she adds.

"And why is that exactly?" Zander smirks, sitting back, placing his hands behind his head, and watching her closely.

"Since Tristan seems to only listen to you, you can be the one to convince him of how dumb this plan of his is," she huffs, glancing at me from the corner of her eye. "Go on."

"Serena . . .," he trails off.

"Tell him he is being completely impossible about all of this, Zander. That his promise to Nox is asinine and not necessary. Convince him," she implores with urgency.

"Stop talking about me like I'm not here. And stop acting like a petulant child who isn't getting her way," I snap out at her. "It's done. I can't undo it, Serena. And even if I could, I wouldn't. Now, let's just fucking move forward."

Zander quickly jumps off the couch when Serena steps toward me, interjecting himself protectively between us when he sees her enraged at my outburst. "Easy, champ."

"We control two great armies, each of which will stand

and die in the name of protection and sacrifice, for kin and realm," she admonishes. "Why won't you believe in what we have at our fingertips? Why must you play the martyr?"

"Could be his huge ego." Zander's reply is directed to no one in particular.

"This is not a typical war," I argue, ignoring my brother.

"Are you not concerned for your kin? Your realms?"

"At the moment, no. I am not interested in preserving the woodland and water realms, princess," I bite out to goad her. "I am no longer the future heir of either. I am, however, your protector, and therefore concerned with your safety and continued existence. That's it. The fucking end."

"Ah shit." Zander clears his throat and rolls his head around his neck. "All right. I have something to do. Some-where . . . anywhere else . . . but here to be, listening to the two of you argue. Again. I'm going to leave and pray to the gods, even the dark ones, that you two don't kill each other," he sighs. "But for the record, if you two do kill each other, then all our problems are solved. Just saying." Zander places a light kiss on Serena's cheek. "Go easy on him, champ," he whispers before turning to me, placing a hand on my shoulder, and leaning toward my ear. "You okay?" he asks, looking over his shoulder at Serena.

Her eyes are hard and her jaw tight.

"I am not afraid of her or her wrath." I straighten and

clear my throat because truth be told, I am a little scared of Serena when she is livid like this. Just the tiniest amount.

Zander stares at me for a moment longer, nods his head, and pats my shoulder before walking toward the door, his voice trailing him. "You'd better beg for mercy, Trist."

14

FIGHT OR FLIGHT

SERENA

Tristan stands and moves toward me, stopping inches from my face, his hands fisted at his sides and his eyes narrow slits of challenge. He doesn't apologize or explain himself as he stares me down, refusing to go back on his agreement with Nox. I realize in this moment that he isn't going to change his mind. Instead, I will have to fight for him. Protect him. At all costs. In order to do that, I'll need to know everything. Everything he has promised Nox and everything he's done.

Straightening my spine, I lift my chin and give him a half smirk, trying to appear friendlier. "Tell me the truth."

His head cocks to the side while he assesses me. "Which one, raindrop? That I love you? That I would die for you?"

I sigh at his dramatics because he isn't being sincere, he's just trying to make a point. A very bad one at that.

"That without hesitation, if you told me to, I would take a dagger to myself and bleed out for you?" He watches me.

Nodding my head, I hold his gaze. "It's nice to know that if I get pissed off at you again, I have dagger options."

"What can I say, I like to live on the edge," he mutters.

I lean toward him. "Just so we're on the same page, as I understand things, you've renounced the throne. Washed your hands of the woodland and the water realms in order to be my royal guard? And as my royal protector, you have bartered your divine soul to a dark-souled deity in exchange for my safety and existence. Have I forgotten anything?"

He offers me a smile that makes my knees weak. "Sounds correct. Like it or not, I am focused solely on your survival."

"It's like you have a death wish," I whisper.

"I did," he replies. "Now, I have a life wish."

"Your actions say differently," I point out.

"You have to learn to trust in me."

I stare into his eyes, wondering if it's pride, or just loyalty in general, that is the reason he's trying so hard to keep me safe. Fear crawls up my throat because one day, I'm afraid he'll discover that I'm more trouble than I am worth.

"Serena?" His smooth voice interrupts my thoughts.

I swallow as tension swirls around us. Tristan's presence

is impossible to ignore, even when he isn't speaking. I shift, hoping it will hide my fear and worry.

"Give me an absolute reason to trust you," I challenge.

Tristan shuts his mouth and clenches his jaw. Then his expression changes, turning peaceful and resolved as his eyes soften. He closes the space between us, cupping my face in his palms. On a deep exhale, he closes his eyes and drops his forehead to mine. My anger extinguishes at the change.

Without opening his eyes, he whispers, "Take my last name." The minute the words leave his mouth, I freeze.

The immediate silence surrounding us is deafening.

"What?"

"You asked for an absolute reason to believe and trust in me." His eyes flutter open. "What if . . . I changed your last name to mine? What's more absolute than a forever with me? An entire existence. You and me. As one."

The roller coaster of emotions I've been experiencing over the last few weeks finally wears me down. Gripping Tristan's wrists, I sink to my knees, taking him with me.

"Are you . . ." I trail off, swallowing. "Proposing?"

His breath catches and I clutch him, needing his nearness. Ten seconds ago, I wanted to kill him. Now . . .

Tristan sits back on his heels, pulling me so that I am sitting on his lap, my knees on either side of him. The room is silent around us, except for our breathing and the crackling fire behind me. Even so, I barely hear him when he says, "Yes. I'm asking you to be mine. Forever, Serena."

"I am yours."

"Are you?"

I draw in a ragged breath and search his eyes. I had missed him so much while I was gone, and now that he is with me, I suddenly don't want to leave him ever again.

"Completely," I whisper with conviction.

Breathing softly, he almost touches my lips, but pauses right before they meet his. His eyes frantically search mine, looking for anything. "Then take my name. Make it official."

Nervousness might be a natural response. Even anger that Tristan is doing this at this moment. But I don't feel either emotion. All I feel is love. Love for this beautifully broken and insane protector in front of me.

"I'm yours. Only yours," I vow. "Until my last breath."

Tristan's eyes close and a hard shudder runs through him. When they reopen, he suddenly looks very nervous. He stares at me, paling. Holding my eyes, he speaks in a low voice. "Serena St. Michael," he breathes shallow and fast, "I promise to love and protect you, every day of my existence, if you will agree to stand by my side. Will you—"

I don't even let him attempt to finish. My lips jump at his, brushing across his mouth in a tender, sweet kiss, full of emotion. Everything that I want to say to him, but can't, is in that kiss.

After a while, I pull back and stare into his eyes as I speak with a shaky voice. "I am so in love with you. I will stand by your side, always," I manage, and he brings a hand up to stroke my cheek with the back of his fingers.

"So, is that a yes?" he waits.

"YES! I will take your last name. Be yours. Yes," I reply through the tears flowing down my cheeks.

The expression on his face makes me even weaker in the knees as my heart races. I try to process everything, but the look of hope in his eyes, mingled with dread and anticipation, has me coming back down to reality quickly.

"What's wrong?"

Tristan winces. "I should have talked to your dad first."

A small smile plays at my lips at the nervousness in his voice. "How utterly traditional of you, Tristan Gallagher."

The raw affection for me in his eyes has me holding onto him tighter. He is the one. Without a single doubt.

"And your uncle, since he is the current reigning king."

"The only acceptance you should be concerned with is mine," I state, annoyed. "This is the twenty-first century."

"My intentions are virtuous in nature, raindrop," he chastises. "We are still of royal bloodlines. There are codes of behavior, formalities to follow when doing this."

"Right," I swallow the lump in my throat.

Emotion overtakes me and I close my eyes, giving myself a moment to absorb everything that just happened.

When my lids flutter open, I'm met with Tristan's warm, loving stare again. And in this instant, he is my entire world. Nothing else even exists to me besides him, regardless of what my clan is going to say, or agree to.

"It doesn't matter what they say, I am yours."

Tristan lets out a soft exhale and kisses me deeply, as if we hadn't kissed in years. The love coming off him is almost too overwhelming, his entire body trembling with it.

His hand shakes as he grabs the hem of my shirt, pulling me even closer to him. I realize he is holding back, forcing himself to go slowly, to remain in control in case I change my mind. Knowing this ignites a fire within me.

I run my hands down his back, feeling every muscle, every defined line under the cotton of his shirt. Tristan groans as I bring my hands around to his chest, placing one palm over his protector tattoo and wrapping the other around the insignia he wears around his neck.

Pulling away from his lips, I tug on his necklace. "You know, you can't distract me with a proposal. I'm still pissed off at you. And if I'm to be the queen by your side, now, more than ever, you need to include me in strategy."

"I love you." His voice is deep, firm.

I stare at his serious expression. "I know."

"I wouldn't survive if you didn't exist."

"I can only exist if you are by my side."

"I will be."

"But what you've promised—"

"I. Will. Be."

His words hit me with such intensity that I stop breathing. Against every fiber shouting from deep within me, I dip my chin and give in, not pushing this anymore.

"Against my better judgment, I'll let you take the lead

on this *plan* of yours." I inhale through my nose. "Until I won't. And when that time comes, out of respect, you will tell me the entire strategy behind your decision. But if we are going to do this . . . be each other's forever, it's going to be on a level playing field. I need to be in the know."

"Understood."

"You do know that Magali is going to tell my clan of your promise to Nox. They'll not hesitate to come for us."

He cocks his head and lowers his voice. "They know."

Confusion rushes over me. "What?"

"The St. Michaels are aware of my deal with Nox."

Studying him, I hold my breath. "And they approved?"

"Yes," he holds my gaze.

I frown at him. Why the hell would my family agree to let him do this? Unless . . . damn them. I clench my jaw.

"Did they coerce you to be leveraged as a scapegoat in order for their heir to continue to exist?" I bite out. "You aren't just their royal protector, Tristan. You are a prince."

"Serena," he tightens his grip on me. "Trust in me."

I release a girlie growl. "Swear to me that my family didn't make you do this? That they didn't con you into this deal with Nox as a form of initiation to be a royal protector."

"I swear," he says, his voice sincere.

I run a finger down his cheek. "I don't know whether to be relieved or pissed off. If they didn't force you, then you really did stupidly do this on your own," I exhale my annoyance. "Now what? What are our next steps?"

"The three of us will meet with Nox and discuss what our plan will be for Asmodeus and Kupuva," he answers.

I look around the room before meeting Tristan's gaze again. "You know, if we can get to the dark army before they attack, we'll have a much better chance at stopping whatever it is they're plotting." I pause for a brief moment before adding, "That requires us leaving Kur. And soon."

Tristan's pierced brow raises. "The dark army is a misguided focus. It's their leaders we need to attend to. It's best of we take advantage of Nox's invitation and remain here in Kur for the time being. Study and train a bit with the Noctis army. Nox invited us to Kur to feel us out. We'll use our time here to do the same with him and his soldiers."

"Invited?" I parrot. "More like took us hostage."

"Rionach taught Zander and I that a leap of faith goes both ways when a mutual end result is desired in an alliance."

"Do you think Nox would turn on us?"

"Yes. Without hesitation."

"Well, that was . . ." I pause. "Blunt."

"Honest," he counters. "He's a dark deity with an enormous ego. We need to be prepared, on all fronts. This isn't just about the peace treaty between Heaven and Hell; it's also about the deities and their desires to gain control and power over the supernatural and human realms."

"Gods and demons. What could possibly go wrong?"

"Nothing, if we do it my way," he watches me.

"And if we don't?" I challenge.

"Realms will fall. Blood will spill. And you and I——"

"We what?"

"Will cease to exist at all."

"Morbid."

"Lucky for us, I have a kick-ass plan."

"And a huge ego."

"That too," he nods. "One that won't allow of any of that shit to happen under my protection."

"You know, if I didn't know any better, I'd say you want to stay here to avoid telling my father about our upcoming nuptials," I tease. "Are we hiding from my dad?"

Tristan helps me stand, stretching his own legs to full height. "Can you blame me? Your father tried to slip me laxatives when I was in London."

I give him a suspicious look. "What?"

He crosses his heart. "In oatmeal raisin cookie form."

My shoulders sag. "He's insane."

"No," Tristan holds my face in his hands. "He just loves and wants to protect you. And who can blame him?"

"In the meantime, it might be best to stop eating his cookies," I reply, and then wince at the double meaning.

Tristan's eyes immediately come to life. "Oh, raindrop, it's not *his* cookies I'm after," he banters.

I push at his chest. "You're still not off the hook with me. However, I will table my concerns and arguments for a bit. So, let's go learn how to kick some demon and deity ass."

Tristan places a small kiss on my lips before pulling back and whispering, "Thank you for trusting me to protect the one thing that will destroy me if it ceases to exist. You."

As I follow him, I stare at his back, ignoring my fight-or-flight reaction to his flowery words. They leave a stale feeling in my gut, because Tristan has forgotten one variable in this protection strategy of his . . . my heart.

What happens to it when it is he who ceases to exist?

15

NOCTIS ARMY

TRISTAN

The three of us stand in front of the open arched windows, staring down into the colosseum where Nox's soldiers are battling. We study the deity military tactics reminiscent of ancient Greece. Each warrior takes on a specific form within a smaller group to execute all of their fight maneuvers. And each subunit works together as a smaller piece of an overall larger strategic picture of deity power.

Metal clanks as they perform tactics with shields. Each warrior holds their shield with their left hand, to protect not only themselves, but also the being on their left. Their wide formation doubles the depth of coverage. *Interesting.*

One notable contrast is that most of the deities use spears; very few use swords when in hand-to-hand combat.

Another difference is the demigods do not like to ambush. Instead, they prefer battling with honor, even the dark-souled demigods. Similar to the Diablo Fairies under Kupuva's leadership. Across the board, honor is everything.

My eyes close for a moment, needing a second to absorb everything going on around me. It doesn't go unnoticed by me that the Noctis army's code of ethics is hypocritical, given they all use their demigod powers to leverage their positions and strengths while fighting.

"Tristan looks pissed," Zander whispers to Serena.

"Why are his eyes closed?" she asks in response.

"Not sure. Is he meditating?"

"How would I know?"

"Don't you know everything about him? His favorite color? Food? If he has tissues and lotion on his nightstand?"

"Sapphire. Pizza. And there are no tissues or lotion on his nightstand," she ticks off haughtily.

Zander huffs. "Please. Every male with blood running through his veins has *tissues and lotion* on his nightstand."

"He doesn't," Serena argues, not understanding.

"Says you," my brother counters.

I open my eyes and throw them both an annoyed look over my shoulder. "The *tissues and lotion* are in reference to masturbation, which Zander is the king of. Now, watch and study the drills. I swear, you two are worse than children."

"Get it now?" Zander bumps his shoulder with hers.

"You're hilarious," Serena moans.

"What can I say? I'm special." Zander flashes her a quick side grin.

"You're *special* all right," she sighs.

I turn back to the training going on below us.

"For the record, if you two didn't drag me away from Magali, who by the way turned me into this shell of a pathetic nymph, I wouldn't have to masturbate. She's fucking ruined me. I can't even look at another female without wistfully thinking of her," he pouts. "Ruined."

"Oh. My. Gods," Serena giggles. "You wanna marry her. And have babies. And buy a house. Oh, and a Volvo!"

Zander pushes at my shoulder so I meet his gaze again. He throws an *is she serious* look my way. "Do you hear this?"

"I'm trying not to," I huff, and focus on the army.

"I never said I wanted to buy a house and Volvo."

"Do you feel the crazy, obsessive, *I will die for you* kind of love for her?" Serena questions with a tease in her tone.

Zander falls silent and blows out an exaggerated breath.

"Maybe," he admits.

Serena squeals and claps her hands in excitement.

"Knock it off," Zander scolds. "I have a reputation."

Serena sighs. "Whatever."

"And for the record, no one said anything about babies."

"M'kay," she draws out. "You totally want to have babies with her."

"Maybe you and Tristan should have babies."

"No." Her answer is quick and clipped.

The speed of her reply catches my attention.

"Why not? I'd be an amazing uncle. Uncle Zan."

I tense as my heart beats wildly in my chest, waiting for her response. I hadn't meant to propose to her earlier, it just sort of happened. I'd always planned to ask her, just not in that way. Or here. Or without following royal protocols.

Looking back, I'm kicking myself for not doing it right. Asking her father for permission, being romantic. Serena deserves better than what I did. She's probably second-guessing her answer. Who could blame her at this point?

"We just got engaged. At least . . . I think we did—"

"WHAT THE FUCK?" Zander shouts, interrupting her. "What the hell is she talking about? Why is Serena *unsure* if she is betrothed to you? Or not? What did you do?"

Turning, I look at both of them. "I asked her to take my name."

"And?" Zander growls out.

"She said yes. Or at least," I stumble. "I think she did."

Zander slides his attention to Serena. "This is like the worst proposal ever. He *thinks* you said yes. You *think* he proposed. Did any of this actually happen?"

"Yes," Serena and I both say at the same time.

"So, you're . . ." my brother prods.

"Officially engaged." I finish for him.

"And telling everyone?" Serena asks.

"And telling everyone," I confirm.

She bites her lower lip. "Except my parents."

I nod. "And your aunts and uncles."

"And your mother."

"Or anyone here in Kur," I add.

"Oh, and Magali. Not yet."

"Definitely not Ryker or Ireland," I continue.

"Or Ethan and Lucas."

"So, basically, you're not telling anyone," Zander points out. He groans loudly. "Great. Another secret betrothal."

Tova approaches us with a wicked grin. "Zander, we are ready for you to train with us. Starting with me. I'm looking forward to getting you on your back again," she seduces.

My brother narrows his eyes at me. "Even that doesn't turn me on. A hot warrior threatening me. RUINED!"

"You've got this, man," I encourage.

He turns to Serena. "Your secret, it doesn't affect us."

Her eyes widen. "No?"

"Nope. You're still my girl, regardless."

"Good to know," she smiles at him.

"Now, give me a smooch for good luck," Zander motions his head to Tova. "I might not make it back from battle."

With an eye-roll, Serena steps forward, looking as though she is going to wrap her arms around his waist. I hold back a growl when she looks up at him with adoration before wrapping her hands around the handle of his sword.

Slowly, she removes it from its sheath. After taking a step back, she smiles and kisses the handle. Winking, she throws it out one of the open windows. It falls the four stories and lands straight up in the dirt floor of the colosseum. "Go get 'em, Zander."

16

PAPER THIN

SERENA

A shiver inches its way down my spine as I watch the strong whirlwind twirl in the desert. The dust from the surrounding land twists in a vertical, upward motion.

"Now *that* is the devil's wind," Nox states from next to me. "With focus, it can grow large enough to pose a threat. As an elemental gargoyle, you need to harness your gifts more. With practice, they can be turned into weapons instead of simply being used as a source of protection."

I stare at the rotating column of wind. Tristan was right—staying in Kur has helped us learn new tactics and skills. Skills that we would not normally be taught at the Royal Protector Academy, as most are considered darker in nature. Like the small tornado of wind and dust I've created.

If I wanted to, I could expand it, increasing its size and intensity, taking down a small army. It's pretty cool.

"Across realms, the devil's wind can produce electrical fields. When it swirls, it picks up small particles, which bump and scrape against one another. As that happens, Serena, they become electrically charged, creating a magnetic field," Nox explains. "Demons and demigods have auras. The magnetic field can deflect and manipulate their auras. You see, elemental gifts are not simply for shifting the wind, or causing the rain. They are great in power when used offensively, instead of defensively, during battle."

My focus shifts to the vast desert around us. Since our supernatural gifts don't work in Kur, Nox has been training me outside of the cavern the past few days. It's hot.

His *unconventional* approach to my gifts has been eye-opening, to say the least. With a drop of my hands, the wind falls, along with specks of sand, which tumble to the ground.

My gaze slides to Nox. "What is it you really want with Asmodeus? Aside from obtaining the woodland and water realms. Our *training* isn't out of the kindness of your heart."

The demigod eyes me coolly. "I have unfinished business with the demon lord."

Ice drenches my stomach at his tone. There are several things I have discovered during our stay in Kur. One of which is that Nox has a reason for everything he does. He's controlled. Calculating. And unforgiving when crossed.

"That makes two of us," I reply.

"Your captivity with him was short, as I understand."

"The length isn't the cause for my vengeance. It's everything that surrounded it. Before and after," I reply.

"The satyr prince?" he surmises.

"Tristan was hurt. Betrayed by those he trusted. Tortured by the unknown. His love ripped away from him."

"Love is for children. Not kings and queens."

"So, I've heard."

Nox steps into my sightline. "He learned a valuable lesson. Trust. Loss of control. Love. These are all weaknesses. Human emotions that are used against us in times of war."

"Funny. Queen Ophelia shares your sentiment."

"Then she is a wise and strong queen," he counters.

"The gods and goddesses don't feel emotion?"

"We feel them. More so than the humans you protect."

"Then aren't they weaknesses for you as well?"

"No. We've learned to harness them into power."

I cross my arms. "Why the need for so much power?"

"As a god or goddess, power is everything. It is prestige. It is honor. It is courage. It is love," he dips his chin. "Without power, demigods are nothing."

"What about peace?"

"Most of the deities are not interested in peace between realms. That is a human desire, not ours. To many of the deities, peace is uninteresting. It doesn't serve a purpose."

"It's odd that you mock peace. When *you* defend it. You, the god of night, rid the realms, including earth, of the darkest souls. You hunt chaos down and end its existence. That is your fate. Why you were created? Was it not to end turmoil, helping to create peace and calm?"

"Do not mistake my purpose," he replies.

Nox's eyes meet mine. I've come to hate his eyes. They're unnatural not just in color, but in lack of emotion. Always cold. To hear him speak always leaves me queasy.

"Do you think Asmodeus will attempt something soon?"

He shakes his head. "It is in his nature to."

"Then we should be more proactive."

"We will be. Tomorrow we leave for Demon Falls."

"What is that?"

"It is his home. Where he protects the nine gates."

"The gates to Hell?" I already know the answer.

"Yes," Nox confirms. "Now, you should practice sourcing lightning again and dispersing the absorbed energy. Remember, lightning is something that most gods and goddesses can't fight against, nor can any demon."

"Even you?" I pose.

A cruel smile taints his lips. "No. I thrive in its energy."

"Of course you do," I mumble under my breath.

"Mortals and supernaturals are not threats to the darker-souled gods," he adds. "A lesson to heed."

I push my shoulders back, meeting his gaze. "Everyone, including you, Nox, has a weakness. Yours may not be physical, but I bet if I search long enough, I'll find it." I step closer to him. "And know this: when I do, I will use it against you to prevent Tristan from giving you his realms."

Nox tips his head respectfully at me.

The action causes me to pinch my eyebrows in confusion, because it's an odd reply to my threat.

"You think like a warrior now," his voice is deep. "Not a protector. You are finally ready to accept your fated path."

———

I STARE AT THE WALL. My breathing picks up as the warm undressed body behind mine shifts. A large hand runs up my spine, causing me to break out in goosebumps.

Warm fingertips slide over my shoulder, curling into my hair, gently guiding it to one side. The strands tickle my bare skin, now tingling and burning from his touch.

Tristan's scruff-covered jaw scratches the delicate skin where his fingertips were just lightly caressing, the harshness after the gentleness soliciting a shiver within me.

I gasp for breath when his lips press against the Sun of Vergina mark behind my ear. His mark. Blessed by the deities themselves, sealing our fates.

His lips move upward until his warm breath tickles my

ear. "You want to keep staring at the wall, or do you want to shower with me? I mean, it is a pretty interesting wall."

"Shut up," I laugh, because the wall is plain white, with nothing decorating it. It couldn't be more uninteresting.

"Are you okay?" he whispers.

I roll onto my back, looking up into his curious gaze.

A playful smile plays on his lips as he hovers over me, his necklace dangling above my chest. I lift my fingers and let the tips trail down his cheek, over his jawline, until they find their way down the leather cord around his neck before reaching the insignia he wears. Gently, I take it between my thumb and index finger, rolling it between my fingertips.

"It's okay to be scared about today. Demon Falls isn't exactly a vacation. And given what happened with Asmodeus, I can understand why you would be apprehensive about going," he speaks quietly. "Seeing him."

"I'm not scared. I'm anxious. I want this all to be over."

His eyes penetrate mine as one of his hands takes my chin between his fingers. "It hasn't even begun yet."

"I know," I sigh.

Tristan's thumb brushes over my lower lip. My eyes slide closed as I bask in the buzz of energy from his touch.

"Serena." His smooth voice invades my peace.

"Hmm?" I relax.

"It's time to get up."

My lids flutter open and I groan. "Five more minutes."

"Come on." He slides out of bed, motioning for me to stand. "We have lots to do. Demons to threaten. Lives to ruin. Demigods to take on. Oh, and after all that is said and done, we need to tell your clan and my mother about our engagement. So . . . up you go. Time to save the world."

"That was super motivational," I whine.

Tristan pulls me out of bed and toward him. I crane my neck and look up at him. Looking down at me, he pushes my hair off my face with both his palms, taking my head between his hands. "I love you."

A loud knock at the door has us both jumping.

"Rise and shine, we have a playdate with a demon lord."

"Why does he sound excited?" I ask Tristan.

"Zander loves this shit," he rubs his hands over his face.

"You guys have five minutes, which for the record is more than enough time for Tristan to finish sexy time."

"Go the fuck away," Tristan shouts. "Idiot," he mumbles.

"Four minutes, fifty-eight seconds before I barge in, slide into bed and cuddle with you both," Zander yells through the closed door.

I frown and meet Tristan's eyes. "You know when we do finally get married, I am going to have to marry you both?"

Tristan's eyes narrow, pulling me closer. "No."

"Four minutes until spooning commences." The doorknob jiggles. "And I need to be in the middle, not on the end like a third friggin' wheel."

I grin up at him. "You sure about that?"

Tristan's brow arches as he stares at the door. "He's going to be living in our basement, isn't he?"

Laughing, I nod. "Yeah, I think he is."

"That's it. You've been warned. I am coming in," Zander shouts, and then snickers. "Hey, did anyone else get that? I am *coming* in . . . doesn't sound like Tristan is though."

"That's it, he's dead," Tristan says, pulling on sweatpants.

"Wait!" I grab the sheet and wrap it around me, just before Zander kicks open the door and saunters in.

With a smug grin, he takes in the room. "So," he draws out. "What are you guys doing in here? Being naughty?"

Tristan lets out a growl. "I'm going to shower."

"You sound frustrated," Zander says with a taunting inflection. "Not having sex does that to a satyr prince."

"Get out." Tristan puts his palm on his brother's chest.

"No can do. I need to talk to Serena. It's important."

"Fine," Tristan mumbles and drops a kiss to my lips. "Be gone, Zander, before I get out," he warns, before sulking off to the bathroom to clean up.

I meet Zander's know-it-all expression.

He grins in amusement. "I could have teleported in. I didn't. I knocked like a good, respectful gentleman."

Tilting my head, I watch him. "What do you want?"

"To cash in on our bet."

I narrow my eyes at him. "What?"

"Our bet," he repeats. "You remember, champ? We bet. You cried. You lost. I won. Now, I want my winnings."

Oh shit. I'd forgotten that he'd challenged me not to cry when we went into the woodland realm to stop Tristan's wedding to Freya. I lost our bet when I cried. And he won. Damn.

"I'm not having sex with you," I murmur.

He laughs. "Tempting, but that isn't what I want."

"And no to grabbing a boob. Or both."

"That is a genuine shame."

"I'm *genuinely* about to stab you with my dagger," I warn. "Whatever it is you want, Zander, it can't be sexual."

He quickly throws his head back and laughs, then walks around me and flops onto the bed on his back, placing his hands behind his head and crossing his feet at the ankles.

"Interesting," he says.

"What is?"

"Are you naked under that sheet?"

"Zander!"

"You might want to reconsider the nonsexual argument. Making it a hard line, you're missing out on having your world rocked. I mean it. Tristan's little pony tricks are nothing in comparison to what I can do to you. Trust me. I am that fucking good. Females for miles lust after me, seeking out my talents. You sure about your rule?"

I roll my eyes and tighten the sheet around me before sitting next to him on the edge so I can look down at him. "I am ten seconds from actually stabbing you in the crotch."

"Violent." He shifts his lower body out of my reach.

"Zander," I grunt out, frustrated.

"Okay. Okay." His eyes brighten as they focus on me. "I know how to get Tristan out of his deal with Nox."

"What?"

"Yup," he pops his *p*. "Want to make out with me now?"

"No. How?"

His smile widens and his eyes become crazy with excitement. "Tristan asked me to train with the deities in order to gain intel and strategic understanding. Well, turns out one of our little gods likes the lady nymphs. One in particular, whom I happen to have a . . ." he searches for the right word, "sordid and detailed sexual past with. Anyway, in exchange for an introduction of sorts, he spilled the beans."

My eyebrows shoot up. "You bribed a deity? Wait, I thought Tristan told you very sternly to stop doing that?"

He rolls his eyes. "I can't help that immortals are gossipy. Besides, Tristan told me to stop bribing the staff in the woodland realm. He said nothing about deities in this one." He pauses for a moment, contemplating before lowering his voice. "And if he asks, I bartered for the information. Not bribed. Understood?"

I chew on my lip. "Before you tell me what it is and I get my hopes up, how trustworthy is this information? I mean, it seems a little strange the god of night would go blabbing about his grand scheme to a mere deity warrior, Zander."

"If you bite on your lip one more time, I am jumping you," he warns. "Nox didn't blab. Nox's *lady friend* did."

My lips part. "Who? Tova?"

Zander laughs. "Not Tova. For the record, Tova is a crazy tiger in bed who rips you apart. Not a lady friend."

"Is there a difference?" I ask, regretting it the second I do.

"Yes. One is a sexual goddess, the other, just a goddess."

"Sounds like you're speaking from experience."

"I am," he wiggles his eyebrows. "Now, focusing. Are you interesting in hearing what I've learned or not?"

My eyes dart between him and the bathroom door. "On account of the fact that I'm desperate to protect Tristan, yes, tell me how we can get him out of this damn agreement."

He hesitates for a moment. "This is the part you aren't going to like, champ. I need to cash in my winnings before I share and impart my newfound knowledge with you."

"Fine," I bite out. "What is it you want?"

Zander's face softens. "Are you and Tristan really going to tie your fates together and get married?"

"Why? Planning on making me marry you too?"

"Just answer me, champ."

At his seriousness, I draw my brows together. "Yes."

"And what about kids?"

"We have you," I tease.

"I mean it, will there be any?"

I exhale. "I don't know, Zander. I mean, we're kind of in the middle of a war between gods and demons at the moment. Kids seems like, far, far off into the way-off future."

"But after, when this shit is all done?"

"We haven't discussed it, why?"

"I want the right to name your firstborn," he states.

"This is a new level of insanity. Even for you."

Zander's expression falls. "My father, he loved Tristan."

My heart stutters and my breath catches. This is the first time Zander has talked about Rionach since his death.

"Rionach loved you both," I whisper.

"He treated Tristan and me equally." His eyes glaze over with sadness. "Rionach didn't care that I was blood, or Tristan was not. We were both his sons, not just me."

"Rionach was amazing," I point out.

He nods absentmindedly. "He was. A respected commander. A loving husband. And the best damn father Tristan and I could have had. It killed him that Tristan was not his biological son. He tried to hide it, but I saw it in his eyes. As a way of forming an everlasting bond, a connection with Tristan, my father planned to gift Tristan a name for his firstborn child, the future heir of the kingdom he loved, fought for, and protected until his last breath. As silly as it is, it was his way of solidifying their relationship, forever."

I uncross my arms and rub my protector bracelet. "It's not silly. That is quite a gift. An honor to receive," I reply.

"In the woodland realm, as you know, it is the highest gift bestowed upon a son from his father," he manages.

The sting of tears appears in my eyes. "I know."

"He never shared the name with anyone. It was his to gift when Tristan's first child was born." Zander's eyes slide around the room and then back to me. "I've never told anyone this, Serena, but that fatal day, before he died," he swallows, "Rionach came to check on the Lion Guard. At one point, he leaned in and whispered the name in my ear, making me promise to gift it to Tristan's child. It's like he knew he wasn't going to be coming home with us."

My lower lip trembles. "Rionach was astute." I shift on the bed, my heart hurting for them. Guilt sets in; I can't deny that Rionach's death was mostly my fault. "All right. If we have a child, I grant you the right to name our firstborn."

"I can't tell you what the name is until he or she is born."

"I understand."

"And you can't tell Tristan about our agreement. I want to fulfill my father's promise, but not at the cost of Gage and Tristan finally having some sort of relationship of their own. Tristan deserves to have his biological father in his life. Rionach would have wanted that for him. Agreed?"

I sniff and nod my agreement, unable to speak.

"Thank you, champ." After a moment, Zander clears his throat. "Now that we have that sorted out," he inhales and when he exhales, he says, "Inanna."

"Zander!" I whisper-shout. "You weren't supposed to tell me the name," I scold him, swatting at his arm while he tries to protect himself. "What is wrong with you?"

His expression turns confused as he shields his face from me. "What?" he asks, then realization dawns on him. "No. Serena." He sits up and grabs my wrists, preventing my attack. "Inanna is the way to get Tristan out of the deal."

After a moment, I blow out a breath, pushing away the strands of hair that have fallen into my face. "Inanna? What is that? A secret code? Or weapon? Or something?"

"Sort of," he replies, releasing me. "*She* is the Sumerian goddess of love, beauty, light, and recently, the Heavenly sky. It's rumored she wields a lot of power past the gates."

I take a moment to consider what he's saying before answering. "Gargoyles deal with the divine for protection assignments. Her name has never come up. Not once."

"The Angelic Council keeps her a secret."

"Why?"

"It's a condition. A directive from Helios."

"Helios? The same god of the sun who bestowed the

Sun of Vergina prophecy on Tristan and me? Nox's brother?"

"The very same one," he dips his chin.

"Since when do the divine take orders from the gods?"

Zander's lips flatten. "Um, since the beginning of time."

"I'm not following. What does she have to do with us?"

"Everything."

"How so?"

"Inanna happens to be the woman Nox loves."

"Wait," I sit forward. "Are you saying Nox, the god of night and the prince of death, the demon hunter son of Lucifer, the darkest-souled of all the demigods, is in love with a goddess of love, beauty, and light? A goddess who is hidden behind *divine* gates?"

Zander grins brightly. "Want to hear more?"

I glance at the bathroom door again. "Give me the short version," I answer. "In case Tristan finishes his shower."

"Inanna has a thing for taking the domains of other deities. Apparently, she also has a fierce temper and a small issue with jealousy. Eons ago, she unleased mass chaos upon the earth. The details are fuzzy, but the story goes, Asmodeus turned her divine soul dark. Nox was sent to seek out her dark soul and destroy it. Instead, he fell head-over-heels in love with her. Rather than ending her existence, he brought Inanna down to Kur. However, Ereshkigal was none too pleased with her son's new love.

Having been the goddess of the earth, she was pretty ticked off that Inanna almost destroyed it," he explains.

"Holy shit."

"Wait, it gets better," he continues. "Apparently, Nox went to all the gods on her behalf, begging them to spare her life. The other deities rejected his pleas. It's said that because of his love for Inanna, Nox couldn't end her existence. Instead, to save him from heartache, Ereshkigal ended it for him. Three days later, Helios mysteriously showed up in Kur. He and Nox held secret meetings."

"What kind of meetings?"

"The kind where Helios brought Inanna back to life, healing her soul with the light from the sun, sky, and heavens. In exchange for life, Inanna had to remain in the sky, behind the gates. And never be with Nox again."

I sit back and take in the story. "Wow."

"I know. Juicy, right? Inanna's attendant had loose lips."

"That nymph must have some amazing skill sets for this warrior to share all of this with you," I point out.

"Truthfully, most of this was during a drunk rambling."

"If this *hearsay* is true, it would explain Nox's statement earlier. He mentioned having *unfinished* business with Asmodeus. I wonder if it relates to Inanna?" I reason.

"Possibly. It would also account for why, when Tristan and I first met with Nox, he agreed to take our meeting. He said it was a *favor* to Helios, mentioning that he owed a debt to his brother," he adds. "Nox's help with stopping Asmodeus and Kupuva is probably Helios's repayment."

I exhale and meet Zander's eyes. "This would also account for why Nox wanted Tristan to promise the woodland and water realms. A form of recompense to his mother for sparing him the heartache of killing his love."

"Everything makes perfect sense now."

"It still doesn't help us, though, Zander."

"It does. Helios is the god who created the Sun of Vergina prophecy, in order to unite the woodland and water realms, keeping the nymphs and sprites safe for the gods and goddesses to share company with, which means he will protect his divination at all costs. Inanna is a divine goddess behind the gates, one that is under Helios's protection."

"And how does all that get Tristan out of the deal?"

Zander sits up, lowering his voice. "What do you think Helios will do to Inanna when he finds out his brother agreed to turn Helios's divination's soul dark? Enabling him to rule over two realms that sustain the earth realm? The very same realms Helios created the prophecy to protect?"

I meet his steely gaze. "Punish him for his betrayal?"

He nods. "Using the one thing that can hurt him."

"Inanna."

"Inanna," he confirms.

A quick breath escapes me. "Okay. You need to go alert Helios of what is happening, then."

"Wait, why me?"

With a wave of my hand, I stand. "I kinda have a lot to do here, Zander. I have a demon lord to threaten, a battle with the Diablo Fairies to prepare for, not to mention a wedding to begin planning. Which, by the way, will lead to a very pissed off gargoyle clan that I'll have to protect Tristan from. Plus, if I *mysteriously* disappear, I'm pretty sure Tristan will notice and have a meltdown."

Zander cracks a smile and starts to laugh. "That is the worst to-do list ever," he teases, patting my arm. "I'll go, *after* Demon Falls. I need to be there today to watch both your backs. Also, demon shit is cool, no way am I missing out on it."

"You're a pain in the ass!"

"But you still love me. Admit it."

"I admit nothing."

Zander stands, pulling me into his arms as he whispers in my ear. "We've got this. We can save him, champ, because in the end, Nox will choose Inanna," he adds.

And there it is.

No matter who we are, our armor is paper thin.

Turns out even Nox has a weakness . . . love.

17

SALT IN THE WOUND

SERENA

M y eyes widen in horror as I stare at the dark, decrepit château in the distance, surrounded by gloom and lit up by electrified bursts of thunder. The unkempt gates that surround it hang off stone walls, squeaking in the harsh wind as the rusted wrought iron sways.

Thunder rumbles in the sky in warning. Everything here is gray and ominous, even the dead grass crawling across the massive estate. The only pop of color are the blood-red flowers peppering the thorn-covered vines, twisting and wrapping around the gated entrance.

They hang in a portentous way, tempting you to enter a place that emanates pure evil.

We make our way up the long walk to the entrance.

"If I thought earth was a shithole, this realm takes the cake," Zander mutters under his breath.

"This is where demons come to fall," Nox states. "It's not meant to be a beach resort. It's the gateway to Hell."

"Sounds about right," Tristan drones.

Once we get to the double doors, they open without being prompted and we enter the lifeless castle. With a slam, the doors close behind us. A deep, arctic chill runs through the air and seeps into my skin.

As we follow Nox, Tova, and Lael through the passageways, I study the old-fashioned wooden lanterns hanging throughout. Their flames flicker, dull and lifeless, providing little light. Everything here is dark and empty, void of life. There are no windows. No warmth. Just castle walls that weep with eerie cries and pleas.

The stench of sulfur mixed with the metallic tang of blood is soaked into every corner of the castle, forcing me to hold my breath a few times to avoid bile rising up my throat.

After a few moments, we reach a set of double iron doors. Nox waves his hand in front of them, causing them to open dramatically. The moment they do, a gush of heat blows over us, a stark contrast from the chilled passages.

Nox leads the three of us into the large, empty room, with Tova and Lael behind us. Nine lit fireplaces surround the chamber. They blaze and burn almost in a threatening manner. Each enormous hearth has a barghest sleeping soundly in front of it. The hellhounds don't stir as we enter.

We step onto an oversized Oriental rug covering most

of the floor. Chills run down my spine when I notice the rug is stained the color of human blood—bright red.

One single black leather medieval chair, with intricate wooden carvings of demons, sits in the center of the room. It's the only piece of furniture in the vast space. Two more hellhounds flank the empty chair, one on each side, sitting calmly, watching our every move, as they protect.

"Why aren't the hellhounds moving?" I ask.

"They sense I am from their world," Nox replies.

"What now?" Tristan questions.

"Now, we wait," Lael replies in a clipped voice.

Nox steps toward the throne and takes a seat, motioning for Lael and Tova to join him. They take their places on either side of the armchair, behind the large wolf-like dogs. The three warriors stare at us before Nox's eyes flick, signaling for us to move behind him. Reluctantly, we do.

"Regardless of what comes out of the demon lord's mouth, no one reacts," Nox orders in his baritone.

Seconds later, the doors fly open and in steps one very entertained demon lord. Cracking his neck, Asmodeus saunters into his chamber, his black irises gliding over us in a calculating and penetrating manner.

"You're in my seat." His voice is low, hypnotic.

"Am I?" Nox replies, bored.

A strange mutual respect filled with hatred hangs between them. I watch their interaction with fascination.

I try not to bristle under Asmodeus's stare as he takes

us all in. While in captivity, I never saw his face. Weirdly, he isn't at all what I expected. With his charismatic good looks, he reminds me of a rock star rather than a feared and powerful demon considered a ruthless dictator of Hell. Asmodeus's chest and shoulders are relaxed under his loose white button-down shirt. The top button is undone and his sleeves are rolled up, revealing his tattoos.

Long, leather-covered legs stand casually as they stretch out underneath him. His worn pirate-type boots are firmly planted on the floor.

Nox shifts, getting more comfortable in Asmodeus's chair. Apparently, he has no plans to vacate it anytime soon.

"Serena." Asmodeus's hungry gaze rakes over me in an unwelcome manner. "You've healed well."

"No thanks to your kidnapping and drugging scheme."

Tristan steps a bit in front of me. "Don't speak to her."

"How chivalrous you are, protector." He tilts his head, his eye excited. "Tristan, right? Yes, that's it—Gage Gallagher's secret love child. Quite the surprise you were. And a satyr prince. What a special bloodline mixture you've got going on there, Trist." His voice has a light lilt. "Are you here to barter for the gargoyle princess's existence?" His expression turns smug, and then cruel. "If so, I'm afraid you are out of luck. You see, you have nothing I want."

"I'm not here to negotiate," Tristan states.

"I rather doubt that," Asmodeus challenges. "I smell

you inside her blood. You've bonded and share a protector link."

"Serena is under my protection," Nox interjects.

Asmodeus lets his words sink in before his expression turns murderous. His eyes flash red. "Interesting."

"As are the woodland and water realms," Nox adds.

Asmodeus's eyes snap to Tristan. "Well, welcome to the dark side. I do believe your father enjoys his time here."

"Fuck off." Tristan steps forward, but I grab him.

"That is enough," Nox warns.

"This wasn't the deal, Nox," the demon lord spits out.

Nox shrugs. "Alliances and deals shift."

The demon lord's eyes narrow, his expression turning into one that is truly menacing. "Is this because of *her*? If so, know that when I get her back, I will end her life. Again. Only this time, I will do it slowly, with pain and suffering. I will torture her as I turn her divine light into darkness."

In an instant, Nox is on his feet, and within seconds his hand is clenched around the demon lord's throat, lifting him off the ground. Asmodeus bats at his arm, but the gesture is pointless; the demigod is too strong for him to escape.

"I will end you." Nox delivers each word harshly.

A howling sound releases from the demon as Nox tightens the vise he has on his neck, crushing his windpipe.

"*She* will continue to be protected behind the divine

gates." Asmodeus's eyes widen at Nox's statement. "Now, are you ready to discuss the reason for our presence?"

I inhale and side-glance at Zander, having a feeling Nox isn't talking about me, but Inanna. By the looks of Zander's wide-eyed expression, I'd say he is thinking the same thing.

"Can't—talk!" The demon gurgles.

Nox drops him and, like a doll, he flails onto the ground.

The demon sucks in quick sharp breaths. He doesn't get up; instead he falls back onto his back, exhausted from not breathing as he rubs his neck where Nox had a hold on him.

Nox makes a guttural sound of impatience with it all.

"What is it you want now?" Asmodeus spits out.

"You to swear an oath to release the gargoyles from your wrath. We both know it's unmerited and misplaced."

"They protect the divine gates," Asmodeus argues. "The St. Michael clan is the reason the two archangels, Michael and Uriel, killed Lady Finella. She was my mate, my love," he announces. "Surely you, Nox, of all of us here, understand the pain the death of one's love brings," his snarky tone is meant as a challenge.

I bristle at the retelling of the story that has more to do with my uncle Asher and aunt Eve than it does me.

Nox crouches next to the demon, lowering his voice so it's barely audible. "The gargoyles are not the only ones who protect the gates, given what is now behind them. If you wipe out the protector race, the deities still keep guard. Your attempt at a divine war and entry is futile, demon."

After a moment of silence, the demon lord falls into a hysterical fit of crazy laughter. "I should have known."

The demigod stands, folding his arms across his chest, as he looks down, watching the demon lord lose his shit.

"What the hell is going on?" Tristan whispers next to me, causing both Zander and I to glance at him. "And why do you two not look surprised by what's happening?"

"Shock," Zander replies quickly. "This is all new . . . crazy . . . nonsensical information, right champ?"

"Right." I swallow and nod my head.

Tristan flattens his lips, obviously not believing us, but with circumstances as they currently are, he won't prod.

Nox's deep baritone voice draws our attention to him again. "Are you done making an ass of yourself?"

"Helios, right?" Asmodeus asks. "He's protecting her?"

Tristan shifts. "What the fuck?" he blows out.

"Shh," I scold.

"I should have known," he sighs. "You'll always protect one another. It's sad and pathetic, really. No matter how much bad you do in the world, how much chaos you create, Helios will always be there to clean up your mess."

Nox smiles down at him before pressing the tip of his boot into the demon's throat. "The protectors and archangels are not the cause of your vengeance. And neither is Serena, regardless of the underhanded deals you have made with the archangels to try to say differently. You are the reason Lady Finella is dead. You used her to manipulate the gargoyles as a façade. You wanted her realm to lure Inanna, playing on her obsession for taking over domains. The fae queen died because of your carelessness for her existence."

"I'll uphold our original deal," Asmodeus returns.

Nox nods like he's agreeing, but grabs the demon by the hair and slams his head against the ground. "No."

"Fuck," Asmodeus groans out. "Fine. FUCK! I said fine, get off of me." He pushes at the demigod, who backs off.

Holding the back of his head, Asmodeus stands wobbling on his feet. The demon peers over Nox's shoulder at me. "You've become more trouble than you are worth."

My hands reach for my daggers, but Zander and Tristan each grab an arm, stopping me from releasing them.

Asmodeus curls his lips at my reaction and locks eyes with Tristan. "I'll never forget how loud Serena screamed that first night at the Midnight Temple. Did you know she called for you, Trist? Over and over. She cried out for you. Vowed you would come for her. Protect and save her," he says dramatically. Then he lowers his voice. "Even when I whispered in her ear at night that you would fail her. How could you not? You have Gage Gallagher's bloodline."

With my breath held, I move closer to Tristan, because his anger is radiating off him in palpable waves. Wrapping my fingers around his wrist, I tighten my grip on him.

"Serena's adamancy became so resolved that one night, after tripling her drug dosage, I went in to the room she was in, gently stroked her cheek and then cruelly broke her ribs and backhanded her so hard across the mouth that your name fell silent immediately on her lips," he yells.

The words have barely finished leaving the demon lord's mouth when Tristan teleports in front of him. His face is dark as his shoulders shake with rage. Tristan's fists use Asmodeus's face as a punching bag, pummeling his flesh.

Black, tar-like blood gushes and flies everywhere. A deafening howl thunders around us, coming out of Asmodeus. Zander and I both run to Tristan, but Tova and Lael hold us back. Nox grabs Tristan and yanks him off.

Asmodeus swears viciously as he lies on the ground panting, wet with blood, and curled in pain. Even for a demon, given the severity of the wounds Tristan caused, it's going to take him a bit to heal himself.

Nox drags Tristan back to me. "Get him under control."

I grab Tristan's face, breathing heavily as I force him to look at me. "Tristan," I whisper, because his eyes are vacant.

His breathing is ragged and he's covered in black blood. After a second, he fixates his eyes on me. "Stay with me."

In an instant Asmodeus is on his feet, his black wings spread out behind him as he seethes at us. "I'll spare Serena's life. And bury all thought of avenging the St. Michaels for Finella's death," he spits blood onto the ground. "Consider it a *welcome to the family* gift. Gage is, after all, bedding my niece, Nassa. And after your reckless attack seconds ago, it's clear that you are your father's son, through and through," he snarls.

Tristan twists to face the demon, but Nox steps in front of him. "And what about Kupuva and the Diablo Fairies?"

"If you bring me my goddess, I will call them off. If not, they're yours to deal with," he snips. "Now get the fuck out."

That's why Asmodeus wanted to attack the divine gates. It was never about revenge against Michael, Uriel, or my family for Lady Finella's death. It was always about freeing Inanna. As protectors, we were simply in the way— salt in a deep wound. And now that he knows the gargoyles aren't the only ones who protect the gates, we are no longer his primary target.

Nox steps into the demon's space. "She isn't yours. She never was. She was always mine. I won't bring Inanna to you. The gargoyles and I will deal with the Diablo Fairies. And when I am done," he lowers his face into Asmodeus's, "I will rip you apart. One piece at a time."

18

WEAK

TRISTAN

I clench my shaking hands to keep from sending them into the closest wall. A furious shudder wracks my body every time I think of what Asmodeus said he did to Serena when he held her hostage. At the thought, I suddenly feel hot and cold all at once. Every breath I suck in leaves me needing more, like I can't catch my breath, no matter how hard I try.

With a frustrated growl, I open the french doors and step out onto the deck. My gaze falls on the lake below as I inhale deeply of the woodland realm's fresh air.

After our visit to Demon Falls, we immediately came to my cabin. Apparently, the raw emotion the demon lord set off in me was enough to trigger my teleporting gift, taking it back from Serena, which enabled us to come here.

Nox and I both agreed we needed a few days to get our realms and armies prepared before going after the Diablo

Fairies. Serena, Zander, and I came back here, to my home in the woodland realm, to do just that. If we are to win, we'll need both the gargoyles and the Lion Guard fighting side by side with the Noctis army.

My fingers grip the poplar railing as I bend over and try to gain control of my anger. Safe. She is safe. And here.

As if she knows I need her, Serena's arms wrap around my waist and she presses her body close to my side. She leans closer and whispers across my ear, "Are you okay?"

"Not yet," I reply in a rough, shaky voice. "But I will be."

Her breath is hot against my neck, her hand sliding into mine. "Come on, I know something that will relax you."

Serena pulls me into the large bathroom attached to the master suite. Arching a brow, I play with my brow piercing as I stare at the empty tub.

"Want to join me?" Her voice is low.

"Yeah, raindrop, I do." I kick off my boots.

Kissing her hand, I let her lead me over to the tub and help her in before I slide in across from her. As we shift to get comfortable, the cold coming off the porcelain seeps through my jeans and T-shirt. Almost immediately, I relax.

Strangely, empty tubs have become our safe space.

"You and Zander knew about Inanna?" I mutter.

Serena nods her head.

"We should discuss this, Serena."

Her long auburn hair falls over her slender shoulders.

The motion causes her flowery scent to swirl around me. "Not now, okay? For twenty-four hours, I just want to be normal. No talk of demons, gods, wars, or anything that resembles any of the above. I want us to just . . . just be us."

I understand why she needs what she does.

"I want . . ."

"What?" I tilt my head. "What is it you want?"

She gives me a pitiful smile. "I want us to have fun."

"Come here," I extend my hand palm up for her.

She grips it like a lifeline as I pull her toward me so she can straddle me. After she does, we stay like this for a few minutes before she leans her head against my shoulder.

"Tristan?"

"Hmm?"

"What if I told you I don't want to do this anymore?"

"Do what?"

"Any of it," she whispers. "That instead, I want to just run away from everything? Does that make me weak?"

"No," I caress her lower back with my thumbs. "Never weak." I reach for her face, pulling it back a little so I can look into her eyes. The very same ones that make me want to say fuck the world and run away and take her far from all this shit. "You are the bravest woman I have ever met."

She laughs bitterly.

"Listen to me. You're beautiful, strong, and brave. There is no one else I'd rather have on my side. Ever." My gaze searches hers. "I swear to you."

Her mouth crashes against mine with so much force it actually hurts. And yet, the pain is intoxicating and addictive. She arches her body as my fingers sneak underneath the cotton of her shirt, digging into the flesh on her back, pulling her toward me. Serena's fingers curl tightly into my hair, and her chest grazes mine as I move my hands to her hips, tugging her closer to my body.

"What's going on in here?" Zander asks smugly from the open doorway.

I groan at his interruption as Serena rears back.

My eyes snap over to my brother. He's leaning on the door frame, arms crossed, wide grin on his face, before I look back at Serena. Her mouth is swollen from our kiss and her big blue eyes framed with thick dark lashes are blinking in both surprise and anger. I swallow, my body still humming from the buzz of her kiss.

"I really have to learn to start closing doors," she moans.

"Yeah you do, raindrop."

Amused, Zander pushes off the frame, walks in, and takes a seat on the side of the tub, frowning down at us.

"You guys do know that you are using the tub wrong, right? Water and bubbles go inside. Clothing, outside," he explains, clearly enjoying himself.

Serena shrugs. "We prefer it this way. It's our thing."

He winks at her. "Kinky, but whatever turns you on."

"What do you want, Zander?" I all but growl out.

"Your kitchen is stocked up for you, you know, since

you no longer have a housekeeper and all," he fake-laughs. "You're welcome, by the way. Also, the Lion Guard has its marching orders and Queen Ophelia will be back from her political tour in three days. I'm getting ready to head out."

"To London?" I confirm.

Zander volunteered to update the St. Michaels and Magali on what happened at Demon Falls. Personally, I think he's just anxious to see Magali. I can't blame him.

"Yeah, but first, I have an errand to take care of, for Serena." He turns his attention to her and she dips her chin.

"What kind of errand?" My focus slides between them.

Serena opens her mouth to speak but he cuts her off.

"Tampons. She needs some. You have none," he deadpans.

Stunned, Serena's mouth drops open.

"Tampons?" I repeat.

"Yeah. The big, absorbent kind. Ultra, right, champ?"

She glares at my brother. "You need professional help."

"Good call. I'm sure *someone* at the store will point me in the right direction once I am there," he banters.

"Stop." Her eyes narrow.

"Oh. I'm sorry," he smirks. "Are you two not there yet in your relationship? Is it still too private to talk about?"

I point to my brother and then Serena. "You are getting my girl . . . tampons? At her request?" I ask, slowly.

"What can I say, I'm swoonworthy," he retorts.

"He's not—," Serena starts, but he interrupts again.

"Oops. That's right. Caught," he shows us his palms. "I'm not just getting her tampons. She also needs hemorrhoid cream too. My bad." He throws a challenging look Serena's way, which makes her roll her eyes at him.

I press my lips together, partly to prevent myself from laughing at the two of them, and partly because it's obvious that something weird is going on between them.

Which makes me wonder why the fuck he doesn't want me to know where he is going at her request?

"She's a hot mess this month," Zander adds.

"You can't heal your," I pause, taking in a breath and trying not to laugh. "Issue yourself? Given your ability to heal?"

She sighs, defeated. "Apparently not."

Zander stands. "You should take better care of our girl."

"MY girl. She's *my* girl."

His arms open. "And yet, I'm the one she comes to for help during her lady troubles and monthly cycle needs."

Her face starts turning red as she closes her eyes and covers them with her hands. "By the grace," she whispers.

I lose it and start laughing, which embarrasses her even more. She removes her hands from her face and opens her eyes, cursing as she glares at the two of us. "You two suck."

"Anyway," Zander draws out, amused with himself and Serena's reaction. "Off to run your errand, champ. Tristan, need anything? Ointment? Floss? Extra small condoms?"

"No," I growl at him.

"M'kay," he waves his phone at me. "Text if you change your mind. See you guys in a few days!"

When he finally leaves, I turn my attention back to Serena's pink cheeks. "Care to tell me why my brother is lying about buying you tampons and butt cream?"

"Because he likes to humiliate me. That's why."

"You did just ask for normal," I wink at her.

"Your brother is anything but normal."

"Where is he really going?"

She meets my eyes. "I can't tell you right now."

"Serena."

"You will just have to trust me on this. Like I did you."

Damn her for throwing that back in my face. "Okay."

She frowns. "I'm sorry he ruined our moment."

I run my fingers down the side of her jaw, memorizing the way her skin feels like velvet. She gasps under my touch.

"Don't be, raindrop. We have a lifetime of moments."

LOVE LIKE OURS

SERENA

From the bed, I stare at the overly bright, larger-than-life moon, envious at how peaceful and far away it is. Millions of miles away from all the drama and chaos that surrounds Tristan and me. For some reason, everything always seems livelier in the woodland realm. Maybe it's because the air and water here are pure and untainted with pollution.

The stars sparkle and dance across the vast darkened sky. Their reflections bounce and leap off the ripples in the lake, reminding me of when I was healing in the forest near the Academy. It's strangely comforting.

Closing my eyes, I silently drift until I hear Tristan's footsteps as he comes upstairs. When I open my eyes again, he is standing in the doorway, watching me.

Words stall on my breath as I stare at him. He's dressed only in pajama bottoms, leaving his chest bare. My gaze runs the length of him before landing on the protector tattoo over his heart, the one infused with my blood, creating our bond. I focus on it as he pushes off the frame and wordlessly walks toward me, climbing into the bed and settling next to me.

We lay in the silence we both need. When Zander left, Tristan and I spent the entire day doing nothing. We swam in the lake, watched a ton of movies and ate a lot of pizza as we talked only about the future, not the present. Our future.

It felt so normal.

Easy.

Peaceful.

And now . . . my heart is racing out of control.

In the strained silence, I'm hyperaware of everything about him. Like the slow, steady breaths flowing between his perfect lips. And the heat radiating off his body, causing mine to suffer with the need to be enveloped in his warmth.

I turn my head and look at him.

He stares back and a shy grin appears on his perfect lips.

"This is . . . so awkward."

"I know!" I screech.

A chuckle falls from him. "Why?"

"I have no idea," I gasp for breath as I giggle.

It feels so good to laugh after everything that has happened. Tristan's laughter joins mine. Unable to stop, we laugh until tears slide down my cheeks. He turns to lay on his side, watching me, causing a flutter to form in my chest.

The sound of his laughter fades as he reaches over and with his thumb, he wipes off a teardrop that settled on my bottom lip. I still, staring at him with a rapidly beating heart as he brings the thumb to his mouth and with his gaze remaining locked on mine, he sucks off the bead, reminding me of when we first met and he gave me my nickname.

"I missed you so fucking much," his voice is low.

Lifting my finger, I trace the tattoo he has of me on his arm. A girl kneeling with wings spread out behind her. In her palm, a single raindrop. "I was always with you."

At my touch, his eyes close and his face relaxes.

"I promise you. I won't let anything else happen to you."

My chest swells as his words fill me with an overwhelming longing. It feels good just lying next to him.

When he opens his eyes again, his fingers brush over mine, interlacing our fingers. It's such a simple thing, but I feel it all the way to my core. His touch sears me.

Licking my lips, I feel my pulse jump as Tristan's other hand lifts to the over-the-shoulder, loose-fitting white T-shirt I'm wearing. He pushes the side that is hanging even lower on my arm. His eyes devour me with each touch.

"I need you, tonight."

"I'm yours," I reply, breathlessly.

He hasn't even done anything to me yet, and already my body is alive with pleasure and need. My skin sensitive.

Tristan's hand disappears beneath the sheet and the sound of lace ripping fills the silence.

I narrow my gaze on him as he brings his hand out from under the covers and eyes my ripped panties. Tristan gifts me a smug grin, the same one that makes me want to scratch his eyes out while at the same time mauling him with my body.

"Pretty," he whispers, and throws them.

"Those were expensive," I pout.

"You should know better than to wear expensive lace."

It's true. This is like the tenth pair he's destroyed.

Damn gargoyle.

He throws the covers off and the cool air bites at my heated skin. Holding my gaze, he slithers down on the bed.

A sweet, slow burn washes over my skin, and I squeeze my eyes closed for the briefest of moments, overwhelmed.

Every inch of me is aware of every inch of him.

The moon's rays bounce off his smooth, muscular back as he slowly crawls over me. His mouth touches my leg, and I tremble with pleasure and whimper when his tongue swirls its way up my thigh. My entire body shakes under his hands as they move up my sides to my hips, holding me in place just as his hot breath reaches me. Tristan's tongue swipes the sensitive spot and I close my eyes and release a hard breath at the contact. The scraping of his scruff against my sensitive skin causes me to tremble again.

Tension soars out of my body as he takes me in his mouth, taking his time.

With a final light kiss, his mouth moves away from me, and he makes quick work of removing his pajama bottoms before sliding his warm body over mine.

One hand cups the back of my neck, squeezing it and holding it tightly as my body arches to meet his. Chills run over my skin as his stomach and chest settle over mine.

I gaze up into his love-filled eyes and my breath hitches.

He drags his mouth slowly across mine before whispering, "I'll protect and love you until my last breath."

I try to push away the unwanted ache that settles in my chest at the way his vow came out like a goodbye.

Instead, I focus on the way his thighs press against mine, and the heat of his skin under my hand.

When I finally reach between us and guide him to where I need him to be, I am completely wrecked. My body is strung so tight that I'm almost afraid to keep breathing. Afraid one breath will set me off before we've even begun.

With the slowest of movements, Tristan slides into me and fills me. Each slow, calculated movement between us causes a delicious friction. He takes his time. Savoring every touch almost as if they were his last, he watches me like I'm the most fascinating creature in the world.

My eyes water as I am overcome with emotion at just how beautiful and intimate this moment is between us. It feels different than all the other times we've been together. Like we have a deeper connection between us.

He shudders at the same time as the beautiful tension he's built in me releases. Blood heats and explodes, running to every inch of my body through my veins.

Tristan holds me firm as my body shivers and writhes beneath him. I stare into the depths of his eyes, seeing an unnerving sadness mixed with love before he blinks it away.

I take his face between my palms and gently kiss him.

Telling him that I'm not ready to let go of him.

Love like ours is rare.

When you find it, you fight for it.

20

FOXFIRE FOREST

TRISTAN

G rowing up the way I did, sometimes I wonder what *normal* actually feels like. If this is it, I don't want anything to do with the fucking word. For me, normal is now overrated.

My heart rams against my chest as if it is trying to break free. I can't remember the last time I've felt this unbalanced and out of control. Taking in a deep breath, I try not to appear outwardly as erratic as I feel inwardly. As it is, I am only about five seconds from completely losing my shit.

"Tristan, are you still there?"

Serena's voice reminds me why I am here.

In the dark.

Trying to get control over my erratic nerves.

Her fingers tighten around my wrists as if I'm her life-line, her savior, her everything. My body immediately responds to her, like she's my gravity. Memories of last night hit me hard. The way she felt underneath me. How for the first time ever in my life, I'd made love to someone.

I look down at a blindfolded Serena and tuck a piece of her loose hair behind her ear, kissing the side of her neck.

"I'm still here," I whisper hoarsely.

"Can I take this thing off my eyes?"

"Nope."

"For the record, when you blindfolded me earlier and said you wanted to show me something . . . well, to be honest, taking me outside in the cold for a hike wasn't really what I had in mind," she whines, annoyed with me.

Her annoyance makes me smile.

"Just a few more steps."

"You do remember that you have your gift of teleportation back, right?" she asks, almost tripping.

I catch her immediately, not letting her fall. "I do. But I didn't want to use it tonight. Plus, you said you wanted to have normal fun. Normal couples hike. They don't teleport."

"Not blindfolded," she argues.

"I've got you. Keep walking, raindrop."

After taking a calming breath, she stumbles over her own feet as I guide her through the dark forest. With my help, she makes her way around the thick brush and vines tangled together on the forest's floor. I guide her to avoid the exposed roots and moss-covered rocks so she doesn't break her neck as I bring her to the perfect spot.

We spent most of today in bed. Tomorrow we will leave for the Academy and meet up with her clan to finish things with Nox and the Diablo Fairies.

Given that I have no idea when I will be able to return to the woodland realm, I decided to take advantage of our last few moments of alone time.

"How long have we been walking?" she asks.

"Half an hour, maybe more. I told you it was hidden."

This place is special to me. My favorite spot across any and all realms and worlds that exist. Which is why I brought her here tonight, because Serena is also special to me.

And what I am about to do should be perfect.

After helping her over a fallen tree, I walk her to the clearing, surrounded by water and vegetation.

Slowly I remove the blindfold, watching as she blinks away the fog in her eyes, letting them adjust as she takes in the dark forest around us. Confused, her gaze flicks to mine.

I bring my finger up to my lips, signaling for her not to speak. We remain quiet and wait for the silence around us to grow even deeper while the forest falls asleep. A few seconds later, I can feel the trees sleeping and the mystical energy rising, as a surreal hush inhibits the noise of even the air around us.

Then it happens. One by one, pieces of the forest begin reawakening as they come to life and produce a dim glow like night-lights around us. The bioluminescent plants cause the still water, leaves, flowers, moss, and other vegetation to glow in the dark in a bluish-green-purplish glow.

Serena turns in a circle, taking it all in with awe.

"Welcome to Foxfire Forest," I speak quietly.

"Why are you whispering?"

"We have to, so as not to frighten the foxfire plants."

"Foxfire, you mean fairy fire plants?"

I nod. "The plants live deep within the trees' bark. When luciferase reacts with luciferin, it emits light. The plant's spores travel in the wind. When they land, they thrive on the moss and water, which is why everything has this dim glow to it."

"This is . . . it's insanely beautiful, Tristan." Her quiet tone is full of amazement. "I've never seen anything like it."

"Come on," I take her hand and we walk towards a larger-than-life tree. Placing my palm on the bark, I conjure a small archway in the trunk toward the bottom. Once it's large enough for us to fit through, I tug her inside the tree.

When the greenish-bluish light appears, I follow Serena's gaze to the top of the tree. It's still, as if frozen, as she takes in the sight of thousands of glow worms waking up to cover the inside canopy with twinkling lights. The worms cling to the roots and vines hanging from the top of the tree, making it appear like a huge glowing natural chandelier.

"It's breathtaking," she whispers.

When I look back down, Serena's penetrating eyes capture mine and instantly, I'm calm. Everything around me disappears, obliterated by her presence.

In this moment, I am physically incapable of taking my eyes off her, and yet, I'm somehow aware that soon a dark, dangerous energy will take my soul from her, leaving her with only my heart, because she owns it.

"You are breathtaking," I reply.

My pulse begins to beat wildly again, stealing the air from my lungs as her gaze drinks in mine.

Exhaling, I take a knee in front of her and hold both her hands in mine, looking up at her curious expression through my lashes as she wonders what I'm doing.

"The moment I met you, you sparked and ignited something somewhere inside of me. The first time I saw you in that field, dancing naked in the rain, I was sure that in my entire existence, I'd never seen anyone so bewitching. And I was right. You are beguiling in both beauty and intelligence. And while our connection started way before you took your first breath, the fact that we exist, as one, takes mine away every single day." I swallow, taking a moment because she is staring at me so intensely. "Even in this moment of madness we are living in, I've never been so certain of anything in my whole life as I am about my love for you. I promise to protect and love you, until the last bit of life leaves my body. I will love only you, forever, in both our physical existences and spiritual eternities."

She exhales loudly as I pull out the ring I had made for

her months ago, when I renounced the throne and took on the position as chancellor of the Royal Protector Academy.

The band is hematite, my protector stone, designed with vines that match her protector bracelet. In the center is a large princess-cut emerald, her protector stone in the shape of the title that she hates, but wears with honor.

Hidden within the stone is a barely noticeable sketch of the Sun of Vergina insignia—our prophecy. Our link.

"Will you, Serena Elizabeth Vivian St. Michael, daughter of Abigail and Callan, princess and heir of the gargoyle race, do me, Tristan Armel Gallagher, son of Ophelia and Rionach, prince and heir to the woodland realm," I pause for a moment, taking in a deep breath before adding, "and son to Gage Gallagher, second in command of the Paris clan of gargoyles"—tears form in her eyes at my acceptance of my gargoyle bloodline—"do me the great honor of being my betrothed?"

With tears streaming down her cheeks, we stare at each other. The moment and silence seem to last forever, before her voice cracks with emotion. "I know of no greater honor that I could have than to be yours. Yes, in every way."

Standing, I step closer and kiss her.

The second her mouth is on mine, I stop breathing.

Serena shudders in my hands, and I release a half growl, half moan from her reaction. I part her lips, deepening the kiss. Memorizing the way she tastes and feels. Her lips are soft, silky. Our kiss slows, becoming something infinitely more intimate. It's so easy to get lost in her, lost in the connection between us. The world—the universe and all its realms—cease to exist.

When I pull back, our breaths come out in rough gasps.

Serena's eyes open slowly, dazed.

I take in a deep breath and slide the ring on her finger.

Serena looks down at it. "It's insanely perfect."

"You're insanely perfect."

She lifts her hand, staring at it. "I already agreed to take your name. All this wasn't necessary, Tristan."

I take her face in my palms so she looks at me. "You deserve everything I can offer you, and more. Especially a romantic gesture and a proper, royal proposal."

"A simple 'will you marry me' would have worked too."

I shake my head. "Not epic enough."

"Well," she laughs. "This is pretty fucking epic."

"The best proposals always are."

She frowns.

"What's wrong?"

"Now we definitely have to tell my parents."

"With a love like ours, what could go wrong?"

21

SILENT ROOM

SERENA

Everything that could possibly go wrong has since we've returned to the Royal Protector Academy. While my family was extremely happy and grateful to see me alive and in once piece, it turns out Tristan was less than upfront with me about just how pissed off my father is at him. It's bad.

"You piece of shit!" he aims a dagger at Tristan's heart.

"Dad, put the dagger down." I lift my hands in the air and jump in between them, frantically looking around Chancellor Davidson's old office for my family's help.

"If my daughter wasn't standing in front of you, I would stab you in the heart," my father threatens.

"Babe." Mom takes a few cautious steps toward Dad.

Once she's next to him, she slides her palm over his arm and pushes his wrist down, so he lowers the dagger.

Gently, she leans into his ear. "Callan, the vein in your

forehead is popping out. You know what that does for your skin complexion. Come sit down. Let's talk, calmly."

Defeated, he nods. "You're right, Abs." His eyes meet mine. "Sorry, pumpkin. I didn't mean to go all Hulk on you."

"Or my fiancé?" I add.

My father points at Tristan. "Don't call him that."

My mother forces a smile that looks more like she's baring her teeth at us instead of calming the situation, as she laces her fingers with my father's and drags him over two chairs before whispering, "You always wanted a son, babe."

With a curse, Tristan walks over to me and grabs my hands. "It's going to be fine, I promise."

"And if it's not?" My voice wavers.

"Then at least we had last night." A smile plays at the corner of his lips before we take the two empty seats across from my mom and dad.

I grab the one in front of my dad, just in case he goes Hulk-green again. Both my uncles—Asher and Keegan—and both my aunts—Eve and Kenna—stand behind my parents with their arms crossed, all watching us with mixed expressions.

Zander and Mags were excused to meet up with our friends Ryker and Ireland, and to debrief the protectors who attend the Academy about the Diablo Fairies and Nox.

Things haven't gone quite how I thought they would

when we shared our engagement news with everyone a few minutes ago. I mean, I didn't think it would go well, but I hadn't imagined my father pulling a weapon on Tristan.

I glance at my father. He has on a T-shirt that reads *DAD*—and then underneath—*a daughter's first and only love.*

Subtle.

Tristan clenches and unclenches his fists next to me.

I shift my focus to the bookshelves behind my family, running the length of one of the walls. Each row is filled with leather-bound books. The sun filtering in from the windows casts squares of light across the rows. Nervously, I count the squares in my head as the silence in the room stretches.

My mom shifts in her chair, catching my gaze before she plasters on a brighter-than-life smile. "What a very romantic proposal," she blurts out, using her nervous tone.

It's the one she uses when she doesn't know what to say or how to respond. I've heard it a thousand times over the years, but it's never been directed at me—until now.

My dad places his hand over his heart, as if in pain.

"And the ring!" Aunt Eve chimes in. Her overly excited voice is loud in the silence of the room, causing all of us to startle. "It's . . . stunning. Really. It's just . . . " she trails off, biting the inside of her cheek. "Stunning."

When she realizes how she sounds, she frowns at herself.

"You said stunning twice, siren," Asher states, amused.

"I'm nervous. This is awkward." Eve replies, trying to whisper-shout, but it's more of a shout-whisper.

"Dad," I prompt.

"I think I am having a heart attack," he says, then looks at my mother. "Abs, can gargoyles have heart attacks?"

"Aw, there you are, Callan. I knew you'd make a come-back." Uncle Asher pats my father's shoulder.

My mom gives my dad a tight smile. "I don't think you are having a heart attack, babe."

He exhales. "I definitely am. Like, a massive coronary."

"Should we get you some aspirin?" Uncle Asher asks.

"Asher!" Eve swats at his arm.

"What? Supposedly it helps prevent heart attack stuff." He waves his arm at his brother. "It thins the blood."

"He isn't having a heart attack," she grits her teeth.

"Callan *is* pretty pale," Uncle Keegan inserts.

"And short of breath," Aunt Kenna points out.

I cringe. "Why is everyone here, again?" I ask my mom.

"Hillary said it takes a village to raise a child. This is our village." Mom grants me her normal relaxed smile.

"I'm raised. And about to get married, so . . ."

Dad makes a strange pained sound in the back of his throat. "I need to lie down," he announces, crawling out of the chair and laying on the floor, on his back, in front of us.

"Serena, I think you stop using the m-word, yeah?" Uncle Asher suggests.

"By the grace. She's pregnant," Aunt Kenna declares.

"I mean, why else would she agree to marry the traitor's son?"

Uncle Keegan shrugs. "Maybe he brainwashed her."

My head falls into my hands. "This family needs to learn boundaries."

Aunt Eve laughs. "Boundaries? Good luck with that. Especially with these two as your parents. Get used to it; they'll be in the delivery room with you."

"I'm surprised they weren't in the room giving pointers and cheering you on during conception," Asher adds.

"I'm not pregnant," I snap out. "Or brainwashed."

Dad reaches for my mom's hand dramatically. "Abs, I think I'm dying. Slowly. That is what this is. All the blood is draining from my heart, which is why I am in pain."

With an exaggerated eye-roll, my mom smiles down lovingly at him, patting his hand. "It's okay, baby. It's almost over. Go toward the light."

"All right. I've had enough," Tristan stands. "I'm done."

I jump up and grab his arm. "Where are you going?"

"Anywhere but here, Serena." He looks down at me.

"Why?"

"Why?" He motions to my dad, who is now pretending to reach for the light. "Do I really have to explain myself?"

"I'm the king, so . . . you kinda do to me," Asher interjects, causing us both to narrow our eyes at my uncle.

He shrinks back, stepping behind Eve. "Just sayin'."

Tristan exhales loudly. "Your family is insane."

I frown. "I know."

Tristan stares at the carpet, his fingers twitching at his side. "You know what? I thought I could do this, but I can't. I'm sorry. You are tied to them by blood and . . . I just—"

My dad's head jerks up, watching us.

I stalk toward Tristan. "Don't do this."

He shakes his head, staring into my eyes. "I want you to know, to feel how much I love you. I would do anything for you, raindrop. Anything. Believe me when I say that."

"But—"

"Anything but them," he whispers.

"So that's it? You're just going to walk away from me? Because of my family? After all we've been through?" I yell.

Tristan closes his eyes.

"Look at me," I demand.

He opens his eyes and stares into mine. "I have given them absolutely no reason not to trust me. I live to protect you. They haven't even given me a chance to show them that. To this clan, I will always be a traitor's son. The protector who put their blood, their heir in danger."

I grab his hand tightly. "I don't feel that way."

"But they do. And they are an extension of you."

"So that's it?"

"This," he motions between us. "It's over. I'm done. I'm walking away. It isn't because I want to, but because I can only handle so much rejection and distrust from your clan."

"You aren't someone who gives up," I attempt.

"They've forced me to give up."

"Fine." With a trembling lip, I pull the ring off my finger and hold it out to him. "I love you," I whisper.

Tristan slowly reaches out to take the ring.

"Tristan, wait a minute," my father says, and gets up off the floor. He walks over to us and takes the ring out of my hand, holding it tightly in his.

"We're all going to die," Asher whispers behind us.

I glance up, looking at Tristan. His eyes narrow.

My father steps slightly in front of me, separating me from Tristan, and folds his arms across his chest. "I'm still pissed that Serena was kidnapped. But not at you. Not anymore. You brought her back safely, and sacrificed your-self to do so. For that, this clan is now in your debt. All that aside, you should have come to me and asked me for her hand. I would have totally said fuck no, but still, I should have been asked."

Tristan dips his chin. "Understood."

"I know we exchanged some harsh words the last time we saw one another." Dad pauses and sighs. "Well more like, I yelled and you took it, but Serena is *my* daughter. My only daughter. I deserve the rights and respect that come with being her father."

"Yes, sir. You do," Tristan agrees.

"Good," Dad nods. "We agree then." Dad turns to

Mom and grins brightly. She gives him two encouraging thumbs up like he's a toddler before he turns back to Tristan, less stern.

"Dad—"

"I'm not done, pumpkin."

"Okay," I exhale.

"At the end of the day, it's Serena's choice. And because the universe has a cruel sense of humor, my daughter picked, and loves, you. Believe it or not, Gage has always been considered a member of this family. The crazy-ass member who drives us all to drink and kill ourselves, but he's still a part of this clan. Which makes you one too. We call him a traitor, but it's done out of love and respect. I know it doesn't always sound like it, but it is. And . . . Abs is right. I have always wanted a son. Granted, in my head his name was Thor, but your name starts with a T, so we can make that work. Maybe you'll let me call you Thor?"

"No."

"As a nickname?"

"No."

"It's a good nickname."

"Still no."

"We'll table it for now."

Tristan exhales roughly. "Fine. Tabled."

"Can you peel potatoes?"

"What?" Tristan asks, taken aback.

"We have family dinners every Sunday. New members peel the potatoes. Ask Gage if you don't believe me."

Tristan looks around, confused. "I guess."

"You guess, or yes, I can peel them?"

"Yes. I can peel."

Dad rubs his thumb over his bottom lip, staring at Tristan for a moment before turning to me.

Leaning in, he lowers his voice to a soft whisper. "Are you positive? You really, really, really want him?"

"I do."

"Forever?"

"Yes."

"This isn't like when you were ten and you wanted to sell Uncle Keegan at your lemonade stand because he sneezed on you. If Thor sneezes on you, you will still have to love him. Forever means . . . forever, pumpkin."

"If *Tristan* sneezes on me, I promise to still love him."

"Even if the sneeze contains a virus and you get sick?"

"Even if I get sick."

My dad looks behind me at my mom. "Thoughts, Abs?"

"I think it's time to let her go, Callan."

My dad's eyes widen. "No fucking way. She's on loan."

"Dad," I push out, and he looks down at me, taking my face between his palms.

"Love is forever, Serena. My love for you is a forever love," he vows. "There is nothing you could do, including marrying Thor, that would make me let you go."

215

"I know, Daddy." His face softens. "And it's Tristan."

"Does he eat fruit-flavored ice cream?"

My dad doesn't consider fruit-flavored ice cream a dessert. It's a big deal in our family if you like it. Don't ask.

"No. He likes chocolate," I lie.

"Good." Dad looks around before turning to Tristan and approaching him. "Do you promise to love and protect her?"

"With every breath I take," Tristan answers honestly.

"Well, then." My dad gets down on one knee in front of Tristan and holds my ring out to him. "Will you, Tristan Thor Gallagher, be my son-in-law?"

Tristan's expression turns shocked as my lips part at what I'm watching. I chance a look at my mother, who has tears in her eyes as if she is witnessing my proposal.

"By the grace, Callan, that is so romantic," Mom says.

"Are you proposing to me?" Tristan asks, snatching my focus away from the craziness that is my mother.

"I am, Thor. Please marry my daughter and take my clan as your own," Dad replies.

Tristan lifts his chin. "Will you stop calling me Thor?"

"I make no promises. It's a badass name."

Tristan meets my eyes and I can't help but laugh.

"Um . . . okay, then. I guess, I accept?" Tristan replies.

My family cheers and claps from behind me, causing us both to laugh and smile at the ridiculous of all of this.

"This family does get weirder with each passing year," Uncle Asher says.

"Not weird. Quirky. There is a difference," Uncle Keegan points out.

Dad stands, taking Tristan's hand in his, placing my ring into his palm and folding his fingers over it. "I'm honored to have you be part of, and protect, my family." He dips his head in respect. "Zhen pri, tu-tim," my father says in Garish, our gargoyle language. "Family first, forever," he adds the English.

"Zhen pri, tu-tim," Tristan replies.

22

MY BEGINNING

TRISTAN

Serena closes both heavy oak doors before turning and facing me. For a moment, we both stand in silence, contemplating what just happened. After a few seconds, we smile at one another.

"You. Were. Brilliant," she beams, hushing her tone.

"I can't believe your reverse psychology plan actually worked on them," I blow out. "I mean, when you first suggested that I pretend to leave you because of your family, I didn't really believe it would work. But . . ."

"But?"

"Your dad just fucking proposed to me."

"I know," she giggles.

"That was weird." I push my hand through my hair.

"It was necessary."

My teeth grind together. "Was it, though?"

"Yes," she steps toward me, taking my face in her hands.

"Then why do I feel guilty about duping them?"

"Don't," she brushes her lips across mine. "They had to come around on their own. We just got them there faster."

"Would they have come around, I mean, had we not pushed them into it with our fake fight?" I ask.

Serena tilts her head. "Gargoyles are fierce because they protect what they love. They love me. And I love you. It would have taken a while, but yeah, they would have come around on their own and honored my love for you."

Maybe it was better this way. At least now I can protect their princess freely instead of having them lock her in a tower. And like with all fairy tales, one day, maybe I can carry her away and we can live happily ever after.

I have a sinking feeling in the pit of my stomach that mine isn't going to be anywhere near a happily-ever-after ending. Even with our small victory today with her family.

My promise to Nox is my fate now.

"All that said, we can never tell them we did this."

I dip my chin. "Agreed." I pull her closer and bask in how good and comforting she feels, clinging to her like a lifeline. Inhaling her scent, I take a moment to appreciate where we are. Asmodeus has backed off. Her family has accepted us. Now, we just have to fight off the Diablo Fairies and I need to keep my promise to Nox.

Then she's safe.

NOX

Forever.

"Close your eyes," I say softly into her ear.

When she does, I teleport us back to her suite here at the Academy. Her lids flutter open and I take a step back.

"What are we doing here?" she asks.

"I have a surprise for you."

"Oh yeah?" her brows raise. "The kind of *surprise* like when you blindfolded me and said you wanted to show me something?" she teases. "Or the naughty kind?"

"Come on," I tilt my head toward her bedroom.

Her eyes sweep down my body. "Naughty it is."

Laughter rumbles out of me. I tug on her hand and pull her down the hallway. When we reach her closed bedroom door, I look down at her. "While we deal with the Diablo Fairies we'll be staying here at the Academy. So, I fixed a few things that were broken." I open her bedroom door and watch as her lips part and she walks into the redesigned bedroom. "I changed out the bathroom door too."

"When? How?" She breathes out in awe.

I step closer, tucking my hands into the front of my jeans. "Zander and Magali helped me while you and I were in the woodland realm the past few days," I admit.

"Tristan, this is . . ." she trails off when she sees the bed.

Holding my breath, I watch her step over to the large four-poster bed, draped in dark gray silk fabrics. Hematite inlays twist around the posts, carved to look as if they are vines. Emeralds have been added, appearing like leaves.

Her fingertips brush over the fabric as she turns and faces me, swallowing. "Is this our stone state bed?"

"It is," I reply, feeling shy all of a sudden. "When we figure out a more permanent living situation, it will go into a chamber, but for now, I thought it best here."

"Tristan." Tears fill her eyes. "I don't know what to say."

For gargoyles, a stone state bed is where we heal in a deep sleep. During the sleep we can astral project or realm jump. The bed is charmed for protection while we sleep.

And only a protector and their bonded partner, or mate, are permitted to sleep in it. Each is designed and enchanted for that particular couple with their healing stone. Since my bloodline is only partially gargoyle, we need both Serena's and my stones inlaid in the wood, instead of just one.

Mates share their stone state bed because, once in a deep stone state sleep, you physically and mentally become one with your bonded partner. It's very intimate. No one will else will ever be able to share the stone state bed but the mates it was created and charmed for.

"How did you do this?" she chokes out.

"Gage. A gift from him to us."

She stills, standing in front of the stone state bed, a look of pure joy radiating from her face. My focus is so intent on her, I've literally stopped breathing. I pull in a shaky breath and watch her as she stares at me.

My body automatically moves toward her. *Mine.* She's been mine since the first day I linked with her. She's been mine since the first time I kissed her. She's been mine since the moment I gave her my heart, and she returned my love.

Seeing her in front of our stone state bed, my body burns in ways I've never experienced before, overwhelmed with the primal urge to claim her. Mark her. Make her mine.

Stepping toward her, I brush my knuckles down her cheek, my stomach muscles tightening when she tilts into my touch, needing more. My fingertips glide over her jaw, taking her chin between my fingers and lifting her head.

I move closer into her space, still leaving a breath of air between our lips. Lazily I drag my fingers down her neck, pausing at the base. Holding her eyes, I gently wrap my hand around the lower portion of her throat so my empath gifts can read her emotions.

Her pulse beats wildly under my touch.

Bending forward, I push her until the backs of her knees hit the bed. Roughly fisting the bottom of her shirt, I drag it over her head, along with her bra. She doesn't flinch.

"I need to make you mine," I growl out.

With a rough exhale, she quickly finishes undressing.

Watching her, I grab my shirt between my shoulder blades and pull it off, then quickly take off the rest of my clothing.

Her gaze sweeping hungrily over me, with a twist of her lips she tilts her head and whispers huskily, "I'm yours."

I don't even realize I've moved until my lips crash onto hers, in a frenzy to claim her over and over again until she begs me to stop. With a feral growl, I lift her and she wraps her legs around me. In one fluid movement, I lay her down on the bed and angle myself perfectly, thrusting into her hard and fast, marking her as mine as I become hers and nobody else's. This is it for me, everything I've always needed and wanted, found in the one girl I never knew I was missing. The past, the future—none of it matters.

Right now, feeling her warmth and desire is everything. I push harder, faster, and she meets me with each thrust, grabbing and pulling me tighter against her as we both find our release, not stopping until we're both boneless and exhausted.

"Holy shit. That was amazing," she groans.

I lift my head and give her a cocky smirk. "Really? You aren't just saying that to stroke my ego, are you?"

Her lips twitch in amusement. "I'm pretty sure your ego is big enough, and doesn't need me to stroke it."

"You should always stroke it," I tease.

The sound of her laughter fills the room and I forget to breathe, because the sound is so fucking beautiful.

"I love you," I whisper, my voice hoarse.

"I love you, too," she replies, brushing my lips.

Obsessed.

I am officially obsessed with this woman. My heart is about to burst out of my chest with love because every time she breathes, I find myself actually being jealous of the air that touches her lips. My lips. The swollen ones on mine.

She is my beginning—my end.

23

FIRE & ICE

SERENA

With a startle, I jerk awake in a cold sweat as tears run down my cheeks. While taking several harsh inhales, I furiously wipe away at the tears and try to catch my breath. The nightmare lingers, leaving a horrible ache in my heart.

It's the third bad dream tonight. All of them ended the same way, with Tristan's lifeless body draped in my arms. I look around the dark room and shift on the bed. This is not exactly the best way to start off our stone state experience.

I swear this bed is cursed, not charmed.

Tristan sits up, worry etched all over his face. Without saying anything, he holds out his hand. I stare at it, and with a final inhale, I reach for him, sliding my palm over his. He squeezes and doesn't let go as he tugs me down into a sleeping position. With our hands pressed together, he curls me into his chest. Protecting me. Keeping me safe.

"Tell me," he mumbles in my ear.

I blink my eyes, stinging with unshed tears. I want to tell him what I dreamt, but I can't, because it's too painful.

"How did Gage survive when Camilla died? How does he go on when the other half of his soul is missing?" I ask in a quiet voice. "I can't imagine how he breathes every day."

Tristan's hands wrap around me tightly. "What other option is there for him? As hard as it is, he has to live and honor her memory."

I nod, silently.

"Their fate isn't ours, though. Do you want to know why, raindrop?" His breath tickles my ear.

This I have to hear. "Why?"

"Well," he shifts, snuggling into me. "First, you are way too stubborn and hard-headed to go and die on me."

"Well, that is true."

"And second, I'm too much of an asshole to let death defeat me. I have too much to live for. Like you."

"Then we agree, neither one of us dies?" I whisper.

"We have a plan. Neither one of us dies."

"Unless it's together. Like in a horrible plane crash or one of those weird house explosions from a gas leak," I add.

"Wow. Both of those scenarios are unromantic and morbid, but yeah, raindrop. We go together or not at all."

"Romantic?" I parrot. "How is death romantic?"

Tristan's voice is low. "Well, if things go badly and I

were to die, I'd want to spend my last moments with you—wrapped in your arms. The last memory I'd want, raindrop, is you kissing me."

An icy feeling crawls under my skin at his words.

"You don't have to do this," I croak out.

"Do what?"

"Give Nox your realms. Turn your soul dark."

His chest rises under my cheek as he exhales. "This fixes everything. Keeps you safe. It's already done, Serena."

"We'll find another way." I tremble in his arms.

"There is no other way." He pulls me tighter. "Nox already dealt with Asmodeus. All we need to do is trap the Diablo Fairies so he can work his dark magic and they can be reborn as part of the Noctis army. Then the threat to you and the gargoyles will be gone. In the end, it all works."

"What about you? Your realms? Queen Ophelia?"

"I've made arrangements for my mother's safety and the realm's. Zander and the Lion Guard will take care of it."

"I. Can't. Lose. You, Tristan." My voice cracks.

"I'm not going anywhere, raindrop. My soul will just be a shade darker. That's it," he kisses my forehead.

"What if it changes you?" I reply.

"It won't. It was already dark."

I sit up and look at him. "No. It isn't. It's pure. And you aren't just gambling with your soul, but my heart too."

"Stop worrying about something that doesn't matter."

By the grace. "You know what? You're right."

"I am?"

"It doesn't matter. You've been careless with my heart. Careless with my love and trust. You keep telling me that you would die for me. Live to make sure I am happy and safe. And yet, everything you are doing says the opposite."

"Serena—"

"No." I twist away from him. Sliding out of the bed, I turn and face him as he watches me. "It's unfair of you to ask for everything I have to offer, knowing that you may not be able to follow through with your end of the deal."

My eyes close against the vision from my dream.

"You died," I blurt out.

He stills. "What?"

"In my dream. You were gone."

"It was just a dream."

My lids flutter open and I look into his eyes. The air around us is thick with tension as we stare at one another.

My hands begin to sweat as I take him in. "A dream in stone state, Tristan, which means it could be a premonition of things to come."

"We haven't completed the bond yet, which means, for now, this is just a bed. And your dream, just a nightmare."

I exhale and say, "Promise me something."

"Anything."

"At some point, when I tell you to move so I can take a dagger for you, promise me you'll move."

He sighs. "You're not going to take a dagger for me."

"Please," I beg. "Please don't be brave or stubborn. Please let me protect what is mine. Let me be your savior."

He shakes his head and swears. "I don't need a savior."

"Let me protect you," I pause. "Please," I soften my tone.

"Fine. Protect me. But if you step between me and a dagger, I will stab the shit out of you myself to keep you from putting yourself in more danger," he growls out.

"Now *that* is romantic."

"I mean it," he says through clenched teeth.

"I believe you."

"We end this and come out of it together."

"Agreed." I nod.

"Come back to bed and try to get some rest."

"Fine." I sigh. "And what about tomorrow?"

"Tomorrow, we light the world on fire."

24

FREE ME

TRISTAN

Regardless of how nonchalant I appear to be about everything, I knew Nox would come for me. The minute I agreed to hand over my realms, I knew there wouldn't be a safe place for me to hide. That is why I am not running.

Why hide from your destiny?

It would be a weak thing to do, and I am not weak.

Last night isn't sitting well with me. I was lying too much to Serena. Honestly, I don't know how else to be about all of this. I know she's disappointed in me. Yet, I can't find it within myself to do anything more, or escape from the promises I've made. Promises owed in blood.

I'm also not going to hide behind her protection, or her sword, even though she begged me to. If her dream was a premonition, I'll face whatever sentence fate has in store for me. Head on. I will not stand by and watch the end of her existence or the fall of the gargoyle race.

There is a certain finality, a harsh realization that it's time—my time. Even love can't twist fate's choices.

"It has been decided that we fight tomorrow," Nox announces. "On the Blood Moon. A truce until."

Asher's eyes lock onto mine. "What do you think?"

"Kupuva has proven herself honorable," I answer.

"While she is dark-souled, she is chief of her tribe," Nox interjects. "The Diablo Fairies have been created in the image of ancient tribal warriors. Honor and ritual is highly important to them as warriors, especially in battle."

Keegan tilts his head at the deity. "And the directive for the army under her command is to go after Asher, Eve, and Serena? Is that still something they honor?" he asks coolly.

"The demon lord and I have come to a new agreement. Asmodeus has decreed they are no longer targets, nor does he hold them accountable for the death of Lady Finella," Nox's deep voice states. "However, the Diablo Fairies are still the gargoyles' concern. He won't call them off."

Conveniently, Nox leaves out that we must fight because he refused to give up Inanna to the demon lord.

"Tristan," Callan meets my gaze. "You were champion for Serena in the Donga fight with the Diablo Fairies, and you fought the demon fairy army within your realm. Is it still the case that they don't have supernatural gifts?"

"Yeah. Since the army was born of black magic, they don't have supernatural gifts. However, they can use dark spells to cast away a gargoyle's power, which makes them dangerous in a different way. Hand-to-hand will be key in gaining the upper hand over them," I answer. "They're fierce about their rituals, so we will be able to pick up on song, dance, or chanting before they spell cast."

"Why the Blood Moon?" Zander asks Nox.

"It is a gray moon, giving demon hunters the opportunity to stalk their prey better at night," the demigod replies. "I chose it for that reason. Kupuva agreed, unknowing that it gives my army an advantage."

"And it's an honorable time for demons to be reborn." A familiar deep male voice booms into the conference room.

We all look toward the door, where the new voice comes from. The five of us arranged to meet Nox, Tova, and Lael in the chancellor's old office to discuss strategy, while everyone else agreed to help Ireland and Ryker prepare the Academy's protectors for battle, even though they are ready.

They have been ready their entire existence, given this battle is why the Royal Protector Academy was created—to fight and keep both the reigning king and the heir safe.

Gage walks in with Helios and a beautiful goddess. She's wearing some sort of white Grecian dress thing. The color matches her white and gold wings. A large crown sits on her head, with two gold wings decorating it.

A gold collar clutches her neck, with gold chains that lead to two gold bands around her wrists. More gold chains dangle from the bands, attached to two lionesses, one on each side.

By the way the animals are standing regally, watching us, I don't think they are her pets.

More like guards.

"Hey," Zander whispers next to me. "Look, she comes with her own Lion Guard."

He laughs, and I throw an annoyed look at him.

"Dude!" Callan turns to my brother. "That was clever."

"Thanks." Zander nods and beams under the praise.

Fury crosses Nox's face as he steps up to them. "Why are you not behind the gates, Inanna?" Nox roars, and the entire building shakes with the god's anger.

The goddess narrows her golden eyes at him. "Quiet your voice in my presence, Nox," she replies.

Her voice is deep and sultry as she pets the lionesses on their heads. I don't know if she is calming them or herself.

They don't move.

Inanna tilts her head, drinking in Nox like it's the first time she's seen him. The movement causes her long dark hair to fall across her slender shoulder. He's still, but his eyes follow the movement in a way that only a man completely in love and obsessed with a woman would.

"I removed her, brother," Helios says.

I take in Zander next to me. His arms are folded casually. He isn't on guard like he normally is, as he watches the scene play out. "Why don't you look surprised by this?"

He shrugs. "Come on, if you didn't see this twist coming, you should re-read your story from the beginning."

"I am not freed, Nox." Inanna lifts her wrists, showing him the cuffs and chains. Her lioness guards remain statuesque. "The lion gargoyle and Helios have granted me a temporary reprieve, though I must remain chained."

Nox takes a step toward Helios. "You've placed her in danger by releasing her from divine protection."

"No, brother. You have." Helios answers calmly.

"Protection?" Inanna spits out. "Prison. It is prison you cursed me to when you allowed Helios to gift me life again."

"Christ." Gage runs his hands over his face.

"Want to fill us in on the family drama?" Asher asks.

The goddess's golden eyes swing to Asher. With her right hand, her fingers touch her heart and she dips her head respectfully. "I am Inanna, Sumerian goddess of love, beauty, light, and the Heavenly sky. And you are?"

"Holy shit," Callan blows out, surprised by her titles.

The clan never knew Inanna existed, even though they accept divine assignments from the Angelic Council.

"Asher St. Michael. King of the gargoyle race," Asher answers her, but it comes out sounding like a question.

The goddess straightens herself quickly. Her lips pucker as if she sucked on a lemon. "Why do you lie?"

Callan chuckles. "We find it hard to believe too. Some days we just humor him and nod. It's easier that way."

The goddess doesn't laugh. "Protectors are soulless. I sense the divine in you. As I do the satyr prince and his brother."

"It's a long story, but my mate awakened the divinity, gifting me a soul. It's rare." Asher's tone is quiet.

Inanna lifts her chin. "You are the Asher of Eve? Protectors of the divine gates? The divine protect you?"

"Yes," Asher answers softly. "Her father is Michael."

"You and your mate are revered behind the gates."

"We are honored to help protect them," Asher replies.

"Why is she here, Helios?" Nox asks, becoming more frustrated. "She is safer in the sky. Not here on earth."

"My protection of her has come to an end," Helios states.

Silence.

"I have heard rumors," Helios continues in an even voice. "Rumors of the war between the Diablo Fairies and the gargoyles. Rumors that you, brother of mine, leveraged a debt repayment and twisted it to darken a divine soul with the intention of taking over two domains. Domains that sustain the earth realm. DOMAINS WHICH ARE UNDER MY PROTECTION!" He bellows the last part.

"Why do you love and protect the earth realm so much, Helios?" Nox asks, seething with hatred. "What pleasure do you get from it? Do you think the realm will bring you Ereshkigal's favor after you gave life to Inanna again?"

"Ereshkigal?" Keegan questions.

"Their mother. The former goddess of the earth," Zander explains.

"Talk about family drama," Callan mutters.

"I do not protect the earth realm. That is for the gargoyles to do. Nor do I seek Ereshkigal's favor. I protect the water and woodland realms for pleasure." Helios calms.

"So this is about your nymph whore?" Nox challenges.

"Watch your tongue, brother. Your favor with me is slipping. Aoife has no part in this. The deities enjoy the pleasures of the woodland and water realms. And they will continue to do so under my protection. If you think otherwise, you are mistaken. If it is war you want between the gods and goddesses, then I accept." Helios pushes Inanna forward. "We have ended our need for one another."

Inanna lifts her chained wrists toward Nox. "Free me."

Wordless and unmoving, Nox stares at the chains.

After a while, Gage sighs. "He can free you, Inanna. But he will never be free *of* you. And that is why he will not grant you your freedom. Once you see the person you love die in your arms, there is no freedom in your existence. You will always be a prisoner to that image." He steps away from the deities, walking slowly until he stands behind me.

Gage's words cause my blood to turn to ice. What he just said is what Serena was trying to explain to me about her dream last night.

"This is the only situation where my love for you trumps my love for my realm, duty, and obligations."

Inanna face falls. "You will not free me then?"

"I cannot," Nox replies. "Your existence fuels mine."

"That is selfish!" she yells, with tears in her eyes.

"I am a dark-souled god. I was created to be selfish."

Helios pulls on her chains, forcing her and the lionesses to him. "Our original terms stand, Nox. She will continue to have my protection so long as you withdraw the threats you have brought upon the woodland and water realms."

Nox growls. "Fine. The satyr prince keeps his divine soul and realms. My debt has been paid to you already. I have dealt with the threat of Asmodeus. The Diablo Fairies are the gargoyles' mess to clean up. Now, take her back behind the gates," he orders. "Where she is safe."

"No!" Inanna shouts and pulls on her chains.

They clank and shift as she fights their hold.

Helios dips his chin. "Our agreement stands. Come, Inanna," he holds out his hand.

She looks at it before her eyes throw daggers at Nox.

"My love for you has ended," she spits out.

"Hate me all you want. I will live out my existence loving you. And know that while you are hating me, I will be thanking the gods that you exist and are safe from darkness and the deities' wrath," he replies.

A sole tear falls down her cheek as Helios drags her away in silence. After a moment of staring at the spot where she was standing, Nox turns and releases his fury on me.

His murderous eyes lock on mine. "Did you bring this heartache upon me, in order to revoke your word?"

"No."

"Our time has come to an end. I have fulfilled my debt to my brother. The Diablo Fairies will be here on the Blood Moon. They are solely your problem. I will not grant deity assistance in their defeat or rebirth," his voice cold. "As for our agreement, my brother's word reverses your promise."

"I am still willing to stand by our agreement," I state.

"Wait." Zander grabs me. "What the hell are you doing?"

I shake him off, stepping to Nox. "For Serena's existence and protection. I give you my soul and realms."

"I will not grant you what you seek." He tips his head toward Tova and Lael, and they disappear out of the office.

Staring at the closed doors, dread and anger flow through me as realization settles in. Everything I worked so hard to put into place these last few months is gone. Disappearing with Nox.

"Are you fucking insane trying to get him to agree again?" Zander pushes at me. "It's over. Helios has spoken."

I don't move, but clench my jaw, grinding my teeth together. "You did it." My voice is low and cold.

Slowly, Zander lifts his eyes to me. "What?"

"You and Serena knew about Inanna when we went to Demon Falls," I accuse. "Was that the errand you did for her? Run to Helios to tell him about my deal with Nox?"

With a sad smile, my brother drops his hands to his sides. "I'd never forgive myself if I allowed you to turn your soul dark and hand over your realms to him. I'd rather kill myself then be the one to watch you, or our people, die."

"Why?"

Zander releases a dark laugh. "Why? BECAUSE YOU ARE MY BROTHER! I LOVE YOU! I PROTECT YOU!"

"Your love and protection of me just ended my continued existence. You've sealed my fate. And Serena's."

"Tristan." Gage places a hand on my shoulder.

I shrug it off. "Why the hell are you here?"

"I went to Gage . . . and asked him for help." Zander explains, as if he's afraid to speak. "With Helios."

Tension settles in around the room.

"I see." I nod, no longer in control of my anger. "So, Rionach is dead. Therefore, you what? Just went to the back-up dad?" The cruel words come out without thought. "You've RUINED EVERYTHING," I roar angrily, "that I just spent months fighting for."

"Tristan, calm down a bit," Gage attempts.

"Fuck you. We aren't friends. Hell, we aren't even acquaintances. We don't know one another," I throw the words he first said to me back at him. "We. Are. Nothing!"

Storming forward, I yank open one of the office doors with force. It squeaks loudly with the intensity of my pull, echoing in the small space, causing a sense of déjà vu to hit me. The scene reminds me of the first time I stormed out of Chancellor Davidson's office, after he told me I was a lot like Gage. I exhale at the fucking irony of all this shit. Because after what just happened, I'm about to become him.

The moment I leave the building and take in a deep breath of fresh air, I realize I was wrong all those months ago when I stood in this very same spot. I thought I was afraid of Serena. Turns out, I'm not. I was afraid of who I would become if I let her into my life. I was afraid of becoming like Gage, a shadow of the being I once was, because I let someone in. Loved them and then had them brutally ripped away. Leaving me to pick up the pieces.

I push away the warmth from the fiery anger that has built in my chest. In its place, ice flows through my veins.

25

IN THE END

SERENA

W ith shaking hands, I swipe the key card and the lock to my suite clicks open. I open the door and close it quietly behind me. Exhausted from training all day, I throw my stuff on the counter and look around the dark suite. My heartbeat stumbles a bit. I thought Tristan would be here.

Gage, my uncles, Dad, and Zander joined the rest of us a few hours into training with the Academy's protectors.

They explained what happened with Helios and Nox.

I assumed that after Tristan cooled off he would join us to prepare for tomorrow, but he never showed up. By the end of the day, I was shaking so badly with withdrawal from not seeing him that I decided not to take our friends Ireland and Ryker up on their offer to spend the night, like Magali and Zander are.

Instead, I came back here, hoping to find Tristan. I was

wrong. I press my lips together and fidget with my protector bracelet. In a lame attempt at calmness, I walk into the kitchen and open and close the refrigerator door several times before noticing the empty beer bottles and pizza box on the counter.

My vision swings behind me toward the hallway and it hits me. With a deep exhale, I slowly walk toward the bathroom. When I get there, the door is open and the lights are off. The moonlight shines in through the window, bathing Tristan's silhouette in a silver-bluish glow.

I lean against the doorframe and cross my arms, staring at him in the dark. He doesn't move. He doesn't speak.

He just sits there, in the empty tub.

When his gaze finally settles on me, the look on his face and in his eyes sends shivers across my skin. And not the lust-filled kind of shivers. It's the kind where I know something bad is about to happen. He's hurt and mad.

"I'm in the tub," his voice is flat.

"I can see that."

"Privacy would be appreciated."

"The door was wide open," I point out.

"An oversight."

His tone is cruel as we mimic our responses from our first tub conversation months ago. Only during that one, I was the one in sitting in the cold, empty porcelain after he took me down in training. I frown, recalling how bruised my ego was, along with my body.

"What are you doing?" I whisper shakily.

"Gargoyles don't have souls." His voice is cold.

The scent of cinnamon, cigarettes, beer, and all things forbidden hits me as I step into the small space. *His* scent.

An overwhelming need to be closer to him starts to take over, but I curb it, knowing he needs his space. I lean against the sink, my fingers curling on the marble counter.

He takes a long pull from the bottle of beer in his hands, and I try to get a hold of the turmoil building inside of me.

Tristan stares at the faucet, mouth slack.

"Your penchant for stating the obvious is mind-blowing," I reply, not really knowing what to say to him.

A dark chuckle falls out of him. "And your and my brother's penchant for scheming behind my back is fucking amazing. Really. I mean, first ending my betrothal, and now my existence. You two should rule the fucking world."

A dark look crosses his eyes, sending a shiver of fear down my back. I swallow, taking him in. He's beyond pissed.

"Why are you sitting in the tub, Tristan?"

"You have no idea what the fuck you two have done."

"We were just protecting you." I argue.

"NO!" he shouts, and I startle. "You just *ended* me."

I take in a deep breath and clench my jaw. "The deal is revoked. Your soul is safe. The water and woodland realms are safe. So, tell me, Tristan, how exactly did we end you?"

He lowers his voice and speaks slowly. "My soul was never in danger, Serena. I have gargoyle blood running through my veins. If my soul darkens, or suppresses, I still can continue to exist because gargoyles are soulless."

My lips part as his words sink in. A hard lump forms in my throat at the meaning behind what he's saying. Tears sting my eyes as realization dawns on me. He's doing the reverse of what my aunt Eve did for my uncle Asher.

She awakened the divinity in his soul, bringing it to life. Tristan was trying to suppress his soul with darkness, putting it to sleep so that his gargoyle bloodline could take over and make him a pure-blood protector. Renouncing not only the throne, but also his satyr bloodline. For me. For us. *Shit!*

"But," I try to breathe. "The realms?"

"Were never in danger of falling. Helios would have always stepped in and protected them. Even if I wasn't king. My bloodline isn't tied to the realm's survival, Serena. My *mother's* is. *Zander's* is. I am only half-satyr, not pure. Therefore, if my soul was suppressed, the realms would have still lived on through them. Helios would have gone to war with Nox before allowing the demigod to take over, because of his love for Aoife and the Sun of Vergina prophecy."

While I try to catch my breath and make sense of this, he pushes himself out of the tub, storming over to me and stepping into my space. With cold, detached eyes, he looks down at me. One hand on each side of me, caging me in.

With a sad, defeated smile he places the lightest kiss on my lips before taking a step away from me. "What you and my brother did . . . was kill me. You've ended my existence."

He throws the beer bottle against the wall and walks out as it shatters into a million pieces on the tile floor.

Along with my heart.

26

THERE IS ONLY YOU

TRISTAN

There was no time for actual wedding plans. Given what Serena and Zander did, it's probably for the best. Feeling the way I do, I most likely would have refused to participate. And I know I am being an ass, but history repeats itself. I just want to get this fight today over with and drown myself in expensive liquor —a lot of it.

It's not her. It's the situation. And love? Well, how the fuck can she still love me, knowing what my future holds?

Ever since I left her in the bathroom last night, I'd been completely unable to focus on anything. I never showed up for training yesterday because what's the fucking point? I'm a dead man walking as it is. And I wanted to blame her. I did.

Then I looked into her eyes last night as she realized what the consequences of her and Zander's actions are, and a piece of me died seeing the darkness take over her gaze. The sadness. Knowing their actions sealed my fate.

Then, I wanted to strangle the shit out of her for being the cause of it. So, I hurt her. Her feelings. Her heart.

I wanted her to feel as devastated as I do right now.

Then I wanted to hold her. Feel her one last time.

But I couldn't bring myself to, so instead, I left.

Christ, I'm a danger to myself and everyone around me.

I pour more brandy and stare into the fire.

The air shifts, and a shadow crosses briefly in front of me. The footsteps are heavy, solid as they approach. "Tristan."

"How the hell did you know I was here?" I drink more.

"I asked myself where would I go," Gage replies in a defeated voice.

He walks over to the bar, grabs the decanter and a crystal glass, and joins me on the leather couch in his Paris loft. With a deep exhale, he fills our glasses and sits back.

"She loves you," he mutters.

"I know."

"They both do."

I take a sip. "I know that too."

He sets his glass on the coffee table and turns to face me.

I brace myself for his speech.

"Sometimes, we do stupid shit to protect those we love."

I let out a heartless laugh. "Are you referring to what I

did, or what Serena and Zander did?" I ask in a quiet voice.

He's quiet for a moment, then whispers, "Friends."

"What?"

"You were wrong. Before. When you were bitching at me in front of the deities. I'd say at this point in the game, you and me, we're friends." His lips draw into a grim line.

"How do you figure?"

Gage waves his hand around his loft. "It seems you always come to me when you are in trouble. Isn't that what friends do?"

I look around. Fuck. He's right. Oddly, his loft has become a sort of safe haven whenever shit hits the fan. And if I am being honest with myself, over the last few months, Gage has been the one I've turned to when I needed help.

And he's always stepped up. Without argument.

I meet his eyes and hold out my hand to him. "Friends."

With a rough exhale, he takes my hand, grips it and nods. "Will you ever be able to not love her?" he asks.

Can I? I think about it for a while. No matter how pissed off I am, she owns me. Every piece of me.

"In the end, there is only her."

"Then you'd better get your ass off this couch and get back to the Academy. It's the Blood Moon and shit is about to go down. And your girl is right in the middle of it."

"Right." I stand and cross my arms, as he stands too.

"Plus, the London clan is gathering in her suite. There is yelling and fighting. I heard something about your balls being removed and thrown down your throat," he adds.

I roll my eyes. "When are they not fighting?"

Gage smiles at me. It's the first time I've seen him do it, and suddenly I am taken aback at how much we look alike.

"They love hard and fight hard. It's what family does," he mutters, and turns to leave.

"Gage," I sigh. "If something should happen . . ."

His eyes dart to mine. "I will protect her with my life."

I dip my chin. "Thank you."

"Don't thank me. You are blood."

My heart stops.

That is as close as Gage will ever get to accepting me as his son. I straighten my spine and give him a half smirk.

He looks confused and extremely uncomfortable.

"One more question." I push my luck.

"One more, Tristan."

"Just how many potatoes am I going to be peeling for the London clan family dinners? Callan said to ask you."

"A shit ton. Your fingers will bleed by the end."

"Really? That many?"

Gage lights a cigarette and chuckles. "I'm just happy to have been finally upgraded to salads."

"How long have you been on potatoes?"

"Since before you were even a thought."

Damn it.

LIKE AN ASSHOLE, I don't apologize or explain myself to anyone when I return to the Academy. Instead, Gage and I enter the chancellor's office—which has been turned into the war room, and without a word to anyone, I change into the protector outfit, which is all black and consists of cargo pants and T-shirts for the guys, and tank tops for the girls.

I'm lacing up my boot when Serena approaches.

"I'm not ready to talk about it," I state, and pause to take a breath. "You should focus more on the fight and less on me."

"I'll do my best." She snips and throws my sword down.

It lands with a hard thud on the carpet at my feet.

I grip it, stand, and meet her hard glare. "I asked for your trust. You said you gave it to me. But then again, you didn't actually trust me to take care of things. Did you? If you had, you and my brother wouldn't have gone behind my back and did what you did. Am I right, princess?" Yeah, I'm a jerk for using the nickname she hates, but I'm seething.

Her lips part, ready to throw out a comeback, but I jump in before she can speak. "Don't. Let's get this shit done with the Diablo Fairies."

"Tristan—" she snaps, as I turn away from her.

I look over my shoulder, meeting her gaze.

With a dramatic huff, she storms off.

Asher approaches. "That went well," he quips.

"I'm not in the mood."

"I can see that," he replies.

"What do you want?" I meet his amused expression.

"Just to share a little piece of advice."

"Wonderful. More fucking advice."

Asher lowers his voice. "Take it from me, Tristan. When you try to hold onto something too hard, you end up breaking it. Eve and I have been through a lot over the years. And the one thing I have learned is that no matter how much I try to protect her, no matter how much I love her, it's never enough. At some point, though, the tables turn. The love and need to protect that is ingrained in your gargoyle bloodline is also in Serena's. You can go thousands of rounds with her over who needs to protect and love whom more, but in the end, it will always be equal. I know this better than anyone else in this room. If you want her to be your happily ever after, then fix this before it's too late."

He pats me on the back and walks over to his mate, placing a very inappropriate kiss on Eve's lips.

I stretch my neck from side to side. *Fuck, he's right.*

Swallowing my pride, I walk up to the weapons wall and grab her daggers before turning and approaching her. She throws an unfriendly smile at me. Deserved.

Composing myself, I hand her weapons to her.

"You sure you want me to have these?"

"I'll take my chances."

I wait for her to clasp her fingers around the daggers and brush my fingers over hers, causing her to flinch.

"Sorry," I whisper.

"For what exactly?"

"Everything. You were just trying to protect me."

"We both were."

"I know."

"I love you."

"I know."

"And you are mine, Tristan. As I am yours."

"I know."

"As stupid and archaic as it is," her lip trembles, "I am a gargoyle. I fiercely protect what is mine. You're mine."

"Understood." I smile at her. "I am yours."

A silent beat passes between us. She's shivering, and I want nothing more than to take her in my arms and surround her with my embrace, willing the nightmare of our lives to go away. But I can't. She needs to remain focused on tonight, stay in warrior mode. In order to fight.

And survive.

"You are the love of my life, Tristan Gallagher."

"No matter what happens," I whisper hoarsely, "I will always love and protect you. Even with my last breath." She inhales in a shaky breath as I step closer and take her face between my hands. "In the end, there is only you."

27

BLOOD MOON

SERENA

Someone once told me that it's always darkest before the dawn. I've never really understood the metaphor. I mean, it seems like a logical statement. Night falls before morning rises.

But tonight, as I gaze up at the dark-gray-colored blood moon, shining minimal light through the black night, I think I finally understand.

Everything that can go wrong, will, before the universe rights itself again. Changes are often preceded by confusion, loss, and pain as things fall apart. But we must honor every setback, every challenge, to strengthen our purpose. Make our future even more clear. And the challenges that we label as dark . . . they resolve themselves in the morning light.

Tonight, I believe in the vision of my future. So many times, over the past few months, I've stopped believing in and trusting in the universe. I've been tested to see how much I believe in myself and my future. I persisted. Tonight, I will close this chapter of my life, and in the morning light, begin a new one. With Tristan.

I look to my right. Tristan and Zander are conspiring with their heads together. The two are thick as thieves once more, after apologies and a lot of awkward hugging earlier.

Gage stands behind them, smoking a cigarette. The way he watches the field, sky, and forest . . . it almost appears as if he has their back. Like he's protecting them. I smile at the absurd thought. It's nice to hope it will be true someday—that Gage will accept Tristan as his son. And Zander too, because we all know they are a package deal.

My eyes meet Magali's. She is standing with Ryker and Ireland. How far they have come. I'm grateful that Magali was finally able to let Ryker go; he belongs with Ireland. And Magali, well, my amazing best friend belongs with Zander. As odd as their relationship is, their love is forever.

Magali narrows her eyes at me when she sees me staring at her, lifting her fingers she signs, "Don't do anything stupid tonight."

I smile at her, signing back, "I'll try."

Even Ethan and Lucas returned from their assignment in Paris to help us. Ethan meets my gaze and dips his chin.

By the grace, I've missed him.

With a deep breath, I turn to my left. The London clan stands tall. As one. Prepared to defend their legacy and protect their future tonight. Regardless of the cost.

The violent stomping of the approaching warriors pulls my attention. Hundreds of them approach, watching us with a fierce display of pride, strength, and unity. The gargoyle army behind us closes in, ready to protect.

Magali shoots me a look to show me she's ready, before turning to face the army.

The warriors materialize from the dark in front of us, with their tongues protruding while they perform their rhythmic body slapping dance, chanting in loud battle cries.

The dark-skinned woman painted with tribal patterns, adorned with gold snake jewelry and small red clothes, leads the Diablo Fairies toward us. Once again, she's wearing a wooden warrior mask. Pink diamond gems decorate the forehead and eye areas. Four horns protrude out of the top and sides.

Her wooden staff, topped by a skull with two horns and red feathers, is firmly in her hands as she and the army get closer to us, stopping just before they reach us.

Kupuva's chin lifts and she slams her staff onto the ground, causing the army to stop their movements. With a snap of her head, one of the Diablo Fairies steps forward and drops a cloth onto the ground. It opens, revealing ten spears, each spearhead tightly knotted with cord onto a stick. The sharp points have been dipped in resin and then glass. I flinch.

"Dambe." Kupuva states, and her warriors cheer.

When we strategized earlier, we went through several

scenarios of what we thought the warriors would call out as a means of battle. Dambe was one of them.

It's where five of your best warriors essentially box, wrestle, and hand-fight five of their best warriors, using spears. Ancient tribes consider it a striking art. Many of the techniques are used in warfare.

Matches last one round. There is no time limit. Only when someone falls to the ground in death is their match over. We assumed they would pick this form of fighting because the only way to end a gargoyle is with a sharp point to the heart. Daggers, swords, knives, or spears all work. The side with three warriors standing at the end is declared the winner of the battle. The ancient warriors respect rituals and rules. And they will abide by the outcome.

"Battlefield," Kupuva orders.

Her warriors clear an area as they gather in a ring formation so they can become spectators. Our protectors follow suit, fighting our instincts not to respect their rules.

"Pick. Five. Hausa," Kupuva orders.

Hausa essentially means boxers, or fighters.

Tristan and I step forward at the same time. We don't look at one another. In my peripheral vision, I see his jaw clench, unhappy that I've chosen to volunteer.

Zander and my father both step in, flanking us.

My uncle Keegan argues with my uncle Asher behind us. "There is already one heir in the ring," Keegan argues.

"I won't sit this out," Asher debates.

"Callan and I will handle this. You remain with the protectors in the event you need to lead them," he reasons.

After a brief moment, my uncle Keegan steps to my father's side. "We have chosen," he announces.

Kupuva dips her head. Dramatically, she walks around the circle of Diablo Fairies and with her staff points at her four desired warriors. Each steps into the ring and stands in front of his preferred opponent.

All but me.

Kupuva turns slowly and takes off her wooden mask, revealing her stunning face and pink eyes. They're the same color as the diamonds on her mask. She throws the mask and her staff on the ground before she takes elegant, dancer-like steps toward me. At her approach, Tristan and my father both growl at the same time. Once she is in front of me, she looks down on me and with a wicked grin, she tilts her head, taking me in.

"I. Choose. You." She says, choppily.

"I'm honored," I dip my chin respectfully.

"You. Die. Honorable." Kupuva replies.

I swallow down my fear. "Good to know," I manage.

"Weapons!" She shouts.

We make our way over to the pile of spears.

Tristan grabs my elbow and leans into my ear. "Are you fucking crazy?"

"Is your question rhetorical?" I try not to show him I am afraid.

He pulls me to a stop, looking into my eyes.

"Remember how Nox trained you. Do not defend and protect. Be the aggressor," he grinds out.

"Got it."

He exhales, annoyed. "And for fuck's sake, don't die."

"I love you too," I whisper.

His face softens before he nods and lets me go.

I wait patiently while everyone grabs their spears before I pick up the last one. They're all the same, so what's the point of pushing and shoving? Once I have it in my hand, I walk back and take my place in front of Kupuva.

We lock eyes.

Around us, the warriors chant with excitement, putting the protectors on edge. Tension fills the air. It's thick and suffocating. Kupuva and her warriors take several steps away from us, causing us to follow suit. As is customary, all the fights will be done at the same time, which in my case is good. This way, I don't watch Tristan. Or my father.

I grip the wooden handle tightly in my hand as Kupuva bends her knees and points her spear directly at my heart. Holding my gaze, she inhales deeply before saying, "Begin."

We circle one another as I focus on her, pushing aside all the fighting and sounds going on around me. Her knees are still bent as she shuffles and shifts on the ground, watching me. My spear is high in my hand, pointed down at her. So she thinks I will drop it down, instead of what I do.

With a roar, Kupuva leaps at me, and I swing the spear

in a circle, twisting it in my hand so the point is up. As she comes down and I face her, I nick her arm, black tar oozing slowly out of the wound.

Angrily, she steps back and circles me again.

To my left, her warrior screams as my uncle Keegan spears him in the heart, ending his life. A small smile plays on my lips as I watch her eye twitch in response to the kill.

Both her hands clutch the weapon like a bat as she twists, aiming for my head. I duck, but at the last minute she changes direction and knocks me down by hitting my ankles. I fall to the ground hard and fast. *Fuck, that hurt.*

Groaning, I try to catch my breath as Kupuva appears above me, her spear aimed at my heart. I wait until she is a breath from piercing me and conjure a hard puff of wind. It pushes the spear away as I scramble to my feet. Wide pink eyes narrow at me, angered at my use of my gift.

Behind me, I hear my father. "Any last words, asshole?"

Silence, followed by the gurgling sounds of blood pooling out of another Diablo Fairy. Knowing my father, he probably slit the demon's throat, letting him die slowly.

I lift my gaze to Kupuva's. "That's two."

She stands taller, lifting her chin at me. Within seconds, her spear is airborne and spinning toward me. Not having enough time to use my gifts, I jump to my left, but the point grazes my shoulder as it flies above me toward Zander.

I shout at him in a scream of pain as I fall to the ground, bleeding badly. Zander grabs the demon he's fighting and spins him, using the demon as a shield so Kupuva's spear enters the warrior, tar gushing from his stomach as the spear sticks out of him.

With a harsh shove, Zander drops the warrior's lifeless body onto the dirt ground and meets my eyes. I try my best to look unhurt so he won't panic. He frowns at my state, but I don't have time to reassure him. I force myself back up as the blood from my wound drips and soaks my right side.

"Three," I breathe heavily at Kupuva.

A warrior from the circle grabs one of the dead Diablo Fairies' spears and tosses it to her. She catches it without taking her eyes off me.

Gritting my teeth, I switch my own spear into my other hand, having lost feeling in the arm attached to my injured shoulder. I try to calm myself and heal my wound, but it doesn't close or stop bleeding.

Confused, I chance a glance at the warrior circle and realize they are using dark magic to take away my gifts.

Which is exactly why I should not have used them in the first place. Fuck.

Angry at myself and Kupuva, I run forward toward her. She does the same, running at me, matching my speed. At the last second, I stop and shift, letting her run by me as I twist and lift my spear, shoving it into her back with a loud scream. Kupuva cries out in pain as she falls to the ground with my spear imbedded in her back. Her breathing is heavy and erratic as I look up just in time to see Tristan shoving his spear into the heart of the warrior he is fighting.

I take in a deep breath, grateful that he won and is okay.

"That's four," I exhale my relief.

Lost in gratitude, I don't see Kupuva push to her knees and grab another spear until it's too late. My eyes drop to her just as the spear is thrown into my side. Deep into my side. With a loud shriek, I fall on my back onto the ground. My vision goes in and out as I lose and regain conscious-ness. Above me, the dark gray moon watches me.

The sick feeling of blood coating my clothes overrides my instinct to get back up. In the distance, as if in a tunnel, I hear a woman's muffled scream. It sounds oddly like my mother. With a hard exhale, I blink rapidly.

Kupuva crawls over to me on her hands and knees. Her face floats above me as she pants and rips the spear out of my body, causing me to almost pass out from the pain.

Tears roll down my face as I try to breathe. She lifts the spear over my heart and everything around me becomes still, silent.

Peaceful.

She tilts her head in awe at how still I've become.

With the last bit of strength I have, I grip the handles of my daggers on my belt and slide them out of their sheaths.

As her spear comes down, my daggers go up. One into

her heart, and the other into her stomach. Her spear pinches my chest right before her widened eyes meet mine.

"Five," I exhale hard.

The life empties from Kupuva's eyes as she drops the spear and falls to the ground. With my hands still gripping my daggers, I yank them out of her, and with shaking hands, force myself to resheathe them. If the warriors see, they will not honor her death, and will attack, because I broke honor and used my daggers instead of their weapon.

"Serena," Tristan appears over me.

I try not to cry when I see the raw fear in his eyes.

"I'm okay," I lie. "Remember, too stubborn to die."

He nods and looks over at Kupuva while I fight for each breath. His eyes dart around before he takes my face between his hands. "Hold on a little longer, raindrop."

Understanding, I nod and squeeze my eyes closed and open. Beside me, Tristan grabs the spear and slides it into Kupuva's dead body in one of the spots my dagger hit. It needs to look like I killed her with the spear.

After a second, his face reappears above me.

"They've stopped pulling dark magic. Try and heal yourself, okay?"

I nod and close my eyes. Within seconds, I can feel my healing energy flow through my body. My shoulder wound closes and the blood gushing out of my side stops.

Unfortunately, it's too deep for me to heal it unless I stone sleep. So that one is going to have to wait.

"Shit!"

I open my eyes and follow Tristan's gaze to my heart.

"It's okay," I croak out. "She pierced the skin, that's all."

"Are you fucking sure?" He rips my tank inspecting it.

"Tristan." He ignores me. "Tristan!" I try harder. Still nothing. "Tristan," I whisper-shout and his eyes meet mine.

"I thought you were dead," he freaks out.

"I am okay." I grab his hand and place it over my beating heart. "I am okay. Still alive, per our plan. No one dies."

"Your plan has a kink in it," Nox suddenly appears.

28

LAST MOMENTS

TRISTAN

My eyes fall, meeting Serena's wide-eyed stare. Zander appears at my side. Tonight's battle will be a dark moment for her, but tomorrow, the morning light will shine, guiding her into her future. In this moment, my heart is full, knowing she will continue to exist. To breathe.

Zander knows what to do. We discussed this at length. He pulls Serena gently into his arms and stands. She's too weak to fight him. Her hand reaches for me, but I don't take it. Instead, I step away from her, knowing it will be the last time I will be in her presence.

I've done everything within my power to save her.

Zander will help her live.

Gage will protect her.

I've always been okay with not existing, until I met her.

Then I was faced with someone else's existence.

The girl who turned my world from one of darkness to light. I never wanted her. But I desperately needed her.

"Tell her I love her. Every day." I don't recognize my own gravelly voice as my brother dips his head, agreeing.

She becomes frantic as Zander carries her toward her clan and I swallow away the pain. What I just did was one of the hardest fucking things I've ever done. It was necessary. I will die for her. And I'll die with peace, knowing my last action had been saving her from the monsters and demons that hunted her. It's over. This war. She is free.

"I'd be doing her a favor by killing her," Nox states.

I throw him an anger-filled look. "I thought you didn't want the warriors reborn into the Noctis army?"

Lael and Tova appear by his sides.

"I changed my mind. Kupuva is dead. Asmodeus is no longer a threat to your love. Or her clan. I have decided to honor my promise and take the army," he says.

"How chivalrous of you." I try to sound bored.

"The Blood Moon is an honorable time to die and be reborn. Wouldn't you agree, satyr prince?" he questions.

I force a smile as I step toward him, unafraid.

"Is that why you are here?"

"I have learned it was your mate and brother who told Helios of our deal. Stupidly, they placed Inanna in danger."

"Inanna is safe behind the gates again."

"Yes, but at what cost?" he challenges. "My brother has

ended our agreement, satyr prince. I may not touch your soul, or realms. He said nothing about your heart."

"Take it," I wink. "It's yours. A gift."

I ignore the commotion behind me, knowing Serena is most likely fighting my brother and her clan to get to me.

"You do not fear death?" He asks, his sword sliding out of its case. The moon bounces off the perfectly polished metal.

"What I fear is not my own death."

"An affliction we both suffer from, then," he whispers.

I dip my chin in understanding. Neither of us fears our own mortality. What we fear is the end of the ones we love.

"In your death, we are even," he says coldly.

I stare him down, holding his eyes, as his sword goes through my heart slowly. My vision begins to blur as I try to keep my eyes open. Oddly, there is no pain. No sound.

There is nothing but stillness and peace.

My body weakens as he removes his sword and disappears. I touch my chest and examine my fingers. My blood is wet and sticky. Slowly, I lose control over my body, falling to my knees. I hear shouting around me, but it seems far way. A strange grunt comes from my lips as my body slumps against the ground. Two arms wrap around me.

Her flowery scent wraps around me, cocooning me.

"I'm s-sorry." My breaths come out sharp.

"Tristan," she whispers, as tears stream down her face.

"R-raindrop." Every gasp hurts, like there is too much pressure on my lungs to keep breathing.

"Don't talk." She cries softly. "You'll be fine."

I slide in and out of focus as she pulls me to her chest.

I nuzzle into her warmth, my cheek on her breast.

"Are you always so . . . welcoming, Serena?" I ask, reminding her of our first meeting.

Her teary eyes finally meet mine.

"Only to those I like," she whispers, playing along.

"So you like me then?" I try to smile, my voice weak.

"Don't flatter yourself." She pulls me closer. "I don't like you at all. I love you. With everything that I am."

"Kiss me," I barely manage. "I want to spend my last moments with you—wrapped in your arms. The last memory I'd want, raindrop, is you kissing me."

When her lips touch mine, I feel my heart stutter to a stop. The shadows of darkness overtake me as I exhale my last breath into her, knowing that I'm gifting her life.

BATTLE SCARS

SERENA

Merciless rain pelts the woodland realm. At one time, I welcomed the rain. It helped fuel my energy and gifts. Now, the drops are just sad reminders of all that I've lost. It feels like it has been raining since that night. The realm weeps.

The clock on the bedside table ticks, echoing around the master bedroom. It never stops ticking, the seconds passing by faster with each day. Each tick a reminder of how time was running out.

Annoyed, I walk over to the clock, grab it, open the french doors, and throw it out into the rain. The wind picks up with my fury, and beads of water push into my face as I watch it soar and fall through the air, staring at the mangled mess after it hits the ground. I imagine that is how my heart looks inside. Mangled and twisted from being torn apart carelessly and thoughtlessly.

Closing the doors, I sigh and curl back into the chair with my favorite blanket in front of the fire.

My gaze flickers over to the stone state bed. Would I have done things differently? Knowing what I know now . . . would I do it all again? Knowing how it ends? I frown.

I'm changing, morphing into something, someone I no longer recognize. When you face death every day, at some point you come to terms with the fact that death will bring peace. It doesn't. To stare into the face of the death of the one you love, knowing that there is nothing in this world or any other that will stop it, brings nothing but turmoil.

"Well, this is depressing," comes a low voice behind me.

I don't need to turn around to know it's Zander.

"Did you bring it?" I keep my eyes trained on the rain.

"Maybe."

I hold out my hand.

"Are you sure you want to know?"

"Yes."

"Maybe we should talk to Callan, or Abby, first?"

"Give it to me." I keep my hand firmly in the air.

The minute the paper touches my fingertips, I snatch it away and hold it tightly against my chest.

Zander takes the seat next to me and crosses his feet at his ankles, appearing relaxed. "Are you going to look?"

"I want to . . . " I trail off, unsure.

"When you're ready."

I take in a deep breath. "Everything is upside down."

"I know." Zander glances back at the bed.

"He'd want this, right?"

"He'd want you to be happy, Serena."

Zander falls quiet as he sits next to me—like he has done every single day since we came here. His sad eyes turn to the glass windows as he looks onto the woodland realm.

We all wear our battle scars differently.

And while my physical scars healed months ago from that dark night, the emotional ones are still raw. For both Zander and me. They're exposed. No matter how much time passes, neither of us feel at peace without Tristan.

I turn and take in the rain-soaked realm outside. After that night, we returned here. I couldn't face anything or imagine being anywhere else. This is the realm Tristan loved. Whether he'd admit it or not. Here, I am surrounded by him. His spirit. His soul. It's a good place to heal.

Zander and Gage had the stone state bed placed in Tristan's bedroom so I could heal in a deep sleep.

Healing my body.

Healing my wounds.

Healing the physical.

My heart, though—

There are holes in my heart that I fear won't ever mend.

I wrap my arms around myself as Zander stares at the

forest; his expression is soft and crestfallen. Missing his brother.

"Queen Ophelia once told me," I turn in the chair and face him, "When love is fated, not even death can break a protector's bond. She told me to search my heart; Tristan will be there. For true love is everlasting, even in death."

He closes his eyes. "And when you search your heart?"

"He's there, Zander," I whisper. "I feel it. It's faint."

"Then keep searching. Wherever he is, find him."

"I will."

Like he does every day, Zander stands and drops a kiss to the top of my head. "Love you, champ. And so does he."

"Today's I love you?" I confirm.

"He said to tell you every day."

I swallow back my tears. "And you have."

"Now, I gotta go beg a gargoyle protector for forgiveness. One who is very pissed off that I blew off our date last night to go skinny dipping with some nymphs."

I hold in a groan. "Why would you do that?"

"Intel. For the Lion Guard," he answers with a sly wink.

I watch him. He reaches for the door handle, before he looks over his shoulder, frowning at the stone state bed.

"Today feels different," I say, and smile.

His sad eyes meet mine, and he winks before leaving.

As soon as Zander is gone, my smile fades.

Standing, I make my way over to the bed and take in

Tristan's sleeping form. Obsessively, I watch his chest as it rises and falls with each breath he takes.

Crawling into bed, I curl up to his side and place my ear over his heart, listening to it beat steadily with strength.

It turns out I should have trusted Tristan all along.

He knew Nox would come for him.

And because of that, he prepared Zander and Gage.

Once Tristan took his last breath, essentially dying in my arms, they immediately teleported us to the woodland realm, where Helios was waiting. Within seconds, the deity gifted him life. Since he died, his soul will be gone, forever, but when he wakes up, he will be reborn as a pure gargoyle.

My lips brush his, pleading with him to wake up.

It's taking even longer than even Helios thought.

Today though, I have a good feeling.

Leaning up near his ear, I open the note Zander handed to me and whisper the name of Tristan's unborn son to him.

FIRST BREATH

SERENA

I bite my lip in nervousness. My heart slams against my chest as I walk down the quiet hall before I open the door. The moment I step foot inside, Gage, Uncle Asher, and my dad turn to face me.

"Hi." I great them.

"Come in, pumpkin." Dad motions me over.

"What do you think, Serena?" Gage asks.

I look around the penthouse. "I love it."

"Do you think Thor will too?" Dad asks.

It's been another month and still, Tristan hasn't awoken.

"It's fully lined with hematite," Uncle Asher points out.

I frown. "No emeralds?"

The three of them fall silent before my dad chuckles.

"What?" I ask.

"When Tristan wakes up, he will be all gargoyle. Which means that once you two complete your bond, your eye color, wings, and healing stone will become the same as his."

"That means hematite," Gage points out.

Uncle Asher steps closer to me, bending down as he studies in my eyes. "Although, I have to say, kiddo. Your eyes are becoming more and more brown and less blue with each passing day. Yeah?"

Gage's gaze rakes over me, and I quickly turn away.

No one but Zander and Mags knows I'm pregnant. And that is the reason I am taking on more of Tristan's traits.

"Anyway," Gage interrupts. "The place is yours if you want it. My personal architect, Everett Weston, helped design it for you. And my firm oversaw the build-out."

"Thank you," I whisper. "Tristan will love it."

"And you?" My father asks, quietly.

"I love it," I assure him before looking out the windows at Paris. I'd love it more if Tristan were here, though.

"If— When," my uncle Asher quickly corrects himself, "Tristan wakes up and he is ready, he will command the Paris clan of gargoyles. With you by his side."

My eyes meet Gage's. "Aren't you?"

Gage lights a cigarette. "No."

"Serena, I know you're hesitant to take over should something happen to me, but I want to assure you of something," Uncle Asher says. "I am full of gargoyle awesomeness. Just ask your aunt Eve. Which means it's going to be, like, thousands of years before you have to worry about reigning." He winks and gives me a cocky grin.

Dad lets out a low whistle. "For a loving uncle, you kind of suck with the sentimental stuff."

Uncle Asher's face turns serious. "I'm not done."

"Oh, sorry." Dad chuckles and waits.

Uncle Asher turns his attention back to me. "As I was saying. When you do finally take over as heir, with Tristan by your side, it will be a proud day for our clan and race."

"Thank you, Uncle Asher." I curl into his hug.

Over my head I sense him sticking his tongue out at Dad, which causes a giggle to fall out of me.

They will never tire of acting like children. I swear.

My father's cell phone goes off and I turn in my uncle's arms to see who it is. When my father's face pales, I know.

Uncle Asher tightens his grip around me so I won't collapse onto the ground as I cling to him like a lifeline.

Within seconds, we teleport to the woodland realm.

NOBODY MOVES or speaks as I walk up the stairs and down the hall. It's quiet, but the air is electric. With a horrifying lump in my throat, I let my fingers linger over the door knobs.

Even though my emotions are in overdrive, I try to

keep calm, not knowing what I am walking into on the other side of the doors. When Zander called, he was vague. All he said was that I was needed here. For Tristan. So here I am.

The moment I push open the doors, I choke, trying to swallow and take a breath at the same time. Instantly, warm cognac eyes meet mine, stealing my breath altogether.

I freeze. Unable to move.

Tristan slowly sits up with help from Zander.

A pained sound escapes me as I stare at him.

I'm torn between wanting to smack the shit out of him or kiss him senseless. As I try to figure out which to do, he tilts his head and his eyes slowly inspect me from head to toe.

He stretches out his hand, reaching for me.

"Serena," Tristan says slowly, drawing it out, like he wants to say it, wants to hear himself say it.

At the sound, tears form in my eyes, and without realizing it, I'm running to him, grabbing his hand with mine before I crawl onto the bed and straddle him.

Zander quietly slides out of the room, closing the doors.

Tristan's hands move away from mine, touching my face, then my hair, sliding down my arms, feeling me, like he's trying to convince himself I'm real. When he places a palm over my side, resting his thumb on my stomach, I completely lose it, as ugly tears fall down my cheeks while I burst into hysterics.

"You're okay?" he whispers, and I realize that he touched my stomach because of the deep wound from the spear during the fight—no other reason. "Are you healed?"

I nod, unable to speak as I sob uncontrollably.

"It's okay, raindrop."

My heart disintegrates at the sound of my nickname, and I move a hand over my mouth to muffle another cry. I try to control my emotions and shaking so I don't scare him.

"Look at me," he demands.

I don't. I can't. I don't want him to see me like this.

Two warm hands take hold of my face, forcing me to look at him. Tristan grips my chin between his fingers, lifting my face so he can look into my eyes. The intensity in his stare is unnerving. He's reading me, my feelings.

Realization hits when he releases my chin. He can't read me anymore. His empath gifts were satyr. He no longer has satyr blood running through his veins, only gargoyle.

"It worked?" he whispers. "Helios brought me back?"

I nod. "Yeah," I hiccup. "You died. In my arms. But Helios brought you back. You've been healing for months."

"Holy shit," he exhales.

I give him a minute to process everything before I grab his face and pull him close, needing to feel him as I drop my forehead to his. "This is . . ." I am barely able to choke out.

"I love you," he says. "Did Zander tell you today?"

I shake my head, because I've been in France all day.

"Good. It's my turn today," he states.

I sniffle.

"I love you," he whispers.

"I love you," his voice gets stronger.

"I love you too," I reply. "What?"

A smirk curves on his lips. "You have sexy in your eyes."

I suck in a sharp breath at the familiar banter.

"I love you." His lips meet mine and my heart shatters all over again at the painful and beautiful way he's kissing me. Like it's our first kiss ever. It's raw and emotional.

My lips tremble as his glide over mine gently. I close my eyes and inhale him as his lips coax mine, as I cling to him. This kiss is deep and heart-stopping, but with an edge of something that fills me with love. I sink into his warm lips as he parts mine, allowing our tongues to explore.

After a moment, he pulls away.

"You stopped," I pant out.

"I need air." He grins. "To survive."

"Don't ever die on me again." I start shaking again.

"I'll try really hard not to," he replies in a sad voice.

"I'm going to kiss again you now." I announce, not giving him a chance to reject me as my lips crash onto his.

With each kiss, he becomes more addictive in the worst way and best possible way. These past few months, I'd been so lost in my own sadness and mourning, I'd ignored the basic need to feel. To be loved. Touched. Held. Kissed.

When he kisses me, my body hums with adrenaline as I feel my blood surge and my stomach drop. Then it hits me.

"Oh shit," I rear back.

"What's wrong?" he frowns.

"I'm pregnant."

Tristan freezes as he stares at me before he bursts out laughing. "I'm not sure how long I've been asleep, but last I checked, kissing does not get one pregnant. I'm good. But I am not that good, raindrop." He smiles at me playfully.

When he realizes I'm not smiling or laughing, his expression turns serious. His eyes search mine. "Seriously?"

I'm breathing so heavy from being nervous that it's embarrassing. I never meant to blurt it out like that. I had a plan. And that plan did not include telling him within ten seconds of him waking up from a long coma after death.

A tear slides down my cheek because I am all over the place emotionally. With his thumb, Tristan wipes it away and studies my face. The way he's looking at me makes my heart clench in my chest. More tears fall, causing him to frown.

"Serena?"

"I don't know how to do this," I confess.

"Do what?"

"I've never told anyone I'm pregnant before."

"I should hope not," he snorts.

Letting out a deep breath, I lean toward him.

Taking both his hands in mine, I flatten them on my stomach. He swallows as his gaze jumps from our hands to my face, and back to my stomach again, staring at me.

"When Kupuva stabbed me, she missed him."

His lips part. "Him?"

His eyes meet mine, full of hope.

"Him," I confirm.

Tristan regards me for a moment. Suddenly, he grabs my hand and pulls me to my feet as he stands.

"Wait, I don't think you should be up," I attempt.

Tristan tightens his hold on my hand and walks us to the french doors, pulling me out onto the deck in the rainstorm. Once we're in the middle of the deck, he lifts his head toward the sky as the cold rain splashes across his face.

When he looks at me, he looks revived and numb at the same time. Something in my chest cracks, watching him embrace the fact that he's alive again. Breathing. He's okay.

Tristan is here with me.

His face finally breaks into a smile as the rain pours down both of our faces, mixing in with my tears. He smiles and reaches for me. When I grab his hand, he pulls me close.

I wrap my arms around his neck, and his warm lips touch mine before he speaks. "I'm not sorry."

"What?"

"I'm not sorry I died, because now I truly get to live."

"Tristan—" I start, but he kneels in front of me.

Speechless, I watch as he brings his lips to my stomach.

"Thank you. For giving me two reasons to exist."

RESCUE ME

SERENA

Tristan tugs me against his chest as we walk back inside. Once we're out of the rain, he peels off his shirt and tosses it to the ground, then shrugs out of his pajama bottoms so he's standing in front of me completely naked.

"What are you doing?" I ask, with a tremor in my voice.

"I've been sleeping for months. And now I am wet. I need a shower. And since we have a new rule . . ."

"Wait, we have a new rule?"

"Let me finish."

"Okay."

"Since we have a new rule, which is that you two never leave my side, you are showering with me," he announces.

Within ten minutes, I've gone from sobbing to gaping.

Confused, I stare at him. "You two?"

"You and my son."

"Oh." I swallow.

"Do you want to get naked? Or shower clothed?"

"Um . . ."

He smiles. "My favorite word, Miss St. Michael."

I bristle. "Don't you think you should rest? Or eat?"

He cups my face. "The only thing I need right now is you. And you know I hate repeating myself. Naked or clothed?"

"Um . . . "

"That is your second *um* of the day. I do hope you will be using the rest of your vocabulary once we're married. And parenting. I think kids need to learn words and shit."

Taken aback by his playfulness, I freeze. "Just give me a minute to catch up here. You died. Slept for months. And then just woke up excited about a baby and marriage."

A choking wave of anxiety washes over me, making me feel like I can't breathe. My head and heart need to catch up.

Tristan stands there watching me. "I have you," he whispers. "I'm here. And I am not going anywhere."

I nod. My eyes follow his every movement obsessively.

Tristan's face breaks out into a gorgeous smile. "You're with child. I should help. Do it for you."

"Do what?" I ask, because he's all over the place.

He tugs my wet dress and bra over my head and moves his hands to my hips, slowly rolling down my panties, waiting as I step out of them. He tosses it all in a pile.

"Tristan, wait . . . I mean, you just woke up," I start, but he stops me with his lips.

After a long, searing kiss, he pulls back.

"I'm fine. Now let me make sure you are, too."

He walks us into the bathroom and twists the faucet, turning on the water. The steam billows out almost instantly with the water. My gaze runs over his body, my mind still trying to grasp that he's awake. He's here. I want to scream with joy and at the same time sob because of the unfairness of everything that has happened to us.

"Hey." Tristan is in front of me. "Stay with me."

"I'm here." My voice shakes.

His mouth meets my ear in a whisper. "Let me take care of you. Let me love you. Show you this is real, raindrop."

Tears pool in my eyes, but I hold them back, because they are no longer tears of sadness. They are grateful and happy tears, and I know if I let them fall, they'll never stop.

"In the tub." Tristan orders.

"What?" I ask, confused.

"New rules. From now on, tubs have water."

Slowly, I walk over to the tub and take his hand as he helps me slide into the warm water. I watch as he slides in on the other side and the water swishes around our bodies, sloshing into my hair and over my shoulders.

"What are you doing?" I ask.

"Isn't it obvious?" He smirks.

He inches forward until he is kneeling over me. His

RANDI COOLEY WILSON

fingers slide along my collarbone and down my stomach until they reach between my thighs. I squirm beneath the pressure of his touch. It's been too long.

"Talk to me," he demands.

I moan in response to the way he massages me. Nearly rising out of the water as he touches me over and over.

"Talk about what," I pant out.

"Tell me what you are feeling, what you felt. What happened. Get all the anger and sadness out so that you won't resent me, resent us, resent the whole fucking situation. We deal with this now." His tone is scary calm.

Leaning forward, his submerged fingers stay beneath the water, as a slow rhythm builds within my body. Images of us, of him, of everything flash through my mind. And the last image, of me holding his lifeless body in my arms.

I cry out both in pleasure and in pain from the image.

"I'm angry!" I whisper. "At you. At the fact that our time together was ruined. That you died, in my arms," I sob. "You took your last breath while I held you." I moan. "I watched you sleep for months, while I mourned. The entire time thinking it was my fault. I'm angry for feeling guilty for blaming you for all the stupid shit that we went through." My voice becomes hoarse. "I hate that I can't function without you. I never, ever want to feel that way again. Ever. I can't. I love you. I lov——"

His mouth slams into mine as he grips my body and pulls me against him, water spilling out onto the floor as I grip the back of his neck, wrapping my legs around his body.

With one hand holding me, and the other pushing against the tub, he stands and steps out of the tub, pulling me with him. Within seconds, I'm on my back in our bed as he slides into me, causing my heart to split into two.

"I'm sorry," he says gruffly.

He thrusts his hips slowly, sliding in and out of me, as his fingers dig into my flesh while he angles my body onto him. His eyes remain locked onto me, and I'm lost. Tears fill my eyes as his mouth finds mine again. With every slow movement of his hips he takes the broken pieces of what was left of me and fuses them back together.

Every ounce of control he has slips, as he hisses through his teeth and begins to thrust into me deeper and harder.

I clench around him, holding on as my body shakes and trembles under him. As he releases inside of me.

He kisses me tenderly and whispers, "I vow never to leave you again."

I exhale and sob against his chest.

Tristan's death and rebirth taught me how to survive through the darkness and emerge once again in the light.

It's always darkest before the dawn.

SACRIFICES

TRISTAN

To sacrifice yourself so that another may live sounds romantic—it's not. Every time I look at Serena, I'm overcome with the need to touch her, love her, please her. The need to erase all the bad of these last few months and leave only the good is overwhelming. She rescued me.

In more ways than one.

It was her smile that had first attracted me to her. The way her entire face lit up, the way her eyes said she'd eat me alive if I wasn't careful. The first time I touched her, and her eyes traced my lips, I stopped breathing—overcome with obsession for this woman. And that first time I left her unprotected, my chest tightened—because without her, I am nothing.

Never in a million years did I think this infuriating and sexy protector would be mine. So many things have changed over the course of our story. But Serena's beauty and fierceness haven't; she is still goddamn beautiful. And with each passing day, my love for her multiplies.

In the split second that I first laid my eyes on her, everything inside me decided then and there that I wanted to be the reason she breathed. Protect her. Be her champion.

And now, I am all these things—as she is to me.

I was never allowed to want her—but I did.

It was always about blood, oaths, and protection—and in the end, it is still about blood, oaths, and protection.

The loyalties and obligations we were both tethered to remain, but now we face them together, as one.

I knew instantly that acting on our attraction would trigger a shitstorm of darkness to fall over both our futures.

What I didn't know is that once we made it through the darkness, it would be pure light on the other side.

"So you're saying it is crazy, obsessive, *I will die for you* kind of love?" Zander asks, pinning me with a look.

I frown. "Did I say that shit out loud?"

"Dude, you're looking at Serena like she's your whole fucking world. It doesn't take a genius to figure out what you're thinking," my brother counters.

"Ready?" Callan clears his throat.

Ready? It's shocking that he's even allowing me to marry Serena, let alone asking me if I am the one ready.

"Hey, I'm wearing my *Callan's Crew* T-shirt under my tux," Zander says. "Memories of an epic bachelor party!"

"Shh." Callan dips his head closer to Zander and lowers his voice. "A top-secret bachelor party; one that Abby and Serena can never find out about. Not ever. I mean it."

Zander nods. "Cross my heart."

Callan stares at him for a moment before dipping his chin. "Who has the rings?" he asks.

"I do," Zander waves them.

Callan gives him a pointed glare. "Don't be an ass and lose them while getting your nymph on. Hey, Thor," he turns his attention to me. "I just want you to know I am going to be the world's greatest father-in-law," he declares.

"Noted." I swallow, feeling a little nervous.

"Seriously. If you wanted to get me a mug, or apron, or something with that on it for the holidays next year, I wouldn't hate the idea," he adds with a serious expression.

"I'll keep that in mind." I shift, waiting.

"In mind, as in, I'll order it after the ceremony? Personalization takes time on gifts. And if you decide to have it engraved, you're adding like six weeks to delivery."

"Again. Noted." I give him a tight smile.

A megawatt toothy grin forms on his lips. "Awesome."

Next to me, Sora, an elder gargoyle from France and leader of the Spiritual Assembly of Protectors, laughs.

"Callan has always been my favorite." She winks.

Nervous, I smile before looking around the clearing.

Abby and my mother stepped in and helped organize everything for tonight. Serena wanted to hold our binding ceremony in the woodland realm, in the foxfire forest where I proposed. So here I stand, waiting for her.

Sora will oversee the binding ceremony and bear witness to us formally accepting our pledge of loyalty to one another's clans and the Spiritual Assembly of Protectors.

Everything stills when Serena appears, holding on to Callan's outstretched arm. I attempt a steady breath when she takes a small step toward me. Callan's eyes brim at the corners as he escorts his daughter down the aisle.

I watch every breath she takes as she locks eyes with me and everything around us fades away. Never in a million years would I have guessed that this is how our story would end.

When they approach me, I take in a deep breath as Callan kisses his daughter on her right cheek, then her left.

"I bless you, on your binding day. May you have a lifetime filled with love and happiness. I love you, pumpkin."

"I love you too, Daddy." She kisses his cheek, and I swear the heartbreak and love on Callan's face almost kills me.

"Thor." He dips his chin at me before taking his seat.

And there goes my Callan moment.

"You look beautiful." I take her hand and she smiles.

"Shall we begin?" Sora asks, and we nod our agreement.

Asher hands Sora a dagger made of my healing stone. The weapon was carved and charmed from the same hematite used in our stone state bed. She places the dagger on an ancient book with intricate Gaelic designs etched into the leather cover. Closing her eyes, she chants in Garish.

"Tristan, if you'll unbutton your shirt so I may gain access to your protector mark," Sora prompts.

I undo the top two buttons and push the material to the side, granting her access.

She finishes her blessing and catches our eyes. "Please hold out your left palms so that I may access the *vena amoris*. The vein of love," Sora instructs.

We do.

Sora takes the sharp tip of the dagger and pricks Serena's ring finger four times, while chanting "in-zen, mánı́, vas-wı́s, ew ter-ort," between each puncture.

"Each represents your mating vows: heart, mind, body, and soul," the elder gargoyle explains with each pinch.

She turns to Serena, handing her the dagger.

"Serena, you must bring the dagger to Tristan's protector mark. Please make a small incision so the wound will open and release his blood."

My heart leaps into my throat. This is it. How we become one, forever, of our own choosing. A heartbeat of silence passes before the tip of the knife caresses my skin.

Serena turns, revealing the deep cut in the back of her dress, exposing her clan's mark on her lower back. It's a dragon, but once we finalize our binding, it will become a lion to match my mark. I brush my fingers over it, calming her before making a small cut. I hand the dagger back to Sora when I am done.

Slowly, I brush my blood-coated fingertip over her mark. Peace floats over me when our blood mixes, binding me to her forever.

"I give to thee forever, Serena Elizabeth Vivian St. Michael," I vow with a strong voice, healing her wound.

She turns, and when her eyes meet mine, they take my breath away, having fully become cognac in color.

Serena lifts her finger to my mark, infusing it with her blood again. This time, of her own free will.

"I give to thee forever, Tristan Armel Gallagher," she whispers, and heals my wound.

Instantly, our heartbeats sync and my mind fills with her emotions and images. My heart feels whole. The mark on my chest comes to life, pulsing and throbbing, recognizing her as my forever.

"The Spiritual Assembly of Protectors and the gargoyle elders have accepted and bless your binding on this day. Serena and Tristan, you each must accept each other's clans as your own family. Are you both prepared to declare unwavering loyalty to each member, to love and embrace them as your own kin of both the St. Michael and Gallagher names?"

"We are." We both say at the same time.

"London clan, do you embrace your new kin?" Sora asks.

"We do," her family says in unison.

"Paris clan, Prince Zander, and Queen Ophelia, do you embrace your new kin?" Sora questions.

"We do." The three say together.

Sora smiles. "No blood ties between clans are required on this day, as we bring two races together. Tristan and Serena, it is my pleasure to announce you are one, forever."

I pull her close and she wraps her arms around my neck and sighs. "Mrs. Gallagher, those sexy eyes you are giving me make me want to maul you right here."

"Kiss me," she whispers.

Just as my lips meet hers, Callan shouts in excitement. "ZHEN EFFING PRI!"

"Must he always scream *family first* at bindings?" Eve asks in a whisper-shout. "It ruins the romance vibe."

"It's kind of his thing." Asher kisses her temple.

"Well, it's fucking annoying," Kenna snips.

"Easy." Keegan takes Kenna's hand and kisses it.

"Listen, cutie." Callan narrows his eyes at Eve. "You loved it at yours just like Serena and Thor love it!"

"Tristan. His name is Tristan, Dad," I sigh.

"But I like Thor better!" Callan whines to Abby.

"Give it time, babe." Abby winks at me.

I look over at my mother. She looks horrified. "Why does Callan want to call Tristan Thor?" she asks Zander.

"Long story. Serena was supposed to a boy named Thor," he embellishes. "Turns out she is a girl."

"This seems highly inappropriate to bring up now," the Queen scolds.

Gage lights a cigarette. "Ophelia, you're tied to the London clan. Forever. I would mentally prepare yourself for a lot of inappropriate moments in the future."

"What's next?" I shoot Serena a smug smile. "Bedroom?"

"Family dinner!" Callan announces.

How's that for romance?

ENDLESS

SERENA

I take in a deep breath as the middle of my dress presses into my stomach, suffocating the two of us. I lay my hand on my stomach, trying to ease the discomfort.

My mother reached out to a designer friend, who carefully designed and skillfully made the ivory, form-fitting gown. It dips low in the back and has two straps crossing over my shoulder blades, designed to appear like vines. Ivory flowers embellish the delicate lace, which cascades, pooling on the ground like water. It's stunning.

And I can't wait to rip it off.

I watch Tristan from across the room. He's laughing with Zander, Ryker, Ethan, and Lucas. I take a moment to just be grateful. Grateful that he's mine. That he's alive and that I get to love him forever.

Both the water and woodland realms are here to celebrate with us, gathered with family and friends, as well as protector clans. Everyone is happy, dancing, and enjoying themselves. For the first time in my life, I truly feel at peace.

Tonight, I look at my clan, at Tristan's family, and at our friends and feel nothing but happiness. I'm no longer naïve; I know with the morning light will come hardships and uncertainties, but now, I get to face them with Tristan.

His gaze lifts and meets mine from across the room. And everything and everyone melts away. From this night forward, we will share everything, because we have a bright, long future to look forward to.

Tristan steps away from the group and walks across the dance floor to me. My breath catches in my throat as I admire him. When he gets to me, he pulls me into his arms.

"You happy, Mrs. Gallagher?" he whispers in my ear.

"More so than anyone deserves to be," I admit.

"We deserve this, raindrop."

I exhale again and he takes me in.

"You okay?"

"This dress is tight. Everything is tight."

"You do realize we are going to have to tell them soon?"

I frown. "I was hoping we could wait."

"Wait?" he laughs. "Until when?"

"He's in college."

Tristan's eyes fill with love. "I think they'll notice."

"You're probably right. How about next Sunday, at family dinner?" I give in.

"Deal. Although let's not tell them it's a boy just yet."

"Why?"

"Your dad will want to name him Thor."

I nod. "Point taken."

"Besides," he drops a light kiss to my lips. "I am looking forward to naming my son."

I swallow. "Um . . ."

Tristan's brow arches. "You know I love that word."

"Actually, you can't name him."

He laughs. "What?"

"Remember how I lost that bet with Zander? I mean," I ramble, "if you think about it, it's really your fault I lost. You made me cry. And I rarely cry. Except that time . . ."

Tristan stills. "Please tell me you didn't hand over naming rights of our firstborn child? To my brother?"

I bite my bottom lip. "Not to *him*, exactly."

"Then who?"

"Rionach."

Tristan stares down at me for a moment as he catches his breath. After a few minutes he nods his head, understanding the meaning behind what I am not saying.

"Do you know the name?" he asks, quietly.

"I do," I smile up at him. "You do too. I whispered it to you while you were in your stone state sleep healing."

He smiles. "That is unfair. I was out cold."

"Shame you don't remember. It's a good one," I tease.

"Knowing Rionach, it would be." His voice sincere.

"It is, I promise."

Tristan brings my hand to his mouth, kissing it. "I trust you."

"Yeah?"

"Yeah," he confirms.

"For the record, I am a pretty badass dancer. Want to dance with me, raindrop?"

"This marriage isn't big enough for you and your ego."

"Guess that means you'll have to go. My ego and I have been together way too long to let a pretty lady get in the way of our relationship."

I smack him in the chest. "How easily you toss me aside, Mr. Gallagher."

"Never." He pulls me tighter against him. "You are the love of my life."

After a searing kiss, we make our way to the dance floor, surrounded by everyone we love and everyone who loves us.

Family.

Friends.

Clans.

Satyrs.

Gargoyles.

Our kin.

Our kingdoms.

For a brief moment in time, all is right in the world.

Legacies are like the wind. They come and go.

Love—love is endless.

THE END

EPILOGUE

TWENTY YEARS LATER

I LET OUT A SHAKY BREATH, staring absently up into Tristan's gaze. My growing love for him causes me to shudder under the weight of his body.

With a wicked smirk, he watches me. "Serena?"

I don't respond. I can't. It's too hard.

He shakes his head, chuckling, understanding my silence. "Raindrop?" I can hear the smile in my nickname.

One eyebrow curves up in annoyance at him as I pinch my lips together, holding back a sigh and sharp response.

"It's time. He's ready."

"He's a child." I pout.

"He's a man."

"He's our son, Tristan."

His expression turns serious. "Which is why he will succeed."

"How can you be sure?"

"Because our blood flows through his veins."

I release a light laugh. "Are you new here? That should be a huge red flag."

Tristan bends down, brushing his mouth over mine in a tender kiss. Even now, years later, my skin breaks out in goosebumps at his touch. When he pulls back, I gasp for air, my fingers tracing the lines of his protector tattoo.

"If you keep giving me sexy eyes we are never going to get dressed and get there in time," he scolds.

"Fine."

Twenty minutes later, we are standing in Chancellor Chasin's office at the Royal Protector Academy.

The gargoyle elder was hand-picked by my uncle Keegan to run the Academy years ago. He's a long-time family friend and a trusted protector among our race.

I try not to fidget as we wait.

Ten minutes later, the doors to the office open.

"You summoned?" Striker mumbles, sounding bored as he walks into the room with his focus on his phone.

Striker's impatience for all things related to his protector duties are much like my own were at his age.

It's annoying.

Tristan turns to our son and cocks his head to the side, assessing him. "Where have you been?"

"Out."

My heart sinks, knowing he was most likely in the company of a female whose name he's already forgotten.

Striker is a mirror image of his father, mannerisms and all. With his good looks, intelligence, and charming personality, it's easy to see why there has been no shortage of female protectors in and out of his life.

A lifestyle that will soon come to an end for him.

It's hard to believe our son just graduated with top honors from the Royal Protector Academy.

It seems like yesterday he was born.

Striker slides his phone into the back pocket of his jeans, and Tristan hands him a folder. THE folder.

"What's this?" Striker asks.

"Your assignment," Chancellor Chasin answers. "You are top in your class, Striker. An impressive feat, despite your bloodline ties to this school. As you are aware, those who graduate top in their class are assigned immediately to their charge. The royal family has provided your protection details in that dossier."

Annoyed, my son opens the file, thumbing through it.

"This assignment is in Spain."

"It is," Tristan confirms.

The eight-by-ten glossy photo falls to the floor and I flinch, knowing what is being asked of him. Striker snatches the photo off the floor and looks at it for a long time before his gaze lifts and slides between Tristan and me.

"You want me to protect a girl?" he asks, confused.

"Her name is Umbria," I reply. "She is the great-granddaughter of a woman named Siobhan."

"Who is Siobhan?" our son asks.

Tristan sighs. "Camilla Gallagher's best friend."

Striker's eyes meet his father's in surprise.

"And Umbria is special."

ISLE OF DARKNESS EXCERPT

A MONSTER BALL ANTHOLOGY STORY

STRIKER

I stand on the stone ledge. The tips of my boots dangle over the edge as I watch the crashing waves below violently slamming into the jagged cliffs. After each wave breaks, a briny spray reaches toward the night sky before falling back into the churning ocean.

Harsh winds whip around me, causing the sea's upheaval. Frustrated, I stretch my neck from side to side, a habit I inherited from my father, Tristan Gallagher, the current leader of the Paris clan of gargoyles. Tonight, like the sea below, I am filled with unease.

Sliding my hand into the front pocket of my jeans, I pull out the crumpled piece of paper and drag my gaze away from the elemental chaos happening all around me. Unfolding the tattered square, I take in its worn edges, damaged from carrying it around with me for so long. With a heavy sigh, I stare at the photo of the being I have come to resent even though we've yet to meet.

My eyes follow her midnight hair as it falls past her shoulders. If you hold the image just right in the light, there are times it appears as if she has dark blue highlights hiding within the black strands. Her long, thick lashes and manicured brows both match the color of her hair.

I look into her turquoise eyes. They stare back at me intently, haunting me. It's almost as if they're trying to see inside me—read my deepest, darkest fears and secrets. It's fucking unnerving. My thumb brushes over her pink lips and pretty face. *She's* unnerving.

The angelic sheen of her fae skin is misleading because Umbria Mendoza is no angel.

In fact, she's the exact opposite—a Caballuca del Diablu—a demon fairy.

And my assignment.

Umbria is someone I have been appointed to safe-guard. I scoff at her photo. No one asked me if I wanted to be her protector, but in my world, the choice isn't mine to make.

Gargoyles were created for one purpose: to protect. We are guardians assigned to beings, realms, or objects, to ward off those with immoral or malevolent intent. And the fae in the photo doesn't know it yet, but I have been given the honor and task of guarding her. Keeping her safe.

The problem is, Umbria's bloodline is dark, not divine,

which means she embodies the very immorality that I was created to protect other creatures and beings from—a dark-souled being.

My focus shifts to my forearm where the Celtic cross tattoo should be. In order to become her protector, I had to renounce and walk away from my oaths and allegiances to the Angelic Council. After graduating at the top of my class at the Royal Protector Academy, a school established to train and prepare gargoyles for their protector assignments, I was supposed to swear my loyalty to the Spiritual Assembly of Protectors, a ruling body that oversees the divine sect of the gargoyle race. Once initiated, we are marked with a Celtic cross and permitted to accept assignments from the Angelic Council.

Since Umbria's bloodline is that of a dark-souled being, my duty and loyalty to her protection places me instead under the authority of the Secular Council of Protectors, meaning I have no affiliation or devotion to either Heaven or Hell. It also means that, like another gargoyle from my clan—one who never swore his fidelity to the Spiritual Assembly—I will be viewed as a traitor amongst my kind. My kin. My race. And as their prince, that is a shitty place to be in.

Regardless, my fate was sealed two generations ago when a human woman named Camilla Gallagher befriended Umbria's great-grandmother. Siobhan was the queen of the Caballucos del Diablu, a title and responsibility that now rests upon Umbria. One that has spilled over to me.

I fold up her picture and return it to my pocket, sensing his approach.

"Do you have it?" I grind out.

"No hello? Or, you're looking quite dashing, as always, Tag," he teases.

I remain silent, unamused and indifferent to my best friend's good-natured banter.

"Contemplating jumping?" he asks. "If so, I'd reconsider. Your wings would save you."

"Fuck off," I growl, and my wings twitch under the skin on my back, begging to be released.

"Shit, Striker. Who pissed in your cereal this morning?" Tag steps to my side.

Slowly, I shift and face my royal protector. Tag and I have been best friends for years. We regard each other more like brothers—blood—than friends. Our easy friendship grants us both permission for constant teasing and prodding. Tonight, apparently, I'm the target. He raises his eyebrows in question at my agitated state. Normally, I'm a bit more carefree and lighthearted.

A light mist of salty sea spray jumps up and covers us. Lifting my hands, I wipe them over my face, removing the spray, and we step away from the ledge. "Sorry. I'm just . . ." I trail off.

Tag shoots me a knowing glare out of the corner of his eye. "I get it. Nevertheless, it's time."

Meeting his gaze, I raise my hands in surrender. "I know," I blow out. "I know."

"Here." He shoves a black garment bag at me. "Your tux."

"Tux?" The word comes out harsh.

"It's a ball. You can't wear your motorcycle boots and T-shirt." He smirks.

"You're enjoying this way too much."

"That I am, my friend. It's my right, having known you all my life."

"And we're sure Umbria will be attending?" I ask.

He dips his chin. "She'll be there. Bronx and Lex confirmed that she's on the list."

"Bronx and Lex?" I repeat. "The identical brothers from New York?"

"The very same. They've been hired as bouncers," he replies, with a slight smirk at the idea.

"Our host acquired gargoyles to watch the door? Interesting," I mutter.

Tag wiggles his brows. "Wait until you see this really cool stone statue trick they do."

"Can't wait," I grumble, eyeballing the garment bag.

With a heavy sigh, I unzip the bag, being careful not to allow any water to get on the fine Italian silk. I feel around, my brows furrowing when I don't find what I am searching for.

I throw a questioning look at Tag. "Where is the invite?"

"On its way."

I eye him and curb my desire to lash out. "You've got to be shitting me," I exhale.

"Patience, Your Highness," he counters.

"This isn't a game," I growl.

"No shit!" he bites out and grabs the bag back, zipping it up. "Christ, you're an asshole today."

With a curse, I begin to pace, attempting to calm my nerves. Ever since being assigned to Umbria, I've been a moody, brooding jerk. I shouldn't be taking out my frustration or anger on Tag. He's done nothing to merit my cruelty. As second in our class when we graduated from the Academy, Tag was assigned as my royal protector. Not only is the appointment an honor, but it's pretty fucking awesome to have him continue to have my back like he always has over the years. And how have I repaid him? By being a complete jackass these past few months.

"Tag, listen—" I begin but get cut off by a bright beam of light that begins to glow between us, appearing out of nowhere. "What the fu—"

"Right on cue," Tag says in a tickled voice.

He grabs and twists my wrist, forcing me to open my palm. Within seconds, the light solidifies and morphs into a brilliant piece of paper, fluttering down and landing in my hand.

My confused gaze meets his with curiosity. "What the hell is this?"

Tag motions with his chin for me to read it. "Your invitation."

I lift up the piece of parchment and read the elegant calligraphy: *The Monster Ball*.

"Flip it over," he orders, and I do.

"Just as the moon has brought me to you, so shall the moon bring you to the ball," I read out loud. Underneath, the date, *October 31st*, is inscribed, and below that, *The Witching Hour*.

Tag tilts his head, assessing me as I examine the piece of paper.

"Why so cryptic?"

"It's how our host does things," he answers and hands me back the tux.

"Who is this mysterious host, anyway?" I ask.

Tag shrugs. "No one knows for sure. I guess that's all part of the fun."

"Peculiar," I mutter, and place my hand on the tux.

As soon as we both are touching the garment bag, Tag teleports us back to my loft in Paris.

I watch as he makes his way into the kitchen, opens the fridge, and grabs a beer. Removing the cap, he strolls over to the couch and flops down onto it, crossing his legs at the ankles. After taking a long sip from the bottle, he tilts it, motioning to the clothing bag still in my hand.

His smirk turns knowing, and with a wink, he says, "You'd better get changed, *Cinderella*. You have a ball to attend and a fairy-demon-queen-girl-being to win over."

With a heavy sigh, I look around my loft. It's all an open space with very little privacy.

"Are you going to watch me undress, or can I get a bit of privacy?"

He crosses his arms and eyes me. Yeah, he's not fucking going anywhere.

"Do you really think I am going to blow off the ball? And my assignment?" I question.

"Yes," Tag responds in an entertained voice.

"Thanks for the vote of confidence."

"That is what you do, Striker." He sits back and studies me. "You run. I chase."

He's right. I run from responsibility. Tag forces me to face it. It's our pattern.

"Hell," I whisper under my breath and jerk off my shirt, tossing it at his face.

With a dark chuckle, Tag settles further into the couch, getting comfortable, and throws the damp shirt to the side. Irritated with this entire situation, I turn toward the hallway to go shower.

Slamming the bathroom door, I turn on the shower and let the steam fill the room around me. For a moment, I glare at myself in the fog-covered mirror. This protector assignment is already grating on my last nerve, and it hasn't even begun. It doesn't help that my best friend is either going to torture me or kick my ass the whole time I am assigned to Umbria.

Meeting my own reflection, I inhale. I'll be okay. As long as I don't let her in, I'm good.

I sift through my emotions, grab every shred of hatred and resentment that I can find in my body, and use it to protect myself. Each becomes a plate of armor to shield me.

Umbria is just an assignment.

I am Striker Gallagher, heir to the gargoyle race. Their future king. And as such, I won't be getting attached to the queen of the Caballucos del Diablu. Ever.

The.

Fucking.

End.

ISLE OF DARKNESS

COMING SOON!

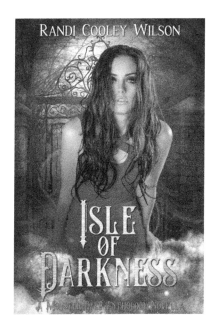

*Before Isle of Darkness Releases, Read Umbria and Striker's
Beginnings in The Monster Ball Anthology*

STOLAS

THE DARK SOUL SERIES

Silence envelops the room as my reflection peers back at me from the windowpane. The bright sun feels warm on my face, but the air surrounding me is chilly.

A deep shiver rolls through my body as I stare vacantly at the outside world.

"There is no reason this has to be difficult, Miss Annandale."

Startled by the voice, I blink rapidly and pull my stare away from the dark figure hiding behind a snow-covered tree. An outwardly undetected quiver of fear shudders from within my soul. The figure's constant presence is the reason my mind has turned dark.

"Miss Annandale?" the inquisitive voice firmly repeats.

I exhale and slowly shift my attention to the warm, vibrant gentleman who is assessing me with a curious expression. "I'm sorry, what did you say?" I manage.

The expensive leather groans under his weight as he sits back in his executive chair, quietly scrutinizing my disposition.

Dr. Cornelius Foster has been silently studying me since I walked through the door, fingers tented under his strong chin.

It's unnerving.

Even so, I don't show my discomfort. I've learned that displaying alarm is cause for medication. And the meds only serve to darken my mind further.

I focus on the prestigious degrees and awards the good doctor proudly showcases on the rich burgundy wall behind his mahogany desk. They're impressive. *He's* impressive.

None of it matters though. He can't help me. No one can. "Let's talk about the voices. Are you still hearing them?" The voices are constant. Never ending. But that isn't what he wants to hear. The hundreds of thousands of dollars he's spent on those framed degrees won't allow the voices to still be there. What he doesn't grasp is, if years of conventional medical treatments and medication haven't helped, one hour in a Swiss "healing spa" certainly isn't going to.

I fake a smile. "They're much quieter now."

Dr. Foster dips his chin. "And the demons? Do you still see them?"

I can't help but notice how bright his crisp, button-down shirt looks against his dark chocolate skin. The white is pure. Ethereal. For a moment, I pretend he's an angel sent from Heaven to protect me from evil. The light to fight the darkness that has settled deep within the corners of my mind.

"Hope?" he prompts, using my name.

"I haven't seen one since landing in Switzerland," I lie.

Dr. Foster's brow furrows and he runs a large hand over his full beard. The gesture causes me to stare at the few strands of gray mixed in with the black. For a man in his early fifties, Cornelius Foster certainly is easy on the eyes. His features remind me of that actor, Idris Elba. Unlike the other doctors before him, he's sharp and seems to be able to read me.

Lost in thought, I suddenly realize he's now leaning on his desk in front of me, muscular arms crossed, gaze calculating.

"Hope," he commands my attention again. "You're safe here. Our patient-doctor relationship only works if you are candid during our sessions. I can't help if you don't truthfully tell me what is going on inside your head. While you are here, I expect open and honest communication. There is no judgment. I'm here to aid in your healing."

An awkward silence lingers between us.

Aid in my healing.

Is that what I'm here to do? Heal? If it were only that easy.

It's been two years since my twenty-first birthday; for two years my mind has been haunted by visions of suffering, pain, and torture. The images are burned into my memory.

They aren't something you *heal* from. Or forget.

I squeeze my eyes closed and attempt to push them away, along with the bile that threatens to rise.

A small knock at the door breaks through our quiet standoff. "Come in," Dr. Foster answers, without taking his gaze off me. I twist my focus to the girl who slides into his office. With her presence, a cold chill spreads through my limbs. The stranger's brown eyes are vacant. Just like mine.

She's young, around my age, and looks to be of Native American heritage. Her straight, brown hair falls to her waist and is parted down the middle. I watch as she robotically flips it over a slender shoulder. The gesture is odd—forced even. There's no feeling behind it. It's almost as if someone programmed her to blink, breathe, and move every few seconds as a way for her to appear human.

"Hope, this is Lore," Dr. Foster says by way of introduction. "She'll be your suitemate during your stay here at Shadowbrook." I frown. "Suitemate? I thought my parents requested a private suite?"

The psychiatrist smirks. "Human nature thrives on community. I believe it's healthy to be social. Having a suitemate will be beneficial to your healing. You'll see."

I don't answer him, as I once again meet Lore's unresponsive expression.

"We're done for the day." Dr. Foster walks around and sits behind his desk. "Lore will show you around the grounds, and help to get you settled in. I'll see you tomorrow afternoon for our weekly private session."

Relieved at the dismissal, I stand and face my new room- mate. She's silent as she opens the door and waits for me to walk through. Maybe Lore doesn't speak. I can understand the desire to remain quiet and keep people at arm's length. Especially in a place like this.

As I pass by her to walk through the doorway, I watch as the inky shadows swirl around her aura. At the sight, my breath hitches. No air moves in or out of my lungs.

Annoyed with my lack of movement, she huffs and steps around me into the hallway, leaving me no choice but to follow at a quick pace.

The sound of a robotic movement pulls me from the shadowy path my mind is wandering down. My gaze lifts and locks onto a small lens with a flashing red light.

"Cameras?" I confirm.

"They're everywhere," Lore says flatly, without a look back. My gaze jumps around, taking in each of the small devices as

we continue to walk down the hallway. The heels of our shoes echo as we step on the elegant hardwood floors.

Shadowbrook feels like a five-star resort. People are relax- ing everywhere—sprinkled around inviting velvet chaises and chairs. They're reading, writing, and using tablets in a mundane manner, as if this is a hotel and they're simply guests enjoying their vacation.

It's all so . . . normal.

331

Unsettling.

Lore and I step into a large open room with vaulted ceilings.

There is a full wall of windows on one side over-looking the retreat grounds and snow-covered mountains, and a baby grand piano on the other side, in front of a roaring fireplace and shelves of books.

The room is warm and cozy, filled with oversized couches and chairs. The walls, furniture, and accents are decorated in shades of tranquil grayish-blues and dark browns. Game tables are set up, and a gigantic glass chandelier hangs from the middle of the room.

I feel my throat tighten a little at the thought of how much like home this room feels. I miss Connecticut, my friends, my parents, and my life—be- fore it all fell apart.

"Do you like it?" Lore asks, uninterested in my answer.

"It's like a modern Swiss chalet." I exhale. "What's not to like?" "This is the game and lounge area," Lore continues monotonously. "Where you come to play games . . . and lounge." She speaks slowly, as if I wouldn't understand.

Is this girl serious? By the blank expression settled across her stunning features, it appears she is. "I can see that," I respond, unable to keep the edge out of my voice.

She ignores me and I follow her quietly as she guides me through more hallways, until we come to a set of double glass doors. We step closer, and with a whoosh, they slide open to reveal a dining hall. The smell of coffee and baked goods assaults me, conjuring up images of my hometown coffee shop, where I'm currently wishing I was, reading a book.

"The dining hall is open twenty-four hours for all of your nutritional needs."

"Nutritional needs," I parrot.

Lore rolls her eyes and focuses on the empty room. "Where are the trays and food windows?"

Her cold glare swings back to me and her brows pinch. "There are servers who take your request and bring it to you once it has been prepared to your liking by our chefs. When you are done, hired staff will remove your used cutlery, china, and glassware for washing."

"So, no KP duty?" I quip.

The last facility I was at required every resident to lend a hand in the kitchen.

Lore's expression turns sour. "We are here to heal, not do dishes. This isn't prison."

Speechless, I simply stand there.

It's obvious she's never experienced a *real* mental health facility. I remain quiet during the tour of the library, outdoor meditation area, spa, and indoor fitness center. At the end, she leads us to our room, which turns out to be a penthouse suite. It has a common area, kitchenette, and two hallways—each leading to a large bedroom on either side of the apartment, with its own private bathroom. It's very elegant.

"The kitchen is stocked with basic needs. Water, fruit,

and the like." Her eyes scan the length of me. "No knives though. If you're planning to commit suicide, you'll need to break a mirror and slit your wrists. Or tie sheets together and hang yourself."

"I'll keep that in mind," I mutter.

After pointing out which room is mine, my suite mate disappears without another word. Alone, I release a deep breath and notice my bags have already been placed neatly on the carpeted floor. My gaze drifts over the luxurious, king-size bed.

There are no hospital sheets here. The white cotton material is without a doubt Egyptian, and a minimum of fifteen hundred thread count. My eyes roam, searching for the restraints, but I come up empty. All that decorate the bed are taupe and steel- blue bolster pillows and fine linens. I look around my luxurious hotel-like surroundings.

"What is this place?" I whisper into the emptiness.

Twisting around, I drop into a wingback chair and trail my focus over the rest of the room. Mirrored side tables flank the large bed, decorated with lamps, vases of fresh cream flowers, and stone Buddha statues. A velvet- cushioned storage bench sits at the end of the bed, most likely holding extra pillows and blankets. It's all so elegant and formal.

An oval glass desk and leather chair have been placed in front of the window, positioned to overlook the meditation gardens.

"No knives, but they're sure as hell is a whole lot of glass," I say to myself.

My attention drops to the circular side table next to the chair. It's decorated with a silver tray holding two glasses, bottles of high-end water, and multiple pill and vitamin containers. A medication schedule outlining when to take the tablets has been handwritten on elegant stationery, along with a printed calendar of my sessions and treatments.

I pick up one of the orange bottles and read the label. A prescription for anti-psychotic medication stares back at me. I shake the full container before returning it to its place.

"Home sweet home."

Standing, I grab my bags and start to unpack. It takes me all of ten minutes to place the few possessions I was permitted to bring into the built-ins located in the walk-in closet. After I'm organized, I waste another forty minutes thoroughly enjoying the rain showerhead in my private bathroom, before getting out and wiping away the beads of water.

Since I wasn't allowed to bring my hair dryer, I squeeze my long, dark strands with a fluffy towel, hoping it will absorb most of the moisture. After a few attempts, I scowl at the clumps and waves forming, and give up, hanging the wet towel on the rack.

Walking to the window, I study the grounds covered in a heavy layer of fresh snow. My stare follows the uphill lines of the breathtaking Swiss Alps. The snow-covered mountains are picturesque. If I wasn't being confined, it would be like living in a postcard.

Just when I start to relax, I'm hit with a sudden burst of cold air. I tense, as a familiar pair of lavish black leather dress shoes stops in front of me, setting off the goose bumps on my arms. I know the drill; I don't look at him. Instead, I inhale deeply and my heart pounds wildly in my chest as I hover over an abyss of fear.

"Not now, please," I exhale, hoping the voices and visions will retreat.

"I've found you," he murmurs, leaning in to place his lips at my ear. "You can run, but you can't hide, little one."

I continue to ignore him and focus on the expensive wing-tip shoes.

Reaching out, he gently touches my hair, letting it spill through his fingers. "You were blonde a few months ago. No?" he asks in a deep masculine voice. "This color suits you. He will be pleased." He moans harshly.

Moistening my lips, I snap my head to the side, pulling my hair out of his hand.

Strong, warm fingers grasp my chin, forcing me to remain still. "The time has come for you to abandon all *hope*."

I lose my breath at his familiar words. Even though it's not the first time he's visited, his warning causes my fear to rise to absurd levels. Attempting to control my panic, I squeeze my eyes closed.

When they reopen, I look around frantically, but the demon is gone.

Trying to calm my heart rate, I pull in deep breaths and talk myself down, reminding myself he wasn't real—he was just a vision. One that keeps haunting me.

When my nerves settle a bit, I turn back to the window, hoping the scenery will keep my anxiety levels even.

I look around the grounds for anything suspicious, but see nothing out of the ordinary, until my drifting gaze stops on a dark form straddling one of the lounge chairs near the pond. The ache of fright is still present in my chest; I pull the sleeves down protectively on my sleeping thermal and curl my fingers around the material to help ground me.

After a few moments of gawking at the figure outlined in shadows, I realize it's a man. Seeing no swirling aura around him, I relax.

Human.

Not demon.

I release a long, grateful breath and let go of my sleeves. I'm just about to step away from the window when he reaches into the pocket of his jacket.

Transfixed, I watch as he pulls out something black. *A crayon maybe?* A few seconds later, he bends his tall frame forward, and mindlessly works his hand over a sketch pad, leaving traces of charcoal with each stroke. Drawn to his swift movements, I follow each shady line marring the pure white paper. I'm too far away to make out what he's sketching, but the intensity with which he draws captivates me.

The rising silver moon highlights his raven hair. It's shaggy on top, and cropped around his neck. Stylish. Sexy even. I notice thick silver rings on each of his middle fingers.

From this viewpoint, it's hard to see his face, but I'm able to make out the sharp angles of his jawline.

The stranger snaps his body back and studies the work on his paper, giving me a fuller view of his face. I lean forward to get a clearer look, hitting my forehead against the glass.

"Crap!" I rub my forehead, not realizing how close I'd moved toward the window.

It's almost as if he's luring me in.

Needing a reprieve from his pull, I twist to grab a bottle of water, but something stops me. Every cell in my body awakens as my gaze slowly shifts back to the window and slams into an intense, emerald-green gaze. The color is so lush and vivid, my heart skips a beat.

I become entranced, swept away with one look. No air moves in or out of my lungs as I hold my breath. A shiver runs bone deep, and my world tilts as everything but him fades.

He looks at me not as though I'm crazy, like most people do, but as if he's fascinated by me. Intrigued even.

I'm hit with a sense of déjà vu when his verdant eyes widen in recognition. Overwhelmed, I grab both sides of the heavy silk drapes and yank them shut. The abrupt motion ceases my trance, allowing me to finally take in air.

Struggling, I search my memories for a spark, trying to remember where I've seen him, but come up with nothing. I shiver at the echo of his stare, feeling his gaze still in my bones.

I stumble over to the orange bottles on the side table. With a shaky hand, I pick up the medication and take the tablets and vitamins as prescribed by Dr. Foster. I convince myself my mind is playing tricks on me again.

I crawl into bed, and it's not long before the medication causes my lids to become heavy. I steel myself, ready for the nightmares I know will plague me throughout the night.

Like every night for the past two years, just as I fall asleep, my dreams turn against me when a familiar deep voice whispers, "*Lasciate ogne speranze.*"

"Abandon all hope," I mutter, as I slip into the darkness of my mind.

READ STOLAS FREE

STOLAS IS FREE WITH KINDLE UNLIMITED

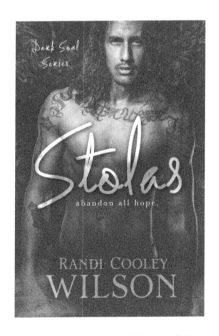

A New Adult Paranormal Romance Series

IF

A CONTEMPORARY ROMANCE NOVEL

I close my eyes and take a few deep breaths, attempting to regain my composure. The crisp evening air fills my lungs but does nothing to soothe my soul. The truth is, tonight, nothing is going to keep me calm—except maybe copious amounts of alcohol.

The brisk fall weather isn't unusual for this time of year in New England. Cooler temperatures hang in the air, chilling even with a jacket. This evening, though, there is another reason for the icy presence deep within my bones.

I shiver and stare at the closed double doors in front of me, knowing what's waiting behind them. Tears threaten to burn the back of my throat. Suddenly, I miss California.

My safe place.

Far away from the memories.

I exhale slowly, staring at the scene in front of me. The plain white church sits unassumingly on the grassy hill.

Like most buildings in Massachusetts, it has a rich history and longstanding secrets. The steeple stands tall against the dusk-colored sky glowing with crimson and auburn hues.

A breeze passes over me, carrying with it the whispers of the ghosts who've passed through the sacred doors. Blue hydrangeas frame the front of the historic building, popping off the white clapboards, which look like they've just received a fresh coat of paint. It's picture perfect. On the outside. What's inside is anything but perfect.

"You ready, Emerson?" a gentle voice asks.

I unglue my gaze from the church and turn my attention to the tall, handsome man beside me, Jake Irons. When my eyes meet his, he smiles effortlessly.

How does he always appear so completely at ease all the time?

It's a gift. It must be. One that I don't possess.

My gaze roams over the tailored black suit he chose for tonight. It's flawless.

He's flawless.

"Ready," I force out, focusing on how handsome he looks.

Jake is easygoing. Calm. Steady.

Exactly what I need to keep me composed.

To keep my façade firmly in place.

He reaches for my hand with his larger one. "You okay?"

No. This is the first time my two worlds will collide, and it's impossible to be *okay.*

Lifting my gaze, I give him a watery smile and nod. "Just happy," I lie.

Jake studies me for a moment before squeezing my hand.

He's always so perceptive.

It's unnerving.

But even he has no idea what we're about to walk into. I've kept it from him, because I don't want my complicated past to tarnish my future with him. I know he senses the sadness at times, the void, but he never pushes. Never asks. He doesn't try to fix the broken pieces or make me whole. He simply accepts that this is the way I am.

With a slight tug of encouragement, he guides me toward the entrance. And with each step closer, my heart lodges itself farther in my throat. The panic crawls underneath my skin, threatening to break through the surface as I try to convince myself that my world won't fall apart the moment I step into the church.

The doors open and a friendly face greets us. "You guys made it!"

Relief crosses my friend Josh's face, and I can't help but smile at his energy.

"Sorry we're late." I step into his warm embrace.

Josh has always been my favorite boyfriend of Kennison's. The three of us went to college together—part of a larger group of friends. And while they've had their ups and downs, it really does make me happy to see the two of them getting married this weekend.

"Where is Kenz?" I ask, hoping to see my best friend. "With the wedding coordinator, going over some last minute details. She'll be out in a minute. Come in. Everyone is already here." Josh steps to the side, letting me by so that he and Jake can shake hands and do their guy greeting thingy.

The moment I enter the church, the air around me jumps with electricity. My chest begins to cave in and my skin feels too tight all over my body. The weight of *his* stare is on me, and my skin heats under it. My head swirls and chaos grips me. I take a deep breath, trying to control what I knew was going to happen the moment I saw him again.

Lincoln Daniels is impossible to ignore.

We are impossible to ignore.

When my gaze lifts, it tangles with a set of steel-gray eyes.

And with one look, I'm gone.

Lost in the memories and heartache.

The *ifs* lingering between us.

READ "IF" TODAY!

A CONTEMPORARY ROMANCE

A New Adult Contemporary Romance Novel

ACKNOWLEDGMENTS

THERE ARE SO MANY PEOPLE TO thank who are a part of this amazing journey I'm on. A simple thank you to them for encouraging and supporting me just doesn't seem like a strong enough show of gratitude on my part.

To my husband and daughter, thank you for loving me and sharing your time with the characters I write and being understanding of my deadlines.

Hang Le, By Hang Le. I love you like I love dancing squirrels. Thank you for always visually capturing my stories on my covers and being my design soul mate.

Sarah Hershman, and Hershman Rights Management, thank you for your ongoing support.

Rick and Amy Miles, and the entire Red Coat PR team, it is a pleasure to be part of RCPR author family.

Liz Ferry, at Per Se editing thank you for polishing these stories so they shine. You're amazing.

Christine Borgford, at Type A Formatting, thank you for making the interiors of my books look badass.

A HUGE thank you to Randi's Rebels. Y'all are the best reader group a girl could ask for. Rebels Rock! Special Rebel shout-outs to: Alexandria Faust for naming Tova and Janean Desmarais for naming Lael! As well as to Misty Mayo for naming Umbria.

Thanks to my family and friends, I love you all.

To the readers, thank you for reading my stories.

Thank you for continuing to take chances on me and the stories I write. Thank you for trusting me with your imagination.

I'm honored to be part of your literary world.

ABOUT THE AUTHOR

Randi Cooley Wilson is an award-nominated, bestselling author of **The Revelation Series**, **The Royal Protector Academy Novels**, **The Dark Soul Trilogy**, **If,** and the upcoming **Knightress Series**.

Randi's books have been featured on *Good Morning America*, *British Glamour Magazine*, *USA Today*, and in the Emmy's Gifting Suite. Her books range in genre, and include contemporary romance, urban/high fantasy, and paranormal romance, for both young adult and adult readers. Randi makes stuff up, devours romance books, drinks lots of wine and coffee, and has a slight addiction to bracelets. She resides in Massachusetts with her daughter and husband and their fur-baby, Coco Chanel.

Visit **randicooleywilson.com** for more information about Randi or her books and projects.

Or via **social media** outlets:

Made in United States
North Haven, CT
03 June 2022

19800730R00202